PART (

Peter Stevenson though   as
too old to cry, but he had   ered
his new school classroo   iis
class knew everyone els   alked
about what they got up to during the long Summer holidays, or
in most cases, what they would have liked to have got up to
during the holidays, and how far they could expand their tales
of encounters with the opposite sex, and still be believed. He
had always been small compared with the others in his school
year, but this new lot were monsters. They couldn't have
grown that much during the six weeks holiday, surely! As
usual, the biggest boy in the class, inevitably called Kevin, was
also the loudest, and his tall tales matched his size. Peter had
not even heard of some of the things that this boy was saying
that he did during the summer, and some of the other things
didn't seem physically possible. Peter looked aghast at what
he was hearing, but the rest of the class were cheering the big
boy on as he gave his sexual master class.

"What's up with you, short-arse?" On Kevin's remark, all eyes
turned to look at Peter. Oh shit! Peter had only just got there,
and he was being bullied already. The room went quiet, and
Peter waited for the punches to arrive. He had learnt from an
early age that being small made it easier to be picked on, but
before the fight started, the class tutor arrived and Peter
watched the youngsters as they ambled to their desks. The
tutor looked over his glasses at the new arrival.
"Stevens, I'm glad you've met Stevenson. He can sit next to
you and you can show him around the school whilst he gets
settled in." The big boy looked Peter up and down.
"Stevenson eh? That makes you my dad then." Kevin
laughed out loud at what he thought passed for humour. Peter
was amazed at Kevin's stupidity. 'God he was thick!' Peter
thought, 'he couldn't even get that right.'
Peter followed Kevin to his desk, and slumped down in
despair. Due to his size, Kevin usually had a desk to himself.
He made no allowance for his new colleague, so Peter spent

1

his time cramped on the edge of the desk. Peter had regular problems controlling his farting, and being scared shitless did not help matters, so he spent the first morning at his new school friendless, frightened, and fighting the urge to cough in his rompers, in case it caused the Neanderthal sat next to him to rip his head off, and plug his bottom with it.

Despite the close encounter with the class moron, Peter's first day at his new school was not as bad as he had expected. The teachers were always stricter at the start of the new school year, and his new school-mates had to concentrate on their lessons to get back in the swing of things, so they were kept too busy to bully him. He knew most of the answers to the questions that the teachers had thrown out at random to the class, but decided to keep that to himself, especially from Kevin, to avoid being picked on. Peter had also learnt at an early age that no-one likes a smart-arse. He breathed a huge sigh of relief as he boarded the school bus home. He sat down and looked out of the window, happily day dreaming about how he'd survived his first day, only to find Kevin throw himself down next to him, crushing Peter against the bus window.

"Hello Dad, guess what?"
"What?"
"Good guess! We haven't had chance for your initiation ceremony yet, have we?"
"In my last school, I did the classes' maths homework for them on the bus home." Peter was getting worried at what was about to happen, and tried to think of a way to get out of it. "I can do it now if you want me to."

Peter had noticed the look on the face of his class mates when the homework question was handed out. It was only a simple decision tree, but as far as they were concerned, it might just as well have been hieroglyphics.

"How are you going to do all that during the journey home?" Aha, there was a chance that Kevin might be persuaded to leave him alone. Peter took his maths book from his schoolbag, and looked at the problem. He took his biro from his pocket and started to draw the decision tree.

"Look, it's a matter of drawing a branch for each possible outcome and the probability as a percentage of each of them occurring, and making all of the possibilities add up to a hundred. It's quite easy really."

"Are you saying I'm thick?"

'I wouldn't say it to your face, big boy, but I would definitely think it!' Peter always had a quick smart-arsed response ready, but a few beatings had taught him to control his tongue, and keep his thoughts to himself.

"No, there's nothing clever about it. I've done these before at my old school." Peter had worked out the percentages in his head, whilst he was drawing the diagram. His new school mates had moved up the bus to look at the result.

"Can I have a copy?"

"I'd pay good money for that: It would take me hours tonight, when I could be watching the telly."

Kevin, always quick to spot an opportunity, could see that there was money to be made. "Who's up for a copy for fifty pence?" He was almost crushed in the stampede. "Double bonus."

Peter looked at Kevin in confusion.

"What do you mean, 'Double bonus'?"

"On the fruit machines in the local pub you increase your winnings when the 'bonus' button flashes, and it's even better when the 'double bonus' button flashes. This is a double bonus because not only is my homework being done for me, I'm also getting paid for it."

It sounded quite logical when Peter thought about it, but what was Kevin doing in the local pub?

"Come on Dad, get drawing as fast as you can. We've got money to make."

Peter didn't want to move to Oxford, but manufacturing jobs were becoming scarce in Northern England, so Peter's father moved the family to the more affluent South when he was made redundant. The redundancy money helped to pay for their removals and a small part of the difference in the cost of the new house in Oxford compared with the selling price of their old house in Newcastle. The mortgage on the new house would take up a large amount of his father's wages from his new job, but the move South would greatly improve his chances of staying employed, and would give Peter a much better chance of success in his future career. Peter was their only child, and had come into the World late in his parents' life. Although his father was too proud to claim unemployment benefit, Peter was the real reason why he carried on working instead of retiring early.

Peter's parents weren't worried about him leaving Newcastle at all, he was always top of the class, and didn't have many friends to lose, anyway. They hoped that it would give him a fresh start away from the bullying that he received at school, which they complained to the head master about, resulting in Peter being so badly beaten up that he was frightened to go home in case it was reported again. Having nowhere else to go, Peter went home late at night; his parents had stayed up worrying what had happened to him, and his mother caught him trying to go upstairs without being noticed.

"Look at the state of you, I'm reporting this to the police tomorrow."

"Why can't you just leave me alone, it was because of your complaint that I was beaten up again."

Peter stayed off school for the rest of the week, only going back when the bruises were no longer visible on the outside; the ones on the inside would never leave him. The bullying increased, and Peter became withdrawn, and suffered in silence.

Peter's parents pointed out to him that they had also left their friends and family behind, and the sacrifice was for his future more than theirs. What they didn't know then, was that Peter's move to Oxford would result in fraud, theft and eventually murder.

Peter spent his last year at school trying his hardest to avoid being beaten up, and providing Kevin with a means to make money. As well as losing his broad 'Geordie' accent, the best way that he had found to reduce the number of beatings was to make use of his ability to impersonate the teachers, which always seemed to make the others laugh, especially when he made topical comments such as "Your dog must be terribly overweight if it has eaten your homework again boy!" Peter was still top of the class and would have liked to have stayed on for his A levels, but his parents needed him to start work to help them with the mortgage. His school lessons did not prepare him for the grim reality of life in the big bad World. He had as much idea about mortgages as any other sixteen year old, or why it was so important to pay so much money each month. His father had told him that the word 'mortgage' was made up from two separate words, mort being the Latin word for dead, and gage meaning social life. Morecombe and Wise needn't be too worried with the competition!

At least the bullying would stop when he left school, but the cretins that gave him the hardest time were those who left school at sixteen anyway. Those who stayed to study for A levels usually did so to get the qualifications to go to University, and were the cleverer ones, who were more interested in studying than putting chewing gum in his hair, or filling his schoolbag with custard.

Kevin, on the other hand, spent his last year at school becoming more of a bastard. His school report was unbelievably glowing, because, when he was in the same class as Peter, it was Peter who did the work to get him the high marks, and it was Peter who provided Kevin with the answers to the tutors' questions. He'd sat next to Peter during the mock exams, and copied his answers. The only new things that Kevin learnt in the whole year was how to belch and say "*bollocks*", a feat of which he was incredibly proud, and that the word 'knob' began with a k. From then on, it became his favourite term of endearment, and Kevin pronounced the word 'ker-nob' to show that he understood the strange spelling convention.

Peter's father had arranged an interview for Peter at the Accounting Department of the Company where he worked. Peter was smart and polite at the interview, and started work the week after he left school. He was taken to the Finance Director's office when he arrived, and was gob-smacked when he found Kevin already there.

"Good morning Peter," the FD greeted him warmly. "I hope we're not going to have any problems with yours and Kevin's surname being so similar. I always like to meet my new staff as early as possible, to get them settled in. We have a busy team here, and the sooner you start producing, the more efficient the office will be. We are taking on two school leavers this year, and both your school reports look very promising". Peter looked at Kevin in amazement at this statement. He couldn't be the only one that thought that Kevin was as thick as shit, surely!

The FD ran through the set up of the Accounting Department, and told them about their duties; learning how to use the computer software, inputting journals onto the computer, reconciling the bank account each month and providing reports for the management board. He also spoke about their prospects and career path within the company, and if they progressed in line with their school reports, the Accounting qualifications that they would be expected to study for, how the company would support them, and the accompanying pay rise and promotion when they qualified. The FD then took them to meet Mark, a qualified accountant, who was their department head.

Peter was full of enthusiasm and hope for the future, but his mood quickly deteriorated when he discovered that his desk was next to Kevin's. No prizes for guessing who was going to do all of the work then.

"How did you get them to believe that you had the attributes to be an Accountant?" Peter still had to be careful with his words, but he didn't expect Kevin to beat him up on their first day at work.

Kevin was surprisingly jovial. "That was the Careers Master's doing. He'd seen the marks that I received for my Maths mock exam, and my homework, and decided that I should use my skills as a mathematician to become an Accountant. He was such a stupid ker-nob, he would probably have offered Stephen Hawking the job of the speaking clock."

"But it was my work that got you the high marks in the first place."

"Well, you'd better keep that up then. You don't want them to find out that you've been helping me to cheat, do you!"

Peter was quick to learn his new job, but was always being dragged back to correct Kevin's regular and simple mistakes. Kevin tried to take the same holidays as Peter, so that he was never left on his own to get caught out. Christmas and Easter was easy, but Kevin had to bully Peter into doing as much work in advance prior to going on his summer holidays.

To broaden their knowledge of accounting procedures, Kevin and Peter spent a few days out of the office every year assisting in the accounts of other local companies. Their first visit was to work with a funeral director, who was a friend of the FD. Kevin, as usual, took charge, and started bossing Peter around.

"The first thing we need to do is to check that the unpaid invoices are accounted for correctly. I'll look through the unpaid invoices in this file, and check that the burials which have taken place but have yet to be paid for are in the Creditors' account. You can check the coffins and count the dead bodies, as they should be in the accounts as 'Work in Progress'."

Peter's bottom lip began to twitch. He suspected that Kevin was talking rubbish, but didn't have the courage to tell him so. He was already apprehensive at working in the funeral parlour, and was horrified at the thought of having to check out the dead bodies. "Look, you know that I'm better at figures than you, so I should check out the Creditors account, and then I'll give you a hand with the Stock Take."

"You're always saying that I need to practice my book-keeping, and this is a good chance to do it. This won't take us long, so I'll go and get some cups and coffee stuff whilst you're doing the Stock Take."

Kevin made a bee-line for the funeral parlour, whilst Peter summoned up the courage to go down to look inside the coffins. The coffin on the table was a bit of a squeeze for Kevin, as although he had stopped growing upwards, he was still growing outwards. He had just managed to slide the top of the coffin into place as Peter entered the dimly-lit parlour. Kevin could hear Peter mumbling to himself as he moved around the room, gradually getting closer and closer. As the lid was lifted off a few minutes later, Kevin shouted "Boo!", and Peter had just enough time to shit himself before passing out. It took until going home time that night until Peter stopped shaking, and all that night he plotted his revenge. The next afternoon, after they had looked through the accounts, Peter put his plan into action.

"Kevin, we still haven't counted the dead bodies, and there's no way that I could set foot in the parlour on my own, so you'll have to do it."

"Fair cop Dad. We're nearly finished here, so I'll do it before we knock off."

"OK, I need to pop up to speak to the Funeral Director, so I'll see you back at the office tomorrow."

Peter went down to the parlour and gingerly climbed into one of the coffins. He felt uneasy as he closed the lid on top of him, and was shaking in the darkness, but contented himself in the thought that he would soon get his own back. After about ten minutes, which felt like an hour, he heard someone enter the parlour, and the sound of coffins opening and closing. Peter's heart started to pound as he made himself ready to spring up, but instead of the top being taken off of his coffin, he heard squeaking noises, and, too late, started to bang on the lid of the coffin as he realised that it was being screwed shut. Peter was left alone in the darkness for what seemed like hours. The odour from his farts was almost overpowering, and the decreasing oxygen level was beginning to make him feel light-headed. Surely everyone will have gone home by now, and he would suffocate all alone during the night. He would have normally enjoyed the irony of actually dying in a coffin, but other factors were occupying his thoughts.

The sound of footsteps entering the parlour, and coffins being opened and closed again brought him back to his senses. He banged as loudly as he could on the lid of his constricted wooden prison, and finally the lid was unscrewed to allow him freedom.

Kevin peered at Peter in mock surprise, fanning his nose to shake away the smell. "I thought you'd gone home?"

"Oh yeah, and this was nothing to do with you!"

"Not me, I've been checking the final parts of the accounts, and came here to count the dead bodies as we agreed. You'd better watch out or you'll end up spending all of your wages on under crackers. It smells like you've shit yourself again."

Peter had no way of proving whether or not that it was Kevin that screwed down the coffin lid, and he was also in the wrong for hiding in the coffin to get his revenge, so he let the matter drop. When he went back to work the next day, he heard Kevin laughing and joking about how he'd scared Peter, and how he'd rescued Peter from the locked coffin.

After two years at work, Peter and Kevin had moved to more important jobs in the office. Mark was completely unaware that all of their work was being done by Peter. He was keen for them both to increase their Accounting knowledge further. As neither of them had A levels, they were both enrolled in the Association of Accounting Technicians course at the local college to obtain a recognised qualification. It took them three years to complete the course, and as usual, Peter found it quite easy, and Kevin copied Peter's homework, work-based assessments and exam answers. Kevin spent most of his time in class chatting up the girls who had enrolled with them. At no time during and after the course did Kevin understand the reason for performance variances, or how to calculate them, but when the final results were received in early August, they had both passed.

"This deserves a proper piss-up." Kevin had already framed his certificate, and it took pride of place on his desk. Peter had drunk more than enough on the night after their final exam. He couldn't remember much of the evening, but his hangover the next day was evidence enough that they had already taken part in one proper piss-up too many.

"A celebration this big needs the proper setting, and that can only mean a weekend at Blackpool. I'm off to see Mark to get his approval for some Team Building funding."

For some unknown reason, Mark thought that the idea of Kevin and Peter, and a couple of the other young lads in the Accounting Department having a weekend away team building in Blackpool was brill, whatever that meant, and the following Friday, Kevin's Mini was coughing and wheezing its way up the M40 towards the land of the never-ending Amusement Arcade. Against his better judgement, Peter had allowed himself to be press-ganged into the trip, and was squeezed in the back seat between Rob Davies, this year's school-leaver, and a couple of bags that wouldn't fit into the boot. Unlike Peter and Kevin's era only a few years ago, the trend for leaving school at sixteen was changing. Rob was eighteen and was waiting for his 'A' Level results. The other member of the gang was Terry, who was larger than Peter and Rob, so sat in the front passenger seat, which meant that, unlike the two in the back, he had a car window that could open enough to let out the smoke from his and Kevin's regular cigarettes. Luckily, as far as Peter was concerned, they were stuck in traffic on the M6 for some time, and didn't make it to Blackpool until late in the evening. After they'd booked into their Bed and Breakfast, they only had time for a bag of fish and chips and a couple of pints before the pubs closed. Despite being a long way from home, it was, as always, Peter's turn to buy the beers before Kevin.

"Hurry up and get the beers in Dad, before we die of thirst." Peter, as usual, was trying to keep his alcohol intake as low as possible. "We have a long day in front of us tomorrow. It would be a good idea if we drank Coke tonight instead of beer."

"Drinking coke in a pub is like shagging a fat girl." The bizarre comment made the other two turn and look at Kevin. "It's okay until someone sees you doing it."

Peter took note of the resounding laughter from all those within earshot of Kevin's remarks, and bought the beers. The lack of beer didn't stop Kevin from keeping them out until two o' clock playing on the racing car simulators in the Amusement Arcade, but at least Peter was spared his usual hangover.

Peter was rudely awakened the following morning, by Kevin kicking on his door, and he was told to get dressed for a day at the funfair. The B&B that they were staying in was a large house that had been divided into several small rooms. There were no windows in his room, so Peter had no idea what time it was. He thought that his watch must have stopped, as it only said half past eight. He jumped into the shower to try to bring his body back to life. When he ventured downstairs to the dining room, Kevin was the only person there, tucking into his full English.

"Come on Dad, get a decent fry-up inside you, we've got a long day in front of us, but keep off the baked beans, I want to attract women, not flies."

They were soon joined by Rob and Terry, and Kevin laid out his plans for the day, which included the morning at the funfair, lunchtime in the pub, the afternoon in the bookies, a trip up the Tower, and the evening doing a tour of the entertainment. If they didn't end up with female company for the night, any remaining energy could be expended on the re-match at the racing cars after the pubs closed.

As they made their way from Blackpool Tower down the Golden Mile, they made regular stops to play table football and other assorted games in the numerous Amusement arcades situated between the pubs and Fish and Chip shops. The others had learnt from the previous night's experience that Kevin was fairly enjoyable company as long as he was winning, so he emerged at the entrance to the Pleasure Beach funfair as the reigning champion of all of the games that they tried. After confirming his mis-spent youth by winning the usual worthless prize at the shooting gallery, Kevin dragged them to the queue for the 'Big One' rollercoaster. Peter tried his hardest to escape, pleading headaches and sickness to offering to buy them ice creams, but Kevin insisted that he went on with them, and Peter was too scared to say no. As they got closer and closer to the start of the ride, Peter became more and more afraid, and he was almost at the point where he was more afraid of the rollercoaster than he was of Kevin, when they were loaded aboard. Although they were all screaming when they went through the corkscrew, Peter's scream was that of complete terror. Kevin was waving both of his hands in the air, trying to get Peter to do the same, but Peter's hands were firmly gripped on the bar in front of him, because he fully expected to be thrown out of his seat to a shockingly painful death. He was too frightened to worry about anything but the imminent break up of his body onto the ground below, so he didn't start throwing up until the ride had stopped, and he'd wobbled very shakily to the exit.

The others were laughing out loud with bravado, and unexpressed relief, and followed the crowd to the presentation of photographs taken during the ride. Kevin couldn't make his mind up which was the most hilarious; the photograph of Peter looking petrified or the sight of him being re-introduced to his sausages and bacon. Although sympathy was in Kevin's dictionary, it was just a word that was between shit and syphilis. Peter's legs couldn't manage to stand back in the queue for a second journey on the rollercoaster, so he waited, propped up against the surrounding fence, trying to get some colour back into his deathly white face, whilst the others rejoined the end of the long queue to have another go. The terror of the rollercoaster was followed by the dangerous combat of the go karts. Peter decided to take a leisurely tour around the few laps of the course, but did not reckon on the buffeting that he received from the others as they flew past him. On the last lap, Kevin cut inside him at a corner, and Peter's go kart finished upside down at the far end of the track. Peter had to be retrieved by the attendants, who swore at him for his poor driving. To add insult to injury, the others had run down to laugh at Peter's predicament, and Kevin had taken a Polaroid photo of the upturned go kart, with Peter strapped in the driving seat. Apart from a small scrape here and there, Peter's lack of speed and his crash helmet had saved him from a serious injury, and he was fit to carry on with what was turning out to be one of the worst days of his life. He handed back his crash helmet and they moved to the delights of the dodgems.

The pubs closed at half past two, so they only had time for a swift two pints in the pubs on the way back from the funfair. Peter could only stomach Coke, which was probably just as well, as he could only drink about four pints before getting pissed, and there was a long night in front of them. When Peter returned from the bar with the drinks, the others were laughing at the photos of him in the upturned go kart, and throwing up next to the rollercoaster.

The next item on their agenda was the visit to the Betting Shop. Peter had never been in a Betting Shop before. Between large gulps of his pint, and pulls on his cigarette, Kevin explained the intricacies of choosing a horse to bet on, and how to place your bet. They left the bright afternoon sunshine and entered the dark smoke-filled bookmakers. Peter looked at the newspapers stuck on the wall, and read the write-ups on the horses involved in the next race. It seemed obvious to him which horse would win, and wrote his bet on the betting slip. Kevin looked at Peter's writing in the same way that he'd copied his course work ever since they'd met at school.

"A pound? You tight ker-nob. Is that all you're going to bet?"

"Is there a limit then?"

"No, you can bet what you want, but a pound's not very exciting is it?"

"I don't really do 'exciting', I'm just putting a bet on, like you told me to."

"Do you expect this horse to win?"

"Oh yes, I don't expect any of the other horses to be anywhere near it at the finish."

"Why not?"

"It's just logical."

Kevin looked at the starting price for Peter's horse. Three to one. Peter was always clever at working things out, and a fiver wouldn't go amiss, so he scribbled his bet quickly on his slip and handed it over the counter, and waited for the race to start. It was only a five furlong sprint, so just over a minute later, Peter's horse had flashed past the winning post yards in front of its rivals.

"Right then Dad. What's going to win the next race?"

Peter looked at the details of the runners in the next race. His eyes were streaming in the smoky atmosphere, and he started to cough. After a few minutes he shakily pointed out his selection, and then rushed outside for some fresh air. Kevin followed him outside.

"Are you sure it's going to win, it's a big price?"

Peter nodded between coughs. "Pay the betting tax on the amount that you are betting, or you will have to pay tax on your stake and all of your winnings."

"How do you know that, you told me that you'd never bet before?"

"There's a chart on the wall. It shows a range of amounts that you could put on, and how much tax you have to pay on the amount that you bet."

Kevin went back inside and wrote out his bet. He added back the amount that the taxman had taken from his winnings from the first race, and put twenty pounds, plus the amount for the tax on the stake on Peter's selection. The other two had been watching Peter and Kevin, and decided that they would like a piece of the action too. The horse romped in at ten to one, and they had just won enough money to pay for the whole weekend, and then more. Envious eyes looked at them as they collected their winnings and went outside to get the next winner from Peter. Peter was still coughing and his eyes were now rubbed red.

"Come on Dad, we're on a roll here. Get back inside and give us the winner of the next race".

Peter was still barely able to breathe, and there was no way that he could go back inside. The others didn't realise that they only had to go to a newsagents and buy Peter a copy of the *Racing Post* so that he could sit outside and look at all of the horses' form to choose the winners, so they had to be content with the small fortune that they had already won, and moved to the closest Amusement Arcade.

Kevin was in a really good mood, and was almost nice to Peter. He was laughing at the postcards and joke badges outside a shop, and went inside to buy some of them, and still laughing, dragged Peter to the closest table-football game, where he beat him eleven nil. Peter staggered slowly back to the B and B to get some rest, whilst the others went up to the top of Blackpool Tower. He had still not fully recovered from the turbulence of the rollercoaster. Lack of sleep from the night before plus the crash in the go kart followed by the smoky atmosphere of the betting shop had wiped him out. He was confused, and had to retrace his steps a few times until he finally found where they were staying. He drank a pint of water, and then fell on his bed for a coma-like sleep.

Two hours later Peter's door was being kicked again.
"Come on Dad, we're going on the pull with the money that we won. Hurry up and get your best kit on."
Peter didn't really have a best set of clothes. As far he was concerned, flared trousers, wide collars and platform shoes had never gone out of fashion, and all of his clothes looked the same. The four inch heels almost made him the same height as his colleagues. He had neither understood nor bothered with colour co-ordination, and it didn't matter what colour his shoes were, as they were completely covered by the large expanse at the bottom of his trousers. He still hadn't had the chance to unpack his bag, so put on whatever was pulled out first.

Peter had lost his breakfast next to the rollercoaster, and had not felt well enough until now to eat anything else, so his stomach was making loud growling noises.
"Are we going for a proper meal?"

"What do you mean, a 'proper' meal?" As far as Kevin was concerned, food was food, and the faster he received it, the better.

"Can we go somewhere for a salad?"

"A fucking salad? I might shag like a rabbit, but I certainly don't eat like one. If you want a salad, you can have one on top of your cheeseburger."

That, apparently, was the end of the discussion about food, and they made their way to the closest burger bar. Suitably fed, they looked for the closest pub, which in Blackpool, was only ever a matter of yards away. Despite the others having won on Peter's horse, he was still pushed to the bar to buy the first round. The pub was already full, and Peter kept being pushed aside by the other customers angling for a position at the bar, so it was some time before he returned with three pints and a coke.

"You're not going to enjoy yourself much on soft drinks."

"I'm just pacing myself, I can't drink anywhere near as much as you can. Also I tend to fart all the time after a few beers." Peter hoped that he wouldn't be made to drink as much as the others, and thought that his comment about the flatulent side effect would put them off, but every time the others bought a round, Peter was given a pint of lager. Whenever it was Peter's turn, which seemed to come round faster than the others, he bought himself a coke. They had a tour of the pubs down the Golden Mile. The holiday makers taking part in the karaoke appeared to have had more than enough to drink, and had trouble keeping up with the words, and the tune. One of the pubs had a Tom Jones impersonator belting out the old classics, whilst the crowd sang along with 'Delilah' and 'It's Not Unusual'. This was quite entertaining, until Kevin decided that it was too noisy in there to arrange a warm bed for the night with one of the many females around, so they moved to another pub. They would have had much more luck had they stayed outside the bars, and chatted to the girls as they wandered up and down the main street, but the bars were where the beer was, so they stayed out of luck until closing time.

They still had plenty of money left from their winnings, and the lap-dancing bar looked interesting from the outside, so they walked unsteadily down the stairs. Terry brought four pints to their table, and they were immediately surrounded by scantily clad young ladies. Peter turned red with embarrassment at their interest in him, so he made a quick call to the toilets, hoping that they would have moved away by the time he returned. Rob and Terry were quite pissed by now, and shared the cost of a bottle of something bubbly for the girls. Kevin was still relatively sober, but was enjoying the attention that they were receiving. Although it was getting late, it was still warm, so the beer was going down quite quickly, even for Peter. He was just about to get another round in, when he suddenly felt incredibly tired. Peter was not used to staying out late in bars, and he also didn't usually go on rollercoasters and go karts. His eye-lids became too heavy to keep open. He slumped in his chair and fell into a deep sleep.

When Peter woke up the following morning, he had a terrible hangover. His head was throbbing, his stomach was churning, and his tongue was far too big for his incredibly dry mouth. He was still dressed, and laid out on top of his duvet. His large heels made it even more difficult to stagger to the sink to get a glass of water. He looked in the mirror, and a pair of sunken, bloodshot eyes stared meekly back. He had no idea how he got back to his bed the night before, but hoped that the others were just as ill as he was, so that he could get undressed, go back to bed, and try to sleep it off for a few hours.

The journey back to Oxford was much quieter than the journey north. They stopped twice for a drink and some fresh air, and Peter went straight to bed on his arrival home, to try to be alive enough for work the next day.

Peter still looked and felt like 'death warmed up' on Monday morning. His eyes were no longer bloodshot, but his face was still pale, with an interesting grey / green tinge. He was well enough to suffer the mental requirements of his job, but still had problems at both ends of his body if he moved too quickly. After one of his numerous visits to the loo, he found an envelope on his desk. His face turned even whiter than it already was when he pulled out the photocopy of a photograph of him at the lap dancing bar. One of the almost naked girls was rubbing herself in an erotic manner against a spread-eagled Peter. Peter locked the picture in his draw, and dragged his body slowly to Kevin's desk. Kevin looked up and smiled at his visibly shaken colleague.

"All right dancing boy? What do you think of the photo?"

"Where's the original?"

"Safe and sound, thank you."

"Well, I need it."

"Oh, I think that I can have much more fun with it than you can!"

"OK, I'll buy it from you. How much do you want?"

"You can give me the name of a winner this Saturday. None of your short-priced favourites, I want a horse that will win at a good price."

"I can't guarantee that."

"I'm sure if you try hard enough you'll come up with a name. Of course, if the horse loses, you'll have to reimburse me with my stake, and then come up with a horse that wins."

Peter went back to his desk and slumped in his chair. Rob had watched him talking to Kevin, and picked up some paperwork and went to Peter's desk, pointing to it.

"Make out I'm asking you about this invoice."

"I'm not in the mood for games."

"I know. He's shown you the photo hasn't he?"

"How do you know about that?"

"Kevin paid the girl to pretend that she was dancing against you, whilst he took the photo. A bouncer came over and threw us out, and we had to carry you home, but Kevin managed to keep his camera."

"I was feeling OK when we went in there. I can't really understand why I fell asleep so quickly."

"Kevin drugged your drink when you went to the toilet." He gave Peter a small bottle. "This fell out of his pocket when he got the money out to pay the girl. There's still a lot left in it."

"Do me a favour Rob, don't tell Kevin what you've just told me, and don't tell anyone about this bottle, OK?"

"Yeah, sure."

Peter knew how difficult it would be to get his own back on Kevin, he'd already tried that at the funeral parlour, and lost badly, so this time he would bide his time, and make sure that his plan was fool proof.

On the Saturday, Peter looked at the racing page of the newspaper, and chose a horse that was eight to one. His head throbbed due to the effort, and he rubbed his temples as he phoned Kevin, and told him the horse's name. Peter watched the racing on television that afternoon, and his horse, naturally, won. He was relieved that he would get the photo back without the humiliation of others seeing it, and he began to feel a little better. He hadn't regained his appetite since the Blackpool trip, but now he finally felt hungry, and went off to make himself a salad.

On Monday Peter went to Kevin's desk and asked for the photo.

"I considered giving you the photo back, but I had such a good night on Saturday celebrating my good fortune at the betting shop, that I've decided to give you the chance to pick me another winner next Saturday."

"It's not that easy, you know. It calls for a lot of concentration, and I end up with a migraine."

"I ended up with a hangover after spending my winnings on drink, but I'm willing to give it another go. I might consider giving you the photo after one more horse next Saturday."

Peter knew that Kevin wouldn't give him the photo, so he had to think of a way to change his mind. On the following Saturday, Peter looked at the racing page again, chose a horse, and wrote its name down on a piece of paper. He put the piece of paper in an envelope and phoned Kevin.

"Come on then, Dad, what's the horse's name?"

19

"I'm not going to tell you over the phone, I need to see you, and the photo."

"I'm just off to the pub, meet me outside of the Gloucester Arms in half an hour. You do remember where the Glock is, don't you? We went there after the final AAT exam."

"Yes, it's next to the bus station."

Kevin, as expected, was late, but Peter was still pleased to see him. He could get back the photo.

"Have you got the photo?"

"Of course I have. What's the horse's name?"

"I'll tell you when you've given me the photo."

"How can I be sure that it will win?"

"Have all of the other horses won?"

"Yeah, but you might not have thought about this one."

"Don't worry, this one will win."

"No, I think I'll have some more fun with the photo. I wonder what the FD will think when I show it to him?"

"He'll think that I'm a single, young man who fell asleep in a lap-dancing bar after too many beers. Do you want this horse's name, or are you intending to stay in tonight?"

"Look, stop pissing about, you ker-nob, and give me the horse's name."

"No, you've had your fun at my expense, and I want it to stop."

Peter was feeling sick, and his head started to swim. He tried his best not to show it, but couldn't stop the inevitable fart from creeping out. A small crowd of people had gathered in the alleyway at the entrance to the pub, and were watching the argument. Kevin took the photo from his pocket and threw it to the floor.

"The joke's started to wear a bit thin anyway. I'll find something else to amuse me next week. What's the horse's name?"

Peter picked up the photo and put it in his pocket, and then gave Kevin the envelope.

"If this horse doesn't win, you're in the shit Dad. You mark my words!"

'I'm always in the shit,' Peter thought to himself. 'It's just the depth that varies.'

Whether it was due to the dull end of the dispute, or Peter's fart, the crowd disbursed into the Glock. Peter caught the bus home, and watched his horse romp home on the TV.

Peter and Kevin's success at AAT encouraged the FD to put them forward for training as Chartered Institute of Management Accountants, or CIMA, as it was better known. CIMA was pronounced See-Ma, so Kevin had trouble spelling it, but Peter joked that he had problems spelling AAT; obviously when Kevin was out of earshot! They were exempt the first year of the course due to having passed AAT, so Peter started another three years of studying, whilst Kevin started another three years of chatting up the girls at the lectures, reading books that he could not understand, scratching his head, and eventually, albeit quite easily, getting Peter to complete his assignments. Their surnames were almost identical, so they were always sat next to each other for their CIMA exams every six months. The large hall in which they sat their exams was always full of students, and, as their surnames started with a letter near to the end of the alphabet, they were seated at the back of the hall. Kevin became adept at getting Peter to pass him his workings and answers or show him his answer sheet without being caught by the adjudicator.

Mark had started to give Peter more responsibility around the office, which was good, but Kevin was also beginning to get more responsible jobs as well, which wasn't so good, for Kevin, for the company, and especially for Peter, who ended up doing more and more work. The resulting pay rise gave Kevin the unexpected chance to buy his own house in Kidlington. House prices in and around Oxford had begun to rocket upwards, and they were a good investment. The high rate of inflation over the last few years had been matched by higher than normal pay rises, so after a few years, the mortgage was not the killer of social life that it used to be. Kevin was not a teenager anymore, and wanted some space when he brought girls back from the pub. There was no way that he could get them into his bed whilst he shared his bedroom with his younger brother. He jumped at the chance to move out of his family's crowded house.

He was still impressed by his father's ability to out drink and outfight anyone in the area, and by the way that his father used his physical presence to get others to do what he wanted them to, including a long string of short-term, and sometimes, long-term relationships with other women, despite always being short of money. The entertainment value of his mother's constant nagging and arguments with his father had greatly diminished, but his father dealt with her as quickly and efficiently as someone who upset him in the pub. The regular black-eyes that his mother sported had ceased to be a badge of honour. They had lived in this house since he had been born, and yet she still managed to walk into one of the doors every time she had an argument with his father.

 If Kevin found that he couldn't afford the mortgage payments he could easily get one of his mates to move into the spare bedroom to ease the burden until his next pay rise, or he could sell the house at a profit, and rent a bedsit like his friends had done when they wanted to leave home. At worst, he could always move back in with his parents.
Kevin smiled when he considered a much better option; he could always find a way to persuade Peter to give him the names of a couple of winning horses.

TWO

The following summer, the school-leaver joining the Accounts Department was a pretty blonde named Susan. Peter thought that she was lovely. He tried to ask her out a few times, but his shyness always got the better of him. Although Kevin moved at his usual snail-like pace, he still made his move before Peter could pluck up the courage to do so. In all the years that Peter had known him, Kevin had only ever relied on bullying and insults to get people to do what he wanted. He was amazed at Kevin's witty chat-up lines, and his easy charm, and Susan giggled at his childish, if smutty comments, and his ability to belch and say 'Bollocks' at the same time. Although she seemed quite posh compared to Kevin, Peter was sure that she would have applauded if Kevin had performed his party trick of setting fire to one of his farts.

Despite her parents' wishes, Susan had left school at sixteen as she felt that she'd had enough formal education. She wanted to be treated as a grown up, and learn from the University of Life. Susan must have been one of the oldest girls in her year at school, because not long after joining them, it was her seventeenth birthday, and they all went to the pub for a few drinks after work.
"Oy Dad, lend me a fiver."
"We've only just got paid. You can't be skint already!"
"It's my round, and I can't find my wallet. She's been drinking double Gin and Tonics, and she's still fucking sober!!"
Peter looked over at Susan. Kevin's interpretation of sober was obviously very different to his. She was starting to look a bit glazed, and had a silly grin on her face.
"I think it's about time she went home, she's only young."
Peter was getting concerned, but Kevin took it as an invitation. Kevin went over to her and put his arm around her. "Are you having a happy birthday?"
Susan smiled at him, and leant towards him and gave him a big kiss.
"This face is leaving in five minutes – be on it."
Susan giggled. "I'd better get my bag."

Kevin had fought off the urge to get pissed with the others so that he could drive, and it was now paying off. They walked back to his Mini, and Susan became more and more unstable as the fresh air took effect.

Susan couldn't remember much about what happened between the time that she left the pub and the time that Kevin dropped her off just down the road from her parents' house the following morning, but as far as she was concerned, Kevin and Susan were now what she called 'an item', and within a few weeks, Kevin had been invited home to meet Mummy and Daddy.

"Why can't we meet them in the pub? I'd feel much more at home in the pub, and not so embarrassed if I do anything wrong."

"All we're doing is having a small supper and chat with them, and then you and I can go out. You're my first proper boyfriend, so they're bound to want to meet you sooner or later."

"But I don't have any posh clothes."

"Just wear your office trousers and a clean shirt. You don't even have to wear a tie, so it'll be less formal than work."

Susan always dressed smartly and spoke with a posh accent. Kevin was worried that he would show himself up, but he knew that unless he agreed, he wouldn't get his end away for the foreseeable future, so had to relent.

"It's not going to be anything posh is it?" Kevin had been brought up on good old plain English food, and didn't like the idea of eating the new cuisine from the continent that was currently all the rage.

"It will be a simple spaghetti, nothing more. If you're lucky, we'll have Ice Cream for desert."

Kevin was so relieved that he didn't notice Susan's childish mispronunciation of dessert. He'd had spaghetti loads of times, but was surprised that a supposedly well-to-do family would serve spaghetti to their darling daughter's boyfriend on his first visit to their house.

Kevin starved himself all Saturday so that he could eat what was put in front of him however horrible it tasted. He usually took his clothes to his mother on Saturday mornings, and received them back washed and ironed later the next day, so he frantically searched through his laundry basket, and found his cleanest dirty shirt.

Susan's family lived in a large house in Summertown. He gave Susan's mother the flowers that he'd bought at the local petrol station on the way, and she took them from him politely. Susan's mother was still a good-looking woman, and wore an attractive summer dress. Kevin's mind immediately conjured up the image of Susan and her mother in a threesome with him, which he had problems getting out of his head, until two small dogs appeared who tried to rip off his trousers at the ankles, whilst bursting his ear-drums with their high-pitched yapping. Susan's father was in the living room, and came out to rescue Kevin from the ferocious pack. "Don't worry about Brahms and Liszt, they'll ignore you as soon as they get used to your smell. Come into the drawing room and have a sherry. Please call me Geoffrey."
Kevin had always thought that dogs had the uncanny ability to read peoples' minds, and were enraged by his impure thoughts about their master's mate. He stifled the urge to kick them away, managed to wade through them into the living room, and accepted the already filled glass from the tray on the coffee table.
"Cheers" said Susan's father.
"Chin up" said Susan's mother.
Kevin, not really sure of what to say or do, sniffed at the top of the glass, then threw its contents down his neck in one go. The lack of food and the warmth of the sherry brought an instant colour to his face, and he was happy to sit down when offered. There then followed half an hour of mind-bogglingly boring conversation about Geoffrey's job in the City and Kevin's prospects, accompanied by two more glasses of sherry, which Kevin had learnt to sip. Although Kevin liked talking about himself in the local pub, he was less forthcoming in this type of company. Susan's mother started to talk about her hobby as the leading lady in the local Amateur Dramatics

25

club, and that she expected Susan to be more involved now that she had left school.

At long last, Susan's mother got up to go and serve 'supper' and they were shortly summoned through to the dining room. Kevin had never seen anything like it in his life. One of the large bowls in the middle of the table contained long, thin worms, another brimmed with mincemeat in a red sauce, and a third bowl contained slices of garlic bread. Susan dished up Kevin's meal, whilst Kevin stared at the food, and the fork and spoon next to his plate. The others started to tuck into their food with great enthusiasm and strange slurping noises, whilst Kevin's mind swam as he tried to think of a way to get him out of his predicament. He stood up and looked at Susan. "I'm sorry, I feel awful. Please excuse me," he stammered. "I can't face food at the moment, I need to leave". Susan and her parents watched open-mouthed as he walked quickly outside and slammed the front door before the two dogs who had rushed after him could have another go at his trousers. His feet had automatically taken him to the closest pub, and when Susan found him, he was tucking into his second meat pie from the pub's hot plate, with a cigarette burning in the ashtray next to his half-finished pint.

"I thought you weren't feeling very well?" Susan looked accusingly at the pie.

"I'm fucking starving, I've not eaten all day."

"So what was wrong with my mother's spaghetti, I thought that it was superb."

"I didn't know what to do with it."

"You said that you'd had spaghetti before."

"Yeah, spaghetti hoops, and alphabetti spaghetti, but not huge worms like those!"

The pie and the pint had made him feel much better, and Susan burst out laughing at what was probably the funniest thing she'd ever heard, and hugged Kevin in sympathy, but backed away at the smell of his cigarette.

"How can you smoke and eat at the same time, it's disgusting. If I had my way people would be banned from smoking in public houses."

"Don't be so stupid. You'd never get a government stupid enough to try to get that through parliament, the voting public would get rid of them at the next election."

"But you'd come home without stinking of smoke."

"It just won't happen."

Not long after the infamous 'Supper', Susan came to Kevin's office with a pantomime script. "We're doing Aladdin this year, and we need two Policemen. We've had the first read through of the script, but there aren't enough men for the cast."

"And?"

"I thought that you would take part?"

"I don't think so. I'm not into that arty-farty crap."

"It'll be fun, and we can spend more time together. I'll make it worth your while."

Kevin re-considered his position on arty-farty crap. "What do I have to do?"

"It's only a few walk-on, walk-off appearances. The two Policemen are very funny, and the audience will love you."

"Two Policemen?"

"Yes, one big one and a small one."

"And which one am I then?"

"Well, the big one, obviously."

"Are you going to be the small one?"

"Not if we can get a man to do the part. What about Peter, he's quite clever."

"I thought that you wanted a man?"

"If you've never done it before, it'll be a lot easier with someone you know."

"Right, leave it to me, I'll tell Dad that me and him are the two Policemen. Are you Aladdin?"

"No, that'll be Mummy. I'll do the make-up."

"She's a bit old to play a young boy isn't she?"

"She still has a good figure, and she'll be wearing lots of make-up."

Kevin had the mental image of Susan's mother with a short skirt and fishnet tights, and had to agree with Susan's comments.

"Why aren't you on stage if it's supposed to be fun?"

"I like doing the make-up for everyone, especially for the panto. Now that really is fun."

Susan skipped back to her office whilst Kevin went looking for Peter.

"Alright Dad, guess what?"

"What?"

"Good guess. Have you ever wanted to be a Policeman?"

"Not really."

"Well, I'm giving you the chance to be one now."

Peter had known Kevin for years, and still didn't have a clue what he was talking about.

"Susan's Amateur Dramatics club are doing Aladdin this Christmas, and we have been chosen to play the two comedy Policemen."

"We're still studying for CIMA. We'll need to learn the lines and spend time that we don't have rehearsing."

"Don't you think that it's about time you started to get out a bit more? When was the last time you did anything apart for work and studying?"

Peter didn't have time to answer, which was lucky, as it was such a long time since he had gone out anywhere, that he couldn't remember.

"Right, I'll pick you up at seven next Tuesday."

Peter was surprised how much he enjoyed himself. As well as getting the chance to spend time with Susan outside work, he was really fitting in well with the people in the club, and despite his natural shyness, was soon on friendly terms with the rest of the cast, especially Susan's mother, Dawn, who was very attractive and charming. Kevin was no longer as charming with Susan as he had been when they first met, and he reverted to form by starting to play his tricks on her. He finally had a chance to use one of the badges that he'd bought at Blackpool and couldn't wait to use it. One night at rehearsals, Susan kept hearing people laughing as she passed them, and eventually clicked on to the fact that it was her that they were laughing at. She was no longer a little girl, and did not like being shown up in front of her mother, and her boyfriend.

28

"Apparently there's a big joke in here tonight, and I'm the butt of it!"

Kevin rushed to her side, and put his arms around her. "Why would anyone want to make a joke at your expense?" He tried to take the badge off of the back of her pullover, but she felt what was happening, and pulled herself away. She took off her pullover and looked at the badge in disbelief. It was a big badge, and she found it quite easily. In the middle it said KEVIN, and around the outside it said SEX INSTRUCTOR - FIRST LESSON FREE. Susan didn't have much of a sense of humour, and could see nothing at all funny about this at all. She stormed out of the hall crying, vowing never to come back.

Peter could not understand why Kevin didn't look concerned at what he'd done. Susan was far too nice for him, but he didn't seem to care.

"Aren't you going after her?"

"No. She'll be back at the next rehearsal."

"She looked pretty pissed off to me."

"You just don't know the first thing about women. Treat 'em mean and keep 'em keen."

The next day at work, Susan stayed in her part of the office, so Kevin went to see her as she usually brought his lunch in, and he was getting hungry.

"Aren't we having lunch today?"

"Do you think that you deserve it?"

"I think that you are over re-acting. Everyone else thought that it was funny."

"Everyone else wasn't being made to look a fool."

"You weren't made to look a fool at all. It was funny."

"No it wasn't, and if you felt anything for me, you wouldn't have done it."

"I feel a lot for you, and you know it."

"You used a strange way to show it."

"How do you want me to show it to you then?"

"Surprise me."

"OK then, why don't you move in with me."

Oh shit! Kevin had no idea why he'd said it, and hoped that she was still pissed off enough with him to turn him down. Susan stopped dead. She didn't expect a surprise this big. "Really! What now? It would be great to have our first Christmas together."

"I think that you'd better speak to your parents before you make a move as big as this."

"I'm seventeen. They couldn't stop me moving out if they wanted to."

"Technically, they can. You need to get their approval."

"It won't be a problem. We can tell them tonight at dinner."

"There's no way that I'm going round to your house for dinner tonight! Your father tries to get me pissed, your dogs attack me, and your mother feeds me worms!"

Susan's mood had changed completely. She had a huge grin on her face, and she laughed at his jokes. Unfortunately, Kevin wasn't joking.

The much-awaited opening night of the pantomime finally arrived. Peter was word-perfect within a few days of receiving his script, and fell into the part with great ease. Kevin hadn't bothered to learn his lines, and was constantly being prompted by Peter, which the audience thought was part of the act. They had a comedy song near to the end of the panto, directing the two halves of the audience to sing against one-another, which enabled the rest of the cast to change into their posh clothes for the final scene. The Policemen wore police uniforms irrespective of what they were doing, so had no need to change their outfits. The song went down really well with the audience. Kevin was completely tone deaf, and out of tune, but the audience thought that this was also part of the act, and a large cheer went up when they made their appearance for the final walk down to the front of the stage at the end of the show.

Susan enjoyed her freedom as head of make-up. Instead of just slapping five and nine face cream over everyone, she spent ages on her mother's face, until she looked as fresh and beautiful as she did twenty years ago. She gave Peter an oriental moustache, and tried to get Kevin to wear a false beard.

"I think that it really suits you, it makes you look more serious and mature."

Kevin considered himself to be too good looking to want to cover up his face, but had to agree that it did make him look more grown-up.

The Amateur Dramatics club had a party after the final performance, and all those involved had a chance to let their hair down after the hard work and stress of the previous three months. Much to Kevin's dismay, Susan's mother, had changed from her short dress to a pair of jeans, so he was no longer able to secretly crane his neck every time that she was in her costume, to get a better look at the tops of her legs. Kevin could never do anything like that too secretly anyway, and had been caught quite often by Dawn, who had started to like the attention that she was getting. After a few drinks, Peter lost his usual shyness and told the cast how busy he was during the day at work, and that he spent his evenings studying for his Accounting qualification, so had to get out of bed really early in the morning to find the time to learn his lines. Susan could never understand double-entendres, so missed the reason why her mother smiled when Kevin said that he often looked forward to the chance of getting up at the crack of Dawn.

Despite Kevin's constant barbed comments, usually about her cooking or her weight, Susan still loved Kevin, and was in love with the fact that she had found someone to live together with. She quite often had to comment on Kevin's table manners, especially the way that he ate his food, and she had noticed that he had started to take more time when he was eating, to keep his mouth closed when he was chewing his food, and not to talk when his mouth was full, something that he usually told her off for when they were in bed together. One thing that she had not managed to do was to get him to wash his hands after having a wee.

"I was taught to wash my hands after going to the toilet."

"Well, I was taught not to piss on my fingers."

After being together for nearly a year, he only seemed to show any feelings toward her in bed, but she expected him to propose in the not too distant future, so was happy with the ways things were. She really missed the companionship of her parents' dogs, and dropped numerous hints that she would like a puppy for her birthday present in the next few weeks. When the day finally arrived, she got out of bed to make the tea, and burn two slices of toast. Kevin no longer had to set the alarm clock as he was woken every morning by the smoke alarm being set off by the toast burning in the kitchen. He dragged himself out of bed to yet again disconnect the smoke alarm battery, and trudged wearily down to the kitchen. He gave Susan a kiss, and a badly wrapped present and card. Susan took off the wrapping to discover a T shirt with a large slogan on the front stating 'FAT GIRLS ARE HARDER TO KIDNAP'. Susan laughed at Kevin's perceived attempt at humour and awaited details of her proper present.

"Am I getting my proper present later?"

"I thought that we could go out for a meal for your birthday." This is usually a bonus choice, as it not only puts Susan in a good mood, but also gives Kevin the chance to have chips, and food which isn't burnt to a crisp.

"What about my puppy?"

"You don't want a puppy, barking all of the time, crapping on the floor, ripping up the furniture, and having to be taken out for walks at all hours."

"My parents' dogs have never done that, and I would be happy to take him for walks"

"My parents' dogs have, and it was always me that had to take them out, especially when I was watching football on the telly."

"But I thought that I was getting a puppy for my birthday."

"I've warned about thinking enough times already. You should leave difficult things like thinking to me."

The T shirt was no longer funny. She threw it to the floor, and rushed upstairs, sobbing her heart out. Kevin heard the bedroom door slam, sighed, and started to scrape the burnt bits off of the toast. He ate half a slice, but even the large helping of Marmite couldn't overcome the taste of the burnt toast. He threw the toast into the bin, and spat on it. 'It will take all day to get the taste out of his mouth,' he thought to himself. He sighed, and followed Susan upstairs. He didn't really care that he was being a bastard, but it was unfair on Susan that she spent the whole of her eighteenth birthday upset. She turned over, away from him and pulled the duvet over her head when he entered the bedroom.

"Listen, if I tell you a secret, you have to act surprised when we meet your parents at the Randolph hotel tonight."

"We're not meeting my parents tonight." Susan mumbled from underneath the duvet.

"That's just one of the secrets. Did you really think that all I bought you for your eighteenth birthday was a T shirt?"

"I didn't know what to think after you were so nasty to me."

"Your parents asked me to keep it all a secret. You know how much they spoil you, and that they would treat you to something extra special on your eighteenth birthday, so they've booked a table for four at the Randolph, and they're picking up the tab." He paused. "They've also paid for a puppy for you to collect tomorrow."

Susan's head sprang out from underneath the duvet. "A puppy? Really? What sort?"

"Look, I've told you too much already. This was all supposed to be a surprise, but I could see how upset you were."

"I wondered why you were being so horrid. Come here, so that you can make it up to me."

Kevin got back into bed. This would make him late for work, but at least it was for a good cause. Susan had wriggled out of her clothes, and pushed Kevin's head down her body. She arched her back as Kevin's tongue made contact, and looked down, smiling at him. Kevin peered back up at her through the expanse of curly hair. "Do you really think that a beard suits me?"

Kevin and Susan arrived at work later than normal. The knowing grins of the office staff matched the huge smile on Susan's face, whilst Kevin had to agree that his thought about not getting rid of the taste of burnt toast had been completely wrong. Mark was waiting with a birthday card and a large bunch of flowers for Susan, and she gave him a hug and a kiss on the cheek.

Peter blushed, wishing that he was the person receiving the kiss, and looked down at the small handbag in her hand, "Have you hidden the cakes?"

"I'll pop out to the shop and get some for the tea break" Kevin's smile disappeared, at the thought of more unnecessary expense that they couldn't afford. "I can't see the need for cakes, she's already had a muffin."

The evening went better than Kevin expected, and Susan showed an unexpected talent for acting by looking surprised when they met up with her parents at the Randolph, and she gave them both a warm kiss on the cheek. Kevin wasn't into all this kissing in public stuff, and hid behind the bag that he had brought with him. Susan didn't really have that many friends, and had been out of touch with them since she'd moved in with Kevin, so she much preferred having a posh meal out with her parents than a wild party for her eighteenth birthday. Although Geoffrey and Dawn had a glass of sherry on their arrival, Kevin ordered a pint of best bitter, which had grown in stature as a posh drink in the Randolph due to the locally-based Inspector Morse TV programmes. Kevin's mind raced when he looked at the menu at their table. He couldn't understand much of the curly words written on the sheet, but the high prices were written in easy to read numbers, and he was greatly relieved when he remembered that Susan's parents were paying for the meal.

"It's a shame there's no spaghetti on the menu," Dawn felt that she knew Kevin well enough to tease him.

"Don't they do proper food?" Kevin had read the menu three times, and was sure that he wouldn't like entrecote.

Geoffrey looked at Kevin from over his menu, "I'm having the steak, but beware, you get a large portion here."

"More than I get at home then!" Dawn smiled at Kevin, and he wished that Susan had inherited some of her mother's quick wit.

The conversation consisted of idle chatter whilst they waited for their food to arrive. Dawn caught Kevin looking at the low-cut top of her dress, which provoked an explanation.

"I was admiring your sun tan," wishing he could find out whether it was an all-over tan. "Did you have a nice holiday?"

"Although some people are now saying that the South of France is becoming passé, we still love it. And if you're wondering, I'm getting too old for an all-over tan these days, so it's only a chicken suntan."

"Oh Mummy, you have nothing to be frightened of to show off your figure."

"I'm not frightened. A chicken sun tan is where the best parts are the white parts."

Geoffrey decided that it was time that he joined in the conversation before it went too down-market. "Are you not going anywhere this year? There's still time."

"Not this year Daddy. Most of our money is still going towards the mortgage."

"We did have a day at Longleat." Kevin thought that he had better show them that he could afford to show their daughter some entertainment.

"It was really good. We went into the Lions' enclosure, and Kevin couldn't remember if he'd locked the boot of his Mini, after we took the picnic out. As the car's getting old, the boot is prone to opening of its own accord unless it's locked. We spent half an hour waiting for the boot to drop open, and for us to end up as the Lions' dinner. After the Lions, we went into the monkey enclosure. Kevin checked the boot lock before we went in there, which was lucky because they jumped all over the car, and would have definitely found their way in if it hadn't been locked."

"They still took off one of the windscreen wipers." Kevin was still upset at the extra expenditure.

"And they tried to rip off the radio aerial." Susan recalled the sight of the monkeys causing damage to each vehicle as they drove quickly to the exit "They really are very naughty animals. Michael Jackson, the pop singer, has a monkey called Bubbles, and my friend told me that he's always spanking it."

The ensuing silence was rescued by the waiter as he returned to their table, with a bottle of posh red wine. They toasted Susan with the wine and wished her happy birthday. Kevin opened the bag he'd brought with him, and gave Susan a large wrapped present. She took off the wrapping to reveal a waxy Barbour jacket. For the first time tonight she looked confused, until her father smiled at her.

"You can't walk a gundog unless you're wearing a Barbour jacket."

Susan managed to keep the look of realisation from her face, and looked under the table for the hidden gundog.

"We've bought a German Short-Haired Pointer puppy for you, to pick up tomorrow morning." Susan squealed with delight, and rushed over to her father to give him a huge hug. She loved Brahms and Liszt, but much preferred a real dog like a GSP. She had problems holding back the tears of happiness, and moved quickly to the wash rooms to repair her make-up before the food arrived. Geoffrey walked with her, struggling to keep up, leaving Kevin alone with Dawn.

"I've had an idea," Dawn looked into Kevin's eyes. "Why don't you pop round one evening, and I'll show you how to eat spaghetti."

Kevin had the feeling that he was been propositioned, and was unsure how to react. "I was going to ask Susan to show me."

"Has she learnt how to cook spaghetti Bolognese since she left home?"

"She hasn't really learnt how to 'cook' anything really. We normally make do with canned food, ready meals or take-aways."

"What are you doing on Tuesday?"

Kevin usually went to the pub on Tuesdays to play darts.

"Nothing I can't miss."

"That's fixed then. Eight o'clock on Tuesday. Don't wear anything too posh, in case it gets sauce all over it. There's no need to tell Susan, it'll be a nice surprise for her the next time that we have spaghetti."

Susan and Geoffrey arrived back at the table as the waiter approached with their food, and the table went quiet for a while, except for the chewing noises and the clanking of silver cutlery on their plates. Everyone remained in good spirits until it was time to leave. Kevin noticed Susan talking quietly to her mother. Susan blushed and giggled, and Dawn gave Kevin a knowing smile.

Geoffrey didn't even raise an eyebrow at the astronomically huge bill, it was worth it to see his daughter so happy. Susan threw her arms around her father, and thanked him again for her present, and Kevin kissed Dawn on the cheek. It was still warm outside, so Geoffrey and Dawn walked home, whilst Kevin and Susan caught a taxi from St Giles. Susan was all over Kevin in the back of the taxi, and he was getting quite embarrassed at her show of affection in public. He just managed to get her inside his house before she pounced on him.

"Go easy, we've got to be up early in the morning to collect your puppy." Kevin's pleas were ignored, as Susan pulled off his trousers.

The usual Saturday morning hangover could not dampen Susan's enthusiasm to get up and out to the dog breeder. There were only two dogs left, one of them coloured solid liver and the other one was liver and white. Both of the dogs wagged their docked tails at their new visitors. The liver and white dog looked the most like the dog in the Barbour advertisement, so Susan chose him. He fitted easily into her hands as she picked him up. "I'll call him Jaeger."

"That's a dress shop isn't it?"

"It's the German word for hunter, except that they use an umlaut instead of the e after the a."

Kevin had no idea what she was talking about, and thought it best to change the subject. He turned to the breeder for some guidance on how to look after the dog.

"What should we feed it?"

"I feed my dogs boiled tripe, but if you don't like the smell of tripe cooking in your kitchen, or you don't have the time to boil it, then he will be OK on tinned tripe dog food."

Kevin hoped that it didn't taste too bad, as it would probably be an improvement on Susan's cooking when he was hungry.

Susan looked up from stroking the puppy. "We were thinking of buying him a cage to sleep in until he's house trained. Is that a good idea?"

"He will probably howl all night if he's locked in a cage. It would probably be better if you put him in the kitchen in a cardboard box for his first few weeks, with a towel in the bottom. I'll give you a piece of his bedding here to remind him of his family. He will be happier if he can walk around, even if he is enclosed in one room. You shouldn't expect a puppy to go all night without having a wee, so just put him somewhere where he won't do any damage, and don't forget to put plenty of newspaper on the floor. He'll be able to move out to the rest of the house after a few weeks. He's had his first injection, but will need his booster before you can take him out for a proper walk."

"Can't he sleep in the garage?"

Susan was mortified at Kevin's suggestion. "I want him to feel part of the family. Brahms and Liszt used to sleep on my bed." She hugged him closer to her chest as she carried him to the car.

Kevin drove back home, with the puppy happily curled up on Susan's lap. They stopped off at the pet shop to buy some puppy food and a small lead and collar, and Kevin picked up a cardboard box on the way out. For the first time in her life, Susan knew what it was like to be really in love.

Kevin was easily second fiddle for the next few days, and was relieved when Tuesday night finally came around, so that he could have a decent conversation, even if it was with Susan's mother. Dawn, as usual, looked very attractive in a thin skirt and blouse as she answered the door. The dogs, as usual, flew at his ankles, and he waded through them to the living room.

"Geoffrey's in London tonight working on a big contract, so you'll have to put up with my company. Dinner is just about ready, so we may as well move through to the dining room." The table was already set for two people next to each other, and two large glasses of red wine had already been poured.

38

Kevin took his seat whilst Dawn went into the kitchen to check the food.

"It'll be another five minutes, but it always tastes better after a glass of wine." Dawn sat next to Kevin, brushing her leg against his. "How are you getting on with Jaeger?"

"I'd rather not talk about the dog, if you don't mind."

"Are you feeling neglected?"

"Neglected isn't the word. It's as if I don't exist at the moment."

"Well, I'm sure we'll make up for that tonight."

Kevin was unsure of how to interpret Dawn's manner, and frowned because he couldn't understand what was happening. Dawn changed the subject to avoid upsetting Kevin further.

"We're about to cast for this year's pantomime. Are you taking part this year?"

"I don't think so. Last year's was fun, but I don't really think that it was me."

"Peter was very good, is he taking part?"

"He probably would if he was asked, but we're very busy at the moment studying for our final Accountancy exams this November."

Dawn went to the kitchen to bring in the plates, and then the spaghetti and sauce, whilst Kevin refilled their wine glasses. Dawn started to fill up Kevin's plate, and looked at him expectantly. "Say when."

"What?"

"No, when!"

Dawn had piled Kevin's plate with spaghetti and sauce, but Kevin doubted that he would have any trouble eating a plateful. It was nice to be able to eat proper home cooked food for a change.

"Right, you can either eat spaghetti with just a fork, or with a fork and spoon."

"A what?" Dawn's posh voice made 'fork and spoon' sound much ruder than she had intended it to sound. He looked at the cutlery on the table, and understood what she meant.

"It's easier if you use a fork and a spoon, like this." Dawn put the tip of the spoon on her plate so that the spoon handle was at right angles to the plate and the bowl of the spoon stood upright. She then pushed her fork into the spaghetti and started to twist it against the spoon. Kevin tried to copy her, but ended up with almost half of the spaghetti moving across his plate.

"No, just select a small amount of spaghetti, and move it away from the remainder, and mix it with some of the sauce."

Kevin was much more successful with his next attempt, and was very pleased with himself. A few strands were left hanging from the fork after he'd put it into his mouth, and with a loud slurping noise, he sucked them into his mouth.

Dawn laughed loudly at this, lifted up her glass, and said "Cheers". Eating the spaghetti took much longer than Kevin expected, and they were well into their second bottle of wine by the time that his plate started to look as if he'd made any progress on emptying it. They had both became noisier and Kevin was laughing much more than he'd ever expected to. He twisted some spaghetti around his fork, and lifted it up to examine his newly-found skill.

"That's really very good" Dawn was impressed at his ability. "Here, you have it."

Kevin pushed the fork towards Dawn, but it unravelled, and landed on her blouse. Quick as a flash, Dawn darted to the kitchen, and took off her blouse, quickly followed by her bra. Kevin arrived in the kitchen, and stood open-mouthed as he took in the picture of a topless Dawn washing her blouse in the sink.

"If I don't get this off now, it'll stain." Dawn looked at Kevin and realised that she could have said anything, and it would not have registered with Kevin. "Have you never seen a pair of tits before?"

"Yes, um, no, er."

Dawn smiled, put her hands on her hips, and turned around to face him. "Do you think my beard would suit you?"

Kevin's mouth went dry, and he felt a sinking feeling in the pit of his stomach.

"Oh God, yes."

It would take him some time to realise that the 'beard' comment was the topic of conversation between daughter and mother at the Randolph, but he did have more pressing things on his mind.

Dawn took his hand and led him upstairs to bed.

Kevin arrived home later that evening, hoping that Susan had retired early. Unfortunately, she was still up watching some drivel or other on the TV, with the puppy sat on her lap.

Jaeger jumped swiftly down, and started to sniff at the bottom of Kevin's trousers, whilst Kevin tried to gently push him away, without arousing any suspicion with Susan.

"I think he wants to go out?"

"Really, he only went out an hour ago."

"You know what the dog breeder said about puppies' bladders."

"Oh yes, of course. Come on Jaeger." Susan opened the back door. Jaeger's young puppy mind tried to work out his priorities, whether to stay where he was and explore the new doggy smell that Kevin had brought in, or discover some more of his new territory in the garden. Susan called his name again, he wagged his tail, and rushed after Susan, whilst Kevin took the opportunity to run upstairs and change into something less incriminating. He took the clothes that he had just taken off out into the garden, and hung them on the washing line.

Susan had put Jaeger into the kitchen for the night, and looked at Kevin when he came back into the living room, intrigued at his unusual actions. "You usually just dump your clothes on the floor for me to tidy up."

"It was best that they were put out to air. If the dog was interested by the smell of my clothes from the pub, he would have probably ripped them up."

"OK, I'm off to bed. Are you coming up?"

"In a minute."

Kevin looked at the sports news on the teletext whilst Susan bumped about in the bathroom, getting ready for bed. He heard her go into the bedroom, and climbed up the stairs to the bathroom to wash his trouser snake, and try to get rid of the taste of Dawn and the Bolognese sauce out of his mouth before joining Susan in bed.

41

Susan snuggled up to Kevin in the bed. "Did you have a nice time tonight?"

"Yes thanks."

"Anything interesting happen?"

"Not really."

"You don't smell of cigarettes as much as you usually do."

"That's because I took my clothes off as soon as I came home."

"I can smell some perfume on you as well."

"What's this, twenty fucking questions?" Kevin was starting to get worried. What did she know?

"No, it's just that it's quite a nice perfume, not the usual cheap perfume that the girls wear in the pub."

"Look, it's only a few months until Christmas, and one of the blokes in the pub had a load of posh perfume that he was selling of cheap, for us to buy for presents. He kept spraying it about to try to encourage us to buy some. I wanted it to be a surprise"

"You're so thoughtful. It is quite nice. It smells a bit like Mummy's perfume. If it's cheap enough, you could buy two bottles, one for me and one for Mummy."

"I didn't have enough money on me tonight. I'll get some the next time I see him."

THREE

The CIMA assignments were getting increasingly more difficult as Peter and Kevin worked their way through the syllabus. At the start of November they were only a few weeks away from their final examinations for their final year. Peter and Kevin were on their revision stage preparing for their exams, and they were given increasingly more and more course work to do outside of the classroom. Kevin needed constant assistance with the coursework, and Peter was his first port of call. Their latest assignment was an exam question from two years previously, and Kevin couldn't understand it at all, so he told Susan to invite Peter over for Sunday lunch. Peter knew that he would have to earn his food by trying to explain the question to Kevin, and then show him how to answer it, but he gladly accepted the invitation because he was still very fond Susan, and he jumped at the chance to spend some time with her. He couldn't believe that someone so nice would live with an ignorant bastard like Kevin, and wanted to be there when she finally saw the light, and gave him the push.

Susan walked into the kitchen with the dog's lead. "Can you take Jaeger for a walk please?"
"I told you I would end up walking the dog. I've got your course work to sort out today, as well as my own"
"I need to start preparing lunch for you and Peter, so I won't have the time to take him out."
"I'll swing for that bloody dog. It's bad enough that I have to do without breakfast."
"He only gets part of your toast, you can't begrudge him that, surely."
"If you want to give him some toast, then make him his own slice, don't keep cutting bits off of mine."
"Will you take him for a walk please, he's bursting, and don't forget to pick up his rattler, you'll get into trouble if you don't."
When Jaeger was a small puppy, Kevin remarked that his short tail wagged like a rattlesnake about to pounce whilst he was doing his business. Susan thought that this was hilarious, and the name stuck. Kevin put a handful of nappy bags into

his pocket, and tried to clip on the dog lead whilst Jaeger jumped up and down, barking in his enthusiasm to get out. "Shut up you stupid dog, or I'll kick you round the park." Jaeger's understanding of English was on a par with Kevin's on a Friday night, after he'd had about ten pints, so he kept barking and jumping up and down, until Kevin had dragged him outside. When they reached the park, Kevin noticed a dead branch on the floor, which was roughly the same diameter and colour of a normal sized rattler. Not wishing to miss an opportunity as good as this, Kevin snapped the branch into rattler-sized lengths and put them into a poo-bag. When the dog eventually went through his business in the bushes, Kevin pretended to pick it up with the bag full of broken branch, and carried it away until he was out of sight, when he could put it back into his pocket, to use it the next time. He was feeling very pleased with himself, and when he was far enough from the road, he allowed Jaeger to run around off the lead. The dog was having so much fun, that he wouldn't come back when he was called, and it took Kevin half an hour until he managed to corner him, and put him back on the lead.

When Kevin arrived back home, his mood had changed from the earlier jollity of fooling everyone with the false poo, to one of great frustration of not getting the dog to do as he was told. He already had a busy day in front of him, and this delay had really pissed him off. He slammed the door on his arrival, and went to look for Susan, to tell her that her dog obedience lessons were not working. The kitchen was full of strange smells and steam from her latest attempt at cooking, with no sign of Susan.

"You were gone a long time. Did you have fun in the park dear?" The sound came from the bathroom. "I'm just getting in the shower, I'll be down in a minute. Could you put the kettle on for a cup of coffee please?" He filled up the kettle, and stormed off outside to the shed.

Despite working in the Finance department, Susan had no aptitude whatsoever for Accounting, so she had started a course at the local college to 'broaden her understanding of life'. For the early part of the course, she had to collect numerous leaves and produce photographs of the insect life that was growing from its egg stage through its pupa stage prior to maturity on the back of the leaves. In exchange for Susan 'cooking' the dinner, Kevin had agreed to place each leaf on a blanket in order of growth of the insect life attached to it, and take the photographs. He opened the shed door to collect the bag of leaves and the blanket, and on the inside wall next to the garden fork and spade that he'd inherited when he bought the house, but had no intention of using, was the biggest black, hairy spider that he'd ever seen. Kevin was never one to miss the chance to get his revenge when someone had upset him, and he blamed Susan for the dog's bad behaviour. He rushed back into the kitchen and grabbed a cup and one of Susan's recipe cards. He went back to the shed and put the cup over the spider. Slipping the card underneath the cup, he carried it back to the kitchen, and placed the cup upside down next to the kettle with the spider trapped inside it, before putting the card back on the shelf with her other cook books. He went out into the garden waiting for Susan's reaction when she discovered his surprise present.

It only took a few minutes until the kitchen was filled with large piercing screams as Susan lifted up the cup and found herself face-to-face with one of her greatest fears. The spider tried to make a hasty escape, but the dog burst into the kitchen to save his mistress, and ate the spider in one quick movement. Susan was still shaking and speechless when Kevin entered the kitchen.
"Oh, did you find that spider, I was going to warn you about that, but I didn't expect you to come downstairs so quickly."
"Make me a G and T before I pass out."
"This is going to be a short day if you're drinking already."
It wasn't until Peter arrived that Susan stopped shaking.

Kevin had just finished sorting through the leaves and placing them in order on the blanket when Peter arrived, with his usual promptness, at two o'clock on the dot. Peter carried his books and his typed up answer to the latest assignment under one arm, and a bottle of 'Blue Nun' in his free hand. Jaeger took to Peter the instant he arrived, and ran around him barking and wagging his stumpy tail furiously. Susan showed Peter into the garden to join Kevin, and they were followed by the dog leaping up and down, and running rings around Peter as fast as he could. Jaeger then noticed the blanket, grabbed hold of one if its corners with his teeth, and ran up and down the garden, spreading the leaves to all corners of the garden. Kevin shouted at the dog, using words that the dog hadn't heard before, and certainly didn't understand (they were probably not physically possible for even a dog to do!). Jaeger could see that the big bloke was angry, and ran off inside to escape him. Kevin closed the living room door to keep Jaeger out of his way, and tried to collect the leaves, but even with Peter's help, they only recovered about half of them. By the time that they had laid them out in order, lunch was ready.

"I hope that you're hungry." Kevin was panting after the exertion of chasing the dog, and picking up the leaves.

"I am now."

"You'll need to be. You won't have eaten food like this before. It takes the human body about twenty four hours to turn food into shit. Susan can do it much quicker than that."

Dawn had bought Susan a Delia Smith cookbook after she'd moved in with Kevin, and today's lunch was one of the recipes from the book.

Susan had placed the bowls of food in the middle of the dining table, and was waiting for Kevin and Peter to join her.

"This is one of my mother's favourite recipes. It's called Spanish pork."

Whatever the Spaniards did with their pork, it was doubtful that it tasted like the Spanish pork served up by Susan. Try as he might, Peter could only eat half of the food on his plate, before making his excuse of being full, despite still being hungry.

Susan could eat almost anything that she cooked herself, and Kevin was starting to become immune from the attacks on his taste-buds, so he had managed most of his plateful.

"You should have eaten more than that, Dad. It'll only get thrown away."

"Can't you give it to the dog?"

"No chance. We gave him some left-overs a few weeks ago, and he spent the next week licking his arse, trying to get rid of the taste."

Luckily, there was a large portion of shop-bought cheesecake for dessert, so Peter managed to fill most of the empty part of his stomach with that.

Kevin looked at Peter's empty dessert plate, and couldn't resist commenting. "I thought you were full up from the main course?"

"I can always make room for cheesecake."

"Why couldn't you make room for some more of the main course then?" Kevin was trying to show Peter up in front of Susan, despite the fact that he expected Peter to help him with his latest CIMA assignment.

"To be quite honest, I don't really like foreign food like spaghetti."

Kevin took a deep breath. What did Peter know about his spaghetti-eating antics? Unsure of where the conversation was heading, he decided to change the subject.

"We need to take some photos of the leaves for Susan to send off with her course work. I've got a Polaroid camera which has been put to good use on a number of occasions." Kevin went into the living room to find the dog with a mangled camera between his jaws. Peter and Susan had both blushed at the thought of the pictures produced by the camera, and were silently pleased at its demise.

Kevin's face went bright red with rage, and he kicked out at the dog. Jaeger was too quick for him and ran out of the living room to sanctuary behind Susan. Kevin stormed into the dining room after the dog, but was stopped in his tracks by a resolute Susan, who would protect her Jaeger with her last breath.

"Don't you dare kick my dog!!"

"I'll do more than kick the useless bastard."

"He's only a puppy, leave him alone."

Kevin went back to the garden and hurled the blanket and leaves onto the roof, and then paced up and down the lawn, swearing and muttering to himself. Whilst Peter tried to hold a polite conversation with Susan, Kevin smoked three cigarettes until he was calm enough to go back into the house, but he was in no mood to go through the CIMA assignment.

"Give me your answer, and I'll send it off as mine."

"But you won't have learnt anything, and it'll probably turn up as a question in the exam."

"Don't be such a ker-nob. You can teach me before the exam, I'm in no mood to concentrate now. Just give me your answer and then piss off."

Peter reluctantly handed over his answer. He could quite easily rework his answer to make them both look different enough to prevent the instructor from discovering that they were both produced by him, but he was upset that he was leaving Susan's company after such a short time.

"You'd better go Peter, Kevin won't be very good company for the rest of the day."

"What about the dog?"

"If he touches my dog, I'll cut his balls off!"

"Thanks for the meal, I hope that we can do it again sometime soon, maybe something a little less continental next time?"

Peter picked up his books, and let himself out of the front door.

Susan had taken the dog out for a walk around the village when the phone rang, and Kevin was relieved to get the chance to speak to Dawn without Susan hearing.

"You don't sound very happy"

"It's that bloody dog. He's ruined my camera, and Susan's gone off in a huff because I lost my temper."

"I think I know something that will cheer you up. Can you get to the amateur dramatics club this evening?"

"If I spent the whole night out I don't think that I would be missed."

"Drop by at about eight o'clock. Bang on the door, and I'll let you in. I've got something to show you."

It was already dark outside, and a normal person would have been worried that Susan had been missing for some time, but Kevin couldn't really give a shit. Susan finally came back from her walk and went upstairs with the dog without speaking to Kevin. Now that Kevin had installed a small television in the bedroom, she would probably stay there all night, so Kevin had a quick wash and shave and drove to the local pub for a swift pint or two, prior to his meeting with Dawn.   At eight o'clock, Kevin drove round for his meeting with Dawn, wondering what it was that would cheer him up. His mind had conjured up a variety of ideas, but none of them included him being confronted by Dawn wearing a skimpy outfit when she opened the door.

"Come backstage, and I'll show you my other dress for Cinderella, I'd like to know what you think."
Kevin could feel his response moving in his shorts as he followed her long legs around the side of the stage to the actors' dressing room, which was full of old comfy chairs and sofas, and numerous wardrobes and racks of clothes. Dawn walked to a splendid long sparkling ball gown hanging next to a tall mirror.
"I'm wearing my normal outfit, which shows how badly I'm treated by my evil Step Mother and her two ugly daughters. This is the posh gown that my Fairy Godmother makes for me for the Prince's ball."
Kevin much preferred the pauper's outfit for obvious reasons.
"How have you managed to keep such a great figure?"
Dawn blushed at the compliment.
"Geoffrey earns so much money that I've never had to work since Susan was born, so I go to the gym most days. I have a personal trainer to make sure that I do the right exercises. The rest is down to luck and dieting."
Kevin had seen the Disney cartoon of Cinderella, so he had a rough idea of the story.
"What happens when the Fairy Godmother waves her magic wand and the ball gown appears?"
"The ball gown is attached to invisible nylon strings, and floats across the stage to just behind me. There's an explosion like thunder and a big flash of lights, followed by a blackout for two or three seconds, in which I take off this and put on the ball gown."

"It'll take more than three seconds to take off the short dress and put on the long one. Can't you just put the long one on over the short one?"

"We tried that, but the ball gown fits tightly and the short dress makes it look too lumpy. What the costume department have done is to make the short dress open out completely using Velcro, so I step off-stage behind the scenery flats, step out of the short dress and my dresser has the long dress ready for me to step into. She then zips me up the back, there's another flash of light, and I step back onto the stage wearing my posh frock."

Dawn turned round to face away from Kevin, and pulled the straps apart. The dress slipped quickly to the floor, leaving Dawn naked in front of Kevin.

"It's a bit risky being naked underneath the dress isn't it?"

"I would normally be wearing a body stocking underneath the dress, this is for your benefit."

Dawn led Kevin to the large sofa, with Kevin tripping over his trousers as he tried to match Dawn's state of undress. They toppled over and landed in a heap on the sofa but disentangled themselves, and Kevin was quickly indulging in his favourite pastime of 'hide the hairy hotdog'.

Kevin eventually had to take a rest, and rolled off of the sofa, onto the dusty old carpet that covered most of the dressing room floor.

"There's a bottle of Coke in my bag, could you get it for me please?"

Dawn had not covered her naked body, and Kevin hoped that they would be able to continue after a short rest. Kevin opened the bag, and noticed a bottle of perfume, which reminded him of their previous encounter after the spaghetti.

"Could you do me a favour?"

"I thought I just had." Dawn smiled wickedly at Kevin

"Could you get me two bottles of your perfume?"

"Two bottles?"

"Yes, Susan wants one for Christmas, and she wants to get you one as well, but it's really expensive, and we just can't afford it. I told her that a friend of mine was selling it off cheaply down the pub."

"You want me to buy my own Christmas present, and give it to you to give to Susan, for her to give it to me?"

Kevin could see no problem with this arrangement, and nodded enthusiastically. "Please make sure that you look surprised when you open the present."

Kevin ambled back to the sofa looking appreciatively at her body, and gave Dawn the Coke. "Is this the casting couch then?"

"I wouldn't know. I don't make a habit of this sort of thing you know!"

Kevin was lost for words, and luckily couldn't think of anything to say to apologise, because he would have only made things worse. The happy mood was broken, and a short period of silence followed until Dawn decided that nothing further was going to happen that evening.

"I really should be getting back. I told Geoffrey that I would only be a short while trying on my dress. How can I get the perfume to you?"

"Could you drop it round in to my house? There's no rush at the moment as Christmas is still weeks away, but I'm taking my final exams in a few days and I'm busy preparing for them, so could you bring it round at the end of the month?"

Dawn had put on her designer jeans and shirt, and tidied away her stage clothing. She walked Kevin to the door of the building and gave him a chaste kiss on the cheek before they parted.

The final CIMA examinations finally arrived. Luckily Peter and Kevin were still on the old syllabus, as there was talk of a change to the exams, and one of the four final exams would entail writing up a huge report in the three hours allotted for each exam. Kevin still didn't really understand much of what he was told by the instructors, but, as long as he could copy from Peter, he was sure that he would get through. As the answers for the final examinations mainly consisted of explanations of business and financial strategies that they would put in place to improve the business, with only a small amount of calculations required, the normal exam technique was to write a brief plan at the start of each question, along with the main factors in the plan, and then write up the plan in full. This made it much easier for Kevin to copy Peter, as he would write up the plan from Peter's paper, and then pad out the answer with explanations of the main factors. The chances of being caught were further reduced because their surnames were a long way down the alphabet. There were about a hundred people undergoing the exams, so their seats were located quite a distance from the adjudicator, who sat at the front of the large hall. Although Peter would get higher marks than Kevin, it didn't really matter, a pass was a pass. You didn't get a larger pay rise to match your marks, and Kevin had made Peter keep his previous results to himself, Mark and the FD.

There were four exams for the final stage, within the space of three days, and each of the exams took three hours, all written in long-hand, so by Thursday afternoon both Peter and Kevin were mentally drained, and their arms and hands ached from over-exertion. Of the thirty members of their class who Peter and Kevin and joined three years ago, there were only twelve left. Some of them had given up due to the difficulty of the course, or lack of time to study the large syllabus, whilst others had failed exams along the way, and had dropped back to classes following them to re-sit their exams in order to continue.

Kevin had persuaded the members of his class that they should all meet up after their fourth, and last, exam and have a pub crawl to (hopefully) celebrate the end of their Accountancy training, and their imminent qualification as Management Accountants. Although they wouldn't get their results until the end of January to confirm their success, the impetus for the celebration would be greatly reduced, and it would be much more difficult to get all of the course members together. Peter, as usual, was very reluctant to take part, but Kevin told him quite bluntly that it would not look good if he didn't take part, as it would make good business sense to socialise with the other class-mates due to the information and contacts that they could provide when they moved to higher profile jobs. Peter knew that the hangover he would wake up to would make his life unbearable the next day, but Kevin told him that he would make his life even more unbearable than the hangover if he didn't turn up, so Peter chose the lesser of the two evils, and was waiting in the Glock with his pint of Coke when they arrived. Although it was still early in the evening, the dimly-lit pub was already half full of the usual young and boisterous customers. He sat close to the door so that he could make regular escapes outside from the smoky atmosphere for a breath of fresh air, which also relieved his ears from the constant noise of the loud rock music played on the jukebox. As usual, it was his round, but these days he could quite easily afford it. Unlike most of the people on the course, Peter still lived with his parents, and his regular pay rises made him quite affluent.

The other class members treated Peter much better than Kevin did, and respected him for his intelligence. They regularly asked him for advice when they couldn't understand the way that the course instructor had explained certain topics, and Peter would always clear up their confusion. Peter, however, was still introverted and withdrawn so they also thought of him as being difficult to socialise with, but he was definitely high on their list of people to network with for work purposes. Kevin was even more outgoing than ever. You didn't need a degree in opthalmics to see that he wasn't as bright as Peter, but they didn't know how much he relied on Peter to get him through the syllabus and the exams.

As the night progressed, Kevin became louder and louder, and his jokes became more and more non-pc. "As I was passing the entrance to the covered market on the way here, I saw three homosexuals in the alleyway having sex in a line, one behind the other. There was a policeman at Carfax, so I reported it to him. "Did you see the man in the middle?" the policeman asked me, "Yes," I said, "Was he a tall man with dark hair and a moustache?" he asked. "Yes, he was," I

replied. "He's lucky at darts as well" he said, and walked away."
The group erupted with laughter, whilst Peter stood with them shaking his head, unable to understand what was so funny.

Kevin had always worked on the principle of letting others buy the drinks for the girls until they were more amenable to his advances, so after a few hours of relatively heavy drinking, he started to chat up two of the girls from the class. It was almost closing time, the juke box was now silent, and about half of the group had already left. Peter noticed Kevin's move, and took his chance to slip off unnoticed whilst Kevin's mind was otherwise engaged. Although he'd drunk less than half of Kevin's alcohol intake, he would still have a far worse hangover, which was another reason he felt that God was treating him unfairly in comparison to Kevin. Tonight, however, he'd escaped after only drinking three pints of lager, and would be able to go to sleep without having to talk to God down the big white telephone in the bathroom. Too late, Kevin looked around for Peter to join him with the girls, so that Peter could buy their drinks. Kevin had to put his hand in his pocket for the first time that night, but it would be worth it if he could get one of them to invite him back to their flat for the night. It would be even better if they both came back, but the chance of that looked quite remote. He'd never got anywhere when he'd chatted them up before, but tonight they'd had much more to drink than usual, and seemed much more welcoming.
"Hello girls, fancy a drink with your favourite uncle Kevin?"
"I've got to get back home. I'm at work first thing tomorrow, and if I don't go now, I won't make it in before lunchtime." She kissed her friend on the cheek, picked up her bag and left. Kevin lifted up his arm and smelt his armpit. "Is it something I said?"
Helen, the remaining friend smiled at him. She thought that Kevin was a bit of a twat, but was usually quite funny.
"No, she really does start work quite early. It's not so bad for me, as I've arranged a day off tomorrow. I thought that I would be too tired to work after a week of exams. I'll have a Vodka and Coke if you're still offering."

Kevin could never see the point of drinking shorts when you were there for a long session, and he could also drink a pint quicker than others could drink a short drink, so he ordered himself another lager, just before they called "time".

Helen picked up her Vodka and smiled at Kevin again. "What are you going to do with your time, now that we no longer have to spend so much time studying?"

"I help out a lot with the local community." Kevin lied. He wasn't going to say that he would be able to spend more quality time with his girlfriend. One because it was completely untrue, and two, it would spoil his chance of getting his leg over tonight.

"What sort of help?"

"Well, there's a single mother who lives just down the road from me who doesn't have much money, so I do odd jobs for her, and she pays me in kind to match the work."

"Really?"

"Oh yeah. Last month, her hand blender was broken, so I fixed it for her, and she gave me a hand job. A couple of weeks ago, her hair dryer was broken, so I mended her blower motor, and she gave me a blow job. I'm going round to see her this weekend to mend her back door."

Unfortunately, Helen had taken a drink just before the punch line, and sprayed Kevin with her Vodka and Coke.

"Oh shit, I'm really sorry!"

"That's OK, I'm sure that you can make it up to me. Just remember, I'm used to being paid in kind." Helen didn't seem too disturbed by his comment, so Kevin's hopes started to grow.

"Did you really see three men in an alleyway by the covered market?"

"Of course I did."

"I didn't think that you could get up to that sort of thing there without being caught."

"It all depends where you go."

"I'll be back in a minute; I just need to powder my nose. Please wait for me."

Most of Helen's drink had ended up over Kevin, and the bar was already closed, so Kevin drank his pint whilst Helen went to the loo before leaving. When she emerged, her nose looked the same as before. She had, however, touched up her lipstick, and had brushed her hair. Another good sign!

"Right, I'm off then."

"Did you want me to walk you anywhere?" Kevin was always courteous if there was something in it for him.

"The covered market sounds good."

Kevin didn't make it to work the following morning. Peter walked round to chat with Susan, and noticed that she was very quiet, and her eyes were red from crying.

"Are you Okay?"

"It's Kevin. He's been really horrible to me since we picked up Jaeger from the dog breeder."

"I know that he was angry when the dog broke his camera, but he has always had a short temper. I should know, I've had to put up with it for years."

"It's not just that. Since Jaeger has been house-trained, he sleeps in the bedroom with us, and when I am on my own, he sleeps on the bed. Kevin came home drunk last night, well after midnight, and when I mentioned the time to him, he started shouting at me, saying horrible things to me, such as I was ruining his fun, and he could come home at whatever time he wanted to. Jaeger growled at him. Kevin swore at the dog, pushed him off of the bed and chased him out of the bedroom."

"You don't begrudge him a few drinks to celebrate the completion of our final exams do you?" Peter couldn't believe that he was supporting Kevin.

"It's not just that. He's been very nasty to me for ages, always criticising everything that I do. And he doesn't pay as much attention to me as he used to, if you know what I mean." Susan blushed as she made the reference to her lack of sex life. "I keep getting the feeling that he's seeing someone else. Was he with a girl last night at the pub?"

"There are a few girls on the course with us, but we were all together."

"I'm sure that he's going to throw me out soon. The mortgage is much less than it was when I moved in, so he doesn't have to rely on my contribution any more. He also spends more time in the pub than he used to. I don't think that he wants to stay in the house with me as much as he did when I first moved in."

"All of his spare time over the last year has been spent studying, so his temper will definitely improve now that we've finished."

"I hope so. I can't afford to live anywhere if he throws me out, so I'll have to go back home to live with my parents."

"I thought that you got on well with your parents?"

"I do, but it's embarrassing to have to go back home after leaving. I would feel such a failure."

Susan burst into tears, and Peter put his arms around her to comfort her.

"I'm sure it's not as bad as you think. Go home tonight and cook him his favourite meal. Now that the exams are over, I'm sure that he'll be in a better mood."

"He'll just complain about my cooking again. I can't buy a take-away, because he'll just moan about me wasting money." Susan paused for breath between sobs. "Although he's quite well paid now, he's still really tight when it comes to spending money on anything except for beer and cigarettes."

"Why don't you get your mother to cook something for you? You're always saying what a good cook she is."

Susan perked up immediately. "That's a great idea."

"You can use my phone to call your mother if you like."

Peter and Kevin's standing in the company had improved recently, and they had been given the privilege of a direct outside line on their phones. Kevin would have preferred a pay rise, but Peter was happy with the recognition for his efforts.

Susan dried her tears and followed Peter back to his office. She had regained her composure by the time she picked up the phone.

"Mummy, could you cook something nice for Kevin and me tonight. I would like to have a romantic meal at home with him now that he has finished his Accountancy exams."

"Any idea what you would like?"

"Something that I can pick up from you, and put in the oven to keep warm."

"How about Chicken in a Lorry?"

She saw the confused look on Peter's face, and put her hand over the mouthpiece of the phone. "Chicken in a Lorry is Daddy's amusing name for Coq au Vin."

"That's a great idea Mummy. When will it be ready to pick up?"

"It would be better for me to drop it off. When will you get home this evening?"

"I expect to be home at about five o'clock, but Kevin will be there all day. He's having a day of rest after his exams."

"I'll pop it round later this afternoon, and put it in the oven on a low heat. Do you want me to prepare the potatoes for some mash?"

"No, that's fine Mummy, I think that I can manage that. Thank you very much."

Susan was smiling again as she skipped back to her office, leaving Peter wondering whether he'd reduced his chances even further of ever going out with Susan. He was always ready with a shoulder for her to cry on, but gave her reasons to stay with Kevin every time she was upset with him.

Kevin had woken up later that morning with only a slight hangover, and a pleasant memory from the night before. He stood under the shower as the hangover washed away, and was feeling good as he got dressed. He said 'double bonus' to himself when he checked his pockets. He found enough cash to buy himself a proper fry up at the café, which improved his mood even more.

Dawn checked Delia's stain covered recipe book, and went to the shops to buy the ingredients, and a posh bottle of red wine for them to drink with it. She completed her shopping with the purchase of two bottles of her usual perfume. On returning home, Dawn started cooking the chicken pieces and small onions, followed by the rest of ingredients from the recipe that she almost knew well enough without having to look at the book. She emptied the cooked contents from the large frying pan into the 'Le Creuset' pot, ensured that the red wine covered the top of the chicken pieces, and put the cooking pot into the oven to cook through whilst she had a quick shower and change.

Despite the oven being set at a low heat, the cooking pot was still too hot to put onto the carpet in the front of the car, so she put two place mats underneath it, along with a large towel, to prevent the contents from spilling onto the expensive floor covering. She tried to keep her mind from thinking of her intentions when she arrived at the house, but knew in her heart that, if the opportunity arose, she would end up in bed with Kevin. It wasn't that she didn't love Geoffrey, or that Kevin was in any way irresistible, but her marriage was beginning to become a little bit stale, and when she thought of Kevin she realised that he makes her feel the way she used to feel.

She parked her car outside Kevin's house and rang the doorbell. The sound of barking drowned out every other noise in the house. Finally the door opened, and a surprised Kevin stood staring at Dawn.
"Didn't you expect me? Susan was going to phone you to let you know that I was bringing over your dinner for tonight."
"I've been out all day."
"No problem. The casserole dish is still hot, but it needs to be put into a warm oven. Could you take it out of the car please?"
Kevin re-entered the house with the casserole dish, followed by Dawn carrying the bottle of wine and the two bottles of perfume.
Kevin put the casserole inside the oven and stood looking at the controls. Dawn turned the heat to low, and gave Kevin the bottle of wine.
"This wine goes really well with coq au vin. You also asked me to get you two bottles of my perfume."
"Thanks for this. Don't tell Susan. She asked me to get it for Christmas, but I wouldn't know how or where to buy it." It

didn't enter Kevin's mind that he should be offering to pay for it.

The dog was still barking and jumping up at Dawn, so Kevin ushered Dawn back into the living room, and closed the dog in the kitchen.

"You only need to boil and mash some potatoes to go with the coq au vin, and maybe some peas and carrots, but you won't need to cook those for some time yet. I'd better be getting back home."

Kevin thought that it would be safer if Susan added some boiling water to a packet of 'Smash', but didn't like to say so in front of Dawn.

"Did you want to look around the house? We're gradually redecorating it, and with your sense of taste, you could let me know where I can make improvements to it."

"Okay, where shall we start?"

"The bathroom hasn't been decorated for donkey's years."

Dawn looked around the upstairs half of the house and found it hard to believe that her daughter was happy in such a small house when you compared it to the mansion which she had moved out of. The bathroom was not a pretty sight. The small radiator doubled as a towel warmer, and a drying rack for numerous pairs of male and female undergarments.

"Maybe the main bedroom would be less of a challenge, we've already started on that."

Dawn followed Kevin into the bedroom shared by him and Susan. The room was tiny. She noticed Susan's female touch in the new wallpaper, and the flowery matching bedcovers and curtains. Scattered on the floor next to the unmade bed were a handful of small cushions and a selection of cuddly toy animals, which she wouldn't expect to be there if Kevin lived alone.

"The bed's quite comfortable. You'll need to take your shoes off before you get in though"

Dawn stared at Kevin for a few seconds, and then sighed resignedly, before getting undressed and into the cold bed. The bed warmed up as soon as Kevin had thrown his clothes onto the floor and joined her.

Susan spent her lunchtime thinking about the romantic evening that she had planned for herself and Kevin, and couldn't concentrate on her work that afternoon. As it was Friday, most of the office staff were packing up early, so she decided to go home and have a nice warm bath in preparation for the evening's adventures.

She popped down to Peter's office humming to herself.
"Wish me luck tonight."
"You won't need it. Have a nice weekend."

The surprised look that had left Kevin's face twenty minutes earlier attached itself to Susan as she parked Kevin's Mini behind her mother's car. Her happy humming stopped dead as she opened the door to the house and was not leapt upon by Jaeger. She could make out some noises coming from upstairs, and hoping that Kevin was not having a go at her dog again, rushed upstairs to rescue her pet. When she threw the door open, the only puppies in view were those belonging to her mother, as she bounced heartily up and down on top of Kevin, quite oblivious to the new spectator.
"MUMMY, HOW COULD YOU!!"
Susan staggered downstairs in floods of tears. On hearing her footsteps, Jaeger had started to bark. Susan rescued him from the kitchen, attached his lead to his collar, and walked briskly to the local park where she hoped the clear air would help her to try to understand what she had just seen.

Dawn pushed herself off of Kevin and started to get dressed.
"There's no reason to rush off is there? We've only just got started."
"I have to speak to Susan. I didn't want this to happen."
"Do you think that you can get her back here for a threesome?" Kevin never did grasp the seriousness of some circumstances.
"You really are a bastard, aren't you!"
Dawn was fully dressed now, and picking up her keys rushed outside to try to catch up with Susan, who was just disappearing out of view at the bottom of the street. Dawn

61

started her car and drove to the park, where she could see Susan and Jaeger. Her maternal need to try to ease her daughter's pain was only just winning the mortal combat against her guilt and shame. She had to run to catch up with Susan, but the hours spent in the gym were put to good use.

"Go away. I hate you!"

"Susan, please."

"How could you?"

"I'm sorry. I didn't want it to happen. It just did."

"What about Daddy? What are you going to tell him?"

The full impact on what she had done became evident to Dawn for the first time. The guilt and shame that she felt earlier reached a new level, and she fell to the ground as if pole axed.

"Mummy, are you all right?" Susan thought that her mother was having a heart attack.

"I'm so sorry. I've ruined everything! Geoffrey will be heart-broken, and I'll have to move out." Dawn had serious problems breathing, and had turned deathly pale.

"Don't tell Daddy. I don't want you to split up. It would kill him"

"What can I do? I've been such a fool."

"We need to go home, and never speak of this again."

"How can you ever forgive me?"

"If the only other option is that you and Daddy separate, then I'll have to."

"What about Kevin."

"I'm better off without him. He's just a horrible, selfish bastard." At least they both agreed on one thing. "Let's go home. I'm sure that I'll start to feel better once I've had a G and T."

"What about your clothes?"

"I can pick those up tomorrow lunchtime when he goes to the pub."

Kevin stood in the living room and contemplated how quiet it was without the dog jumping up and down, and barking at everyone as they passed by the window. The telly, or the T.V. as Susan called it, would have a night off from its normal diet of soaps and associated crap. He went into the kitchen and looked at the casserole bubbling away in the oven. He only had to boil a kettle and add the boiling water to a packet of 'Smash' and he had enough food to last him the weekend. It got even better when he noticed the bottle of posh wine, and the two bottles of perfume on the kitchen worktop. His standard of living had improved dramatically during the last year, and, despite Susan's cooking, so had the quality of food that he had been eating. He had also learnt how to eat proper spaghetti. He no longer felt out of place when he socialised with the senior management. He didn't despise his parents, or the way that they lived their lives, but even they had noticed the change in him. Kevin was also glad to be free of Susan, and he wouldn't take Susan back, even if she begged him to. He still felt that he was too young to spend most nights with the same woman?

FOUR

First thing on Monday morning, Peter walked down to Susan's office space, to find out how her weekend went, but was met by an empty chair. Mark came out to meet him.

"Peter, could you come into my office please?"

"Is Susan ill?"

"No, she phoned in this morning. She no longer lives with Kevin, and doesn't want to work here anymore."

"What has Kevin said?"

"Nothing, he's not in yet. I've never agreed with office romances. They normally end badly, and then one of them has to leave, as they can't bear to work with their ex."

Mark carried on talking, but everything was a blur. All Peter could think about was Susan. It had been bad enough that she lived with Kevin, but at least he saw her most days. Kevin came in later than normal, his shirt not properly ironed, and he looked more hung over than usual for a Monday morning. Peter had wished for months that she would move out from Kevin's house, but now he realised that you need to be careful what you wish for.

"You've heard about Susan moving out then?"

"She spoke to me about it on Friday."

Kevin was surprised that Susan would mention anything that had happened on Friday, even to Peter. "It was nice when it lasted, well sometimes, but I can't say I'm too bothered."

Peter couldn't believe that Kevin was so unconcerned about Susan moving out. He was unable to concentrate for the rest of the day, and went home early, still in a daze. He couldn't bring himself to eat anything for two days. On Wednesday evening his mother made him beans on toast. It was his favourite, but was normally banned due to the resulting odours. Peter managed to eat two slices but it tasted of cardboard. He kept trying to phone Susan, but hung up before he'd finished dialling her number, and as each week passed, it became more and more impossible to bring himself to call her.

Peter's mother was getting concerned about his state of mind. It was nearly Christmas now, and Peter was still mooching around like a love-sick teenager.

"It's the pantomime this weekend, why don't you go and watch it. You might get a chance to speak to Susan."

Peter brightened up immediately. Why hadn't he thought of that? He hadn't really been thinking too cleverly just recently, but his mind became crystal clear on his mission. He booked a ticket for the Friday night show, and spent all of Friday afternoon in an expectant buzz. He arrived early, and bought himself a coke from the bar, but the foyer was almost empty. The girl behind the bar recognised Peter from when they put on Aladdin.

"Is Susan about?"

"She'll be busy in make-up."

"Could you ask her to meet me out here in the interval?"

"I'll tell her as soon as the curtain goes up."

Peter stood around the foyer for the next half hour, too shy to go backstage himself on the pretence of wishing them all to "break a leg". The doors opened, and the audience went inside to their seats as the small band started playing 'Another Opening of Another Show.'

The bar closed, and the girl went backstage to pass on Peter's message. Susan was stood next to Dawn in the wings, who was waiting for the opening song to finish so that she could make her entrance.

"Peter's in the audience, and would like to meet you in the foyer during the interval."

Susan went into 'panic' mode, and gripped her mother's hand for support.

"I'm not going to speak to him. He'll want me to go back to Kevin. Tell him I'm too busy."

Peter enjoyed the first Act, especially the Ugly Sisters. Dawn looked really attractive in her tatty clothes. The interval finally arrived, and Peter rushed out to the bar to meet Susan. The girl behind the bar looked quite sad as she passed on Susan's message.

"If she's too busy now, could she meet me after the final curtain?"

"I think that she's going to be too busy for some time, Peter. I'm sorry."

Peter left the theatre and went home, feeling as despondent as he did when he first found out that Susan was no longer working with him. It was the worst Christmas of all time, not only for Peter, who had lost Susan forever, but also for Susan who was still angry with Kevin, and upset with her mother, and Dawn, who was still ashamed at her behaviour, and worried that Susan would let the cat out of the bag. Geoffrey was pleased with the extra interest he was receiving in bed, but had put that down to Dawn trying to get an extra special Christmas present.

The third weekend in January finally arrived, and with it came the CIMA exam results. Peter received the usual high scores, and Kevin managed to scrape in just above the fifty percent mark for each of them. Susan could never understand that it was possible to get half of the answers wrong and still pass, and Kevin had long since stopped trying to explain the marking system to her. It also didn't bother him that his marks were much lower than Peter's, there was no reason to get excited, a pass was a pass, and he would soon get a large pay rise.

Mark called them into his office first thing on Monday morning to receive the expected good news.

"I can see that you're both happy. How did you get on?"

Peter was as modest as always. "Somewhere in the high sixties."

Despite the fact that Kevin still thought that Provisions were the pies, beer and cigarettes that Susan used to buy for him each Saturday, and an Embedded Derivative was a sexual position, he was full of himself. "Anything over fifty is a waste of effort. The diploma will state that we are qualified accountants, with no mention of the marks."

Mark smiled at Kevin's comments, and was overjoyed that they had both passed first time. There had been previous trainees who had failed on numerous occasions, and he was glad that these two would be able to concentrate their efforts on the business from now on, instead of taking more time away from work to repeat their studying and re-sitting their exams.

"Well done. The FD was expecting you both to pass. You need to write up your 'Record of Practical Experience' log and send it off to CIMA. When CIMA agree that you have enough relevant accounting experience to be qualified accountants, and send back your diplomas, we will increase your responsibilities at work, and also increase your pay accordingly."

They left Mark's office smiling. Kevin, as usual, expected Peter to complete the logs for both of them. They'd been doing the same sort of work since they left school, so it didn't make sense for them both to write up the same information. "Have you completed your log yet?"

"I've been writing it up since we started studying, like the instructors told us to."

"Good, you can print me off a copy, and I'll get mine in the post as soon as it's signed off by Mark and the FD. The sooner we get the diploma, the sooner we get our pay rise." Peter was still too frightened to say no to Kevin, but took the opportunity to ask him about Susan. He'd not had many chances since they'd finished studying, and Susan had moved out.

"I've not seen or heard from her since she left. She came and picked up her belongings whilst I was out the following day. She didn't even leave a note, or her share of the mortgage."

It didn't take much for Peter to write up two copies of the logs, saying the same things with different words, and within a few weeks, they were fully qualified accountants. Peter's mother went to Boots and bought a posh frame for the diploma, and hung it proudly in place in the living room. Kevin found a picture frame that Susan had left behind, the frame contained a picture of them from their visit to Longleat during the summer. Kevin took out the photo and discarded it without a second thought, replaced it with the diploma, and hung it in the downstairs bog. Although Susan had left this photo behind, she'd managed to find all of the Polaroid photos that he'd taken of her.

The following month, Mark called them both into his office. "There's a two-day seminar in London next month. It covers diversification, expanding the business, including funding expansions, accounting for new branches in the business and fraud awareness. There's a get-together and a meal for the attendees and the presenters on the first night, which will give you a good chance to network with accountants from other companies, and other types of business. It will carry on until late so we've booked you in a bed and breakfast for the night in Putney, close to the seminar. You need to be at the B and B by eight thirty on the first morning of the seminar. I know it's short notice, but one of our main suppliers, Burridge's, is having financial problems, and the Board are considering buying their company. We had to move fast to get you places."

Peter, as usual, was pleased that he was being treated as an important member of the company, Kevin thought that it might be a good chance to get his end away with someone different than the girls in the local pub.

They caught an early train to Paddington, and the tube to Putney, and arrived at their digs in good time. They carried their bags to the front door, and Peter rung once, politely, on the door bell. There was no answer, so Kevin hammered on the door, expecting this method to be more successful. An unexpectedly attractive woman, dressed in a short bathrobe, answered the door.

"You're early. I was in the shower." Kevin's mind switched to 'shag' mode, and all he heard was "glah glah glah glah shower". Kevin liked showers.

"I run a dress shop, and I'm out tonight until late at a meeting with buyers. That's why I wanted you here at eight thirty. You'll be back here before me tonight, so I needed to give you a door key and show you the burglar alarm code before I left for work."

Kevin was still unsuccessfully trying to get a glimpse of wet flesh underneath the bathrobe, as the woman showed them the alarm box, hidden in the downstairs loo. Peter listened intently at her instructions, whilst comparing the woman with

Susan. Although he hadn't seen Susan for over three months, he still used her as the benchmark for his model female.
"Follow me, I'll show you your rooms."
Kevin held Peter back, and waited at the bottom of the stairs to obtain a better look at the woman's legs as she went up the stairs. Peter was unsure what was happening until he looked up to the top of the stairs. He took a large intake of breath and dropped his bag onto the floor. The woman turned around quickly to find out what had caused the noise and her bathrobe flapped open, giving Peter and Kevin a full view of her hairy clam. Despite his age, Peter was still inexperienced in the wonders of the female body, and his initial thought was that it was a strange place to keep a hedgehog, as he dropped his bag again.
"Come on Dad, stop acting like an old pervert." The woman scowled at Peter whilst Kevin pushed him up the stairs. Peter blushed deeply, and wished himself anywhere but where he was.

The first day of the seminar was really interesting, and Peter took copious notes to discuss with Mark on his return. Kevin spent most of his time doodling, and eyeing up the females present, to calculate his best chance of a legover. There were many people present at the seminar that Kevin and Peter knew from their CIMA studies and previous presentations, but unfortunately for Kevin, his companion on his late night visit to the Covered Market at Oxford on the last night of their exams was missing.
The questions from the attendees came thick and fast, especially for the final presentation of the day, which was for Fraud awareness. Peter had drawn up a list of questions, both before and during the presentations, and had raised his hand yet again, but was forced to withdraw as Kevin elbowed him wickedly in the ribs.
"Put a sock in it, you ker-nob, the rest of us are hungry". The large amount of questions caused the first day's presentations to finish so late, it was almost time for the evening buffet and get-together, and Kevin's belly was starting to growl in anger. Peter farted loudly in response to the elbow, and the crowd

quickly dispersed to the function room. Peter picked up his notes, and followed them, keeping a lookout for the Fraud presenter, in order to complete his questions. The presenters didn't follow the crowd into the function room, so Peter mingled with the other attendees, sharing comments about the presentations as well as finding out why they were present, and how they were using the time that had previously been filled with studying. He was interested to find the different ways their companies funded their branch businesses, and how they accounted for them, Peter and Kevin filled up their plates from the expansive buffet and found a place to sit, Kevin wolfed his food quickly, and made a second circuit of the table, and sent Peter up to get him another glass of beer. The presenters finally joined them, over an hour later. Peter caught a glimpse of the Fraud presenter, surrounded by a large number of the attendees, so he sat where he was, adding the Branch Accounting information that he had received to his notes, until the crowd had decreased. Kevin, still looking around the room for a possible playmate for the night, noticed a bored looking woman standing next to the Fraud presenter, as he talked to the surrounding group.

"Come on Kevin, the Fraud presenter's free. We need some information from him for Mark". Kevin wasn't bothered about talking to the Fraud expert, but it could be worthwhile getting some information from his female companion. They both moved towards the Fraud expert, with both of them looking at their own specific target.

"Could you please tell me why there is a fraud presentation mixed in with a forum regarding expanding the business?" Peter tried to sound as professional as possible, and succeeded quite well.

"Once you start increasing the amount of different areas of the business, you increase the opportunity for fraud, so it is a very relevant part of the presentations that you need to be aware of."

Peter was impressed by the answer. It was something that he hadn't considered, and he would report this back to Mark.

"If the accountant is the only person who knows how much they should expect from their branches each month, the management won't know if their money is going missing. Are you two thirty years old yet?"

"Do I look that old?" Kevin aimed his answer at the Fraud expert's companion, trying to open a conversation with her. No response.

The Fraud expert continued. "And are you both still single?"

"Yes, we're both single." Kevin's answer followed the same plan.

"Staff start to be promoted into important positions in the business when they get to thirty. People work in generalisations, and the way that they look at it, if you're thirty and still single, there's the possibility that you prefer the company of boys in your bed to the girls, or you drink more than is good for you." Before Kevin could argue, the Fraud expert carried on with his explanation. "If you're in an important position, and you fill either of these criteria, this leaves you way open for exploitation, or even worse, blackmail, and before you know it, you've defrauded the company, and have nothing to show for it. Senior management also need to take note of their members of staff who have money or gambling problems. As well as increasing the possibility of defrauding the company, it also affects their performance at work"

Peter had always expected that he would be married by the time that he reached thirty, but was still only interested in Susan. And he definitely didn't drink too much, his hangovers saw to that.

Kevin finally had the chance to respond to the comments about his sexuality. "I have no inclinations towards boys, I'm quite happy with the opposite sex, and they've always been more than happy with me. I also have no problem drinking either." Kevin could sense that the woman stood next to him was taking an interest in his unsubtle hints.

A new crowd had surrounded them, and were waiting with their questions. The Fraud expert handed Peter his card. "If you have any further questions, call me anytime. Please excuse me, I need to share my time between everyone." He didn't think that Kevin was particularly interested enough to have any follow-up questions, and turned towards his new audience.

Kevin watched the woman's face drop when the man started to talk to his new audience. "Would you like a drink, there's beer or wine?"

"A white wine please, I might as well, there's nothing else to do is there, my husband's busy talking."

Kevin sent Peter for the drinks whilst he continued his conversation with the woman a little way away from her husband. "Do you attend a lot of these functions?"

"Too many. Richard always likes me to accompany him, but he knows that I'm not interested in listening to him saying the same things over and over again."

"What would you do if you weren't here with him?"

"I've heard Richard's talks about company espionage, and I think that I would be quite good as bait to lure an unsuspecting man into giving up business secrets."

"You've certainly got the looks for it. I'd tell you anything that you wanted to know."

"You seem to think that you have a way with women yourself."

"I find that they usually respond to a stiff talking to, but I'm particularly interested in practising my probing and penetration skills. I have a room just around the corner if you're interested in helping me."

"Do you always move this quick? I'm a married woman."

"I find that if I want something, it's always good to let people know. It saves any confusion, and reduces the chances of missed opportunities."

"But you don't even know my name." Unlike the attendees, the woman did not have a name badge on her chest.

"I'd vote for every attendee wearing name badges, it would have given me an excuse to look at your breasts. If that's the only thing stopping you from leaving here with me, you'd better introduce yourself."

"I'll leave it to you to find out during your interrogation."

Peter couldn't believe his eyes as he returned from the bar, and saw Kevin and the woman leave the function. He looked over to Richard, who was still deep in conversation with his audience, and oblivious to his wife's actions.

Kevin unlocked the front door and ushered the woman inside and upstairs to his room, and had barely started his inquisition when the burglar alarm started attacking his ears.

Peter noticed that the crowd around Richard had finally dispersed, and he had started to look around for his wife. Peter was worried that Richard would connect Kevin with him, and put the blame of his missing wife on him. He walked to where Richard was standing, and started to ask further questions regarding fraud in the hope that Kevin would return before Richard would find out what was happening.

"How do you know so much about fraud, and how it's carried out? You can't learn that from books surely?"

"I have contacts with a large number of people who have been convicted of fraud. Some of them are no longer active, and work with us to assist Businesses and the Insurance Companies to reduce the amount of fraud committed."

"So you could commit fraud quite easily and get away with it?"

"If I was that way inclined, I probably could. I get my rewards by preventing crime; I'm also well compensated by the Companies for whom I save money and I also save their ideas and plans from getting into the wrong hands."

The room fell quiet, and Peter noticed that everyone was looking towards the main entrance. Two policemen stood at the entrance with a white-faced Kevin and an embarrassed-looking Richard's wife. Richard took a deep breath, and walked quickly to the new arrivals.

"What's happening, this is a private function."

"Is this your wife, sir?" one of the policemen asked.

"Yes, what's the problem?"

"She was in a house in Putney with this gentleman, and the alarm was sounding off. Neither of them knew the alarm code, or could prove why they were there."

Peter looked through his notes, and found a copy of the details of the house that Mark had given him. "Was it this address?"

The policeman looked at the piece of paper. "Yes, it was."

"That's where we're staying tonight. We're here for a two-day seminar. They've obviously forgotten the burglar alarm code. I don't have the contact details of the house owner, as she's at a business meeting until later tonight."

The policeman looked happy with the explanation. "The householder will have to deal with the alarm company. They don't like being called out to reset alarms due to poor memories. At least no damage was done."

The police left, and the noise in the room returned to its normal level.

Kevin breathed a large sigh of relief, but hadn't reckoned on Richard's reaction.

"What the hell were you doing there with my wife?"

"Nothing."

Richard turned his stare to his wife. "Well!"

"I was bored. You shouldn't keep bringing me to these places where I don't know anyone, and have nothing in common with them."

"You seem to have found something in common with him." Richard poked Kevin's chest sharply with his finger. Although Kevin was much bigger than Richard, Richard looked quite menacing. "You'd better leave now. If I see you again, I'll fucking kill you."

Richard dragged his wife away, and Peter and Kevin left in silence.

Kevin had his mind on many other things throughout the following day's presentations, and his heart wasn't really in it when he dug his elbows into Peter's ribs to prevent him from asking too many questions. He wondered what Mark would say to him on his return, and sat waiting for Richard to arrive with a gang of heavies to exact his revenge for leading his wife astray.

Peter took copious notes to report back to Mark, and asked question after question to increase his account of the presentations. It wasn't until they were on the train back to Oxford that Kevin realised that he should have some idea why he had spent the last two days at an accounting seminar.

"Why does the board think that we'll be more successful at running the Company that we're buying out than they are? We don't know anything about their business, and we don't have any contacts like they already have."

"The middle management will have that information, and they will be keen to keep their jobs."

Kevin was still not convinced. "Why would our company benefit from buying one of our main suppliers, if all we do is get what we already receive?"

"If we can get Burridge's to produce the goods at a cost lower than the price that they charge us, our company will be better off. The board will run the Company from Oxford, so we won't have to pay their Chairman's and Directors' salaries or the shareholders' dividends. Burridge's overall expenditure will reduce, so the average cost of production will be less than the price we currently pay. That will reduce our production costs, we will be able to lower our selling price, and our sales will increase. This will result in an increase in the company's profit."

Peter spent the evening at home typing up his report, and printed off four copies for the next day's meeting. First thing the next morning Kevin met Peter before they went Mark's office to update him with their report. Kevin took the copies of the report from Peter, read it through and gave Peter back one of the copies.

"I think this covers everything that we spoke about, don't you? Let's go and see Mark." Kevin kept hold of the three copies until he had handed two copies to Mark.

"That's quite a report, well done Kevin. I'll give a copy to the FD and discuss it with him. Hopefully he can convince the board to buy the suppliers. We also had information about a problem with a burglar alarm in Putney."

"That was Peter. He was so distracted by the householder of the B and B in her short dressing gown, that he gave me the wrong code for the burglar alarm. I went back to the house early as it had been a long day, whilst he stayed at the function. The Police arrived, thinking that I was a burglar, and the security firm came out to reset the alarm."

"Unfortunately, there was a call out charge which the householder says that we should pay, so I expect you to send her a cheque, Peter."

Peter was gob-smacked, but still sent off the cheque to cover the bill.

The board were almost as sceptical about the idea as Kevin, and took so long to make their decision, that the suppliers were bought up by another company. To make matters worse, the new owners of the suppliers told the board that they would have to increase the cost of the parts supplied in order for them to survive. The Company had little option but to pay the increase. They had a 'Just in Time' arrangement with the supplier, meaning that they did not have to hold large amounts of stock, and it would take them too long to find another supplier, and get a new contract in place without causing huge disruption to their manufacturing.

Peter had learnt a lot in the last few days, the least of which was that if you need the board to make a decision quickly, you need to communicate the benefits clearly and concisely, and show how the risks can be averted or mitigated. He also learnt that when producing a report on which an important decision would be made, he had to ensure that the risks, dangers and consequences involved in the 'do nothing' option were clearly explained, as 'doing nothing' was usually the easiest course of action. In this case, the board's decision not to purchase the suppliers resulted in a reduction in the company's profit due to the increase of the new supplier's costs. He had also been sharply reminded that, after all of these years, Kevin was still a bastard.

Kevin didn't learn anything, and was out on the prowl for women, married or otherwise, as soon as he got back to Oxford.

For the following three years Peter tried to forget his heartache from losing Susan by burying himself in his work, looking for ways to improve the business. He was working at home one Sunday evening, preparing for the following week, when he received the phone call that he had given up all hope of ever arriving.

"Hello Peter, it's Susan."

Peter stopped breathing, his mouth went dry, and he could hear his pulse thumping in his head. He had rehearsed on numerous occasions what he would say to Susan if he met her in town, so that he would sound cool, and successful, but his body went into severe shock and he was unable to speak.

"Peter, can you hear me?"

Peter coughed, and his body jerked back into life. He searched frantically for a reason for not answering, and the delay only made it harder for him to respond. He took a deep breath.

"Hello Susan. How are you?"

"I'm fine thank you. We're thinking of putting on a comedy called 'Outside Edge', and we need a man to play the part of a small cricketer. I remembered how good you were in Aladdin, and said that I would ask you if you were interested."

Peter would play the part of a small cricket ball, if it resulted in the chance of spending time with Susan. "I would love to."

"Are you sure you're not too busy?"

"I'm always busy, but my mother keeps telling me that I need to get a hobby, and meet more people."

"We're meeting backstage on Tuesday for the first read-through. Although this is an audition, we're so short of men at the moment, that any male who turns up will get a part. I'll look forward to seeing you at about seven thirty. Bye."

The phone clicked, and Peter stood open-mouthed listening to the dialling tone.

Peter was too excited to sleep, and spent the night thinking about Susan and what he would say to her. He lay in bed tossing and turning, counting down the minutes. He tried his hardest to get to sleep to make the time pass quicker so that he could get to work and tell everyone his good news, but no matter how many times he relaxed his body and counted sheep, his mind was far too over-active, and the elusive sleep would not arrive. He wasn't sure how Kevin would react, as he'd never mentioned Susan since she'd gone back home to her mother, so Peter decided to let him find out via the office grapevine. He eventually admitted defeat on getting any sleep at six o'clock, and got ready for work. Arriving at work even earlier than usual, greeting the few people in the office with a huge smile, he was certain that nothing could spoil the way he felt, and was only slightly concerned when he noticed that Mark was already waiting for him.

"Burridges is up for sale again."

"So I hear. I'm surprised it's taken the new owners so long to realise it's not a going concern as an independent business. Are we interested this time?"

"The FD wants to talk to us about it as soon as Kevin gets in."

Kevin arrived after nine o'clock, bleary-eyed, and still hung over from a long weekend spent trying to drink the pubs in Oxford dry. He had resolved the problem of arriving at work unshaven by growing a full beard, more out of laziness than for aesthetic reasons, but he did have to admit to himself, that a beard did suit him. Mark called him into the FD's office, so he grabbed a quick coffee, and followed Mark and Peter. The FD looked at the three Accountants on the other side of his desk and sighed heavily.

"The company is just about to go through a period of great change, and unfortunately, I won't be with you to join in." Peter sharply resurfaced from his day dream where he was walking hand in hand with Susan, whilst Kevin just nodded in blind indifference.

"I'm overdue retirement, and have given my notice to the board. Mark will take over from me, but his current duties will change, and increase to cover the extra work due to our purchase of Burridges, which will be completed soon. We've had another look at your previous report, and I don't expect any problems with the take-over, as we've been dealing with them for years. We will have to complete Group Accounts from now on, and one of you two will need to be closely involved with the new part of the business." The FD looked at Peter and Kevin. "This isn't going to be easy, as the last two owners have found out."

Peter's face went white with the implication of having to spend his time in Newcastle. He wouldn't have time to take part in the play, which meant that he wouldn't have his chance with Susan. He had to make sure that the one who would be closely involved with Burridges would be Kevin, and started to devise a plan to get Kevin to work in the frozen North.

"I've helped other companies around Oxford with their Group Accounts, and it's not an easy job." Peter looked over at Kevin to see if his comment had registered, but Kevin was still blowing out the alcohol-induced cobwebs from his rarely used brain.
"That's why we pay you so much money." The FD replied. "That's all I was going to say, Mark can take it from here. The news of my retirement will be common knowledge shortly, I just wanted to tell you personally, and to thank you for all of your hard work and support."

Peter and Kevin followed Mark to his office. It was much smaller than the FD's office. As well as the desk and filing cabinet there was a small round table and four chairs. There wasn't much room for any paperwork on the desk due to the large computer covering its surface. The walls were covered in graphs and charts showing the profitability of the company, and future cash flow projections. A decision tree showed the probability of profit from the purchase of Burridges, but the details were still lost on Kevin. They sat around the table to discuss the future arrangements.

"When I move into the FD's office, we'll re-arrange this office so that you can both work in here, when you're not in

Newcastle. It should be quite easy to put in a new desk and a computer."

Peter had always hoped that this would be his office one day, and dreaded the thought of having to share it with Kevin, who would take up all of the space in the filing cabinet, and cover the round table with his rubbish. This made it even more imperative that Kevin spent as much time as possible in Newcastle.

"Kevin's much better at working with people than I am. It wouldn't be a good idea to send me to Newcastle to work with the team there, as I would be too shy to dictate our instructions to them. It would be more beneficial for the company if I stayed here, to complete the Accounts, and work on the business strategy."
Mark agreed with Peter's points.
"What do you think Kevin? How do you fancy working in Newcastle on a regular basis?"
Peter had another thought. "I used to live in Newcastle. The girls all wear really short skirts and always buy the beers when it's their round." 'That should clinch it' Peter thought.
"Why eye, that soonds good to me canny lad." Kevin gave his best Alan Shearer impersonation, but sounded more like Alan Hansen.

"We need to work out a way to ensure that this part of the business becomes profitable, and remains so. This will be the second time in three years that it's been sold because it was losing money, so we'll have to carry out monthly performance analyses on all aspects of the business. The workforce will remain, as will the production manager and the supervisory staff, who will be really happy to keep their jobs. The chairman and directors were the previous owners, and they are all leaving. I have a breakdown of their current Income and Expenditure, and they have been losing money for the last year. They tried to increase their prices with us again, but we learnt our lesson from when they took the company over three years ago, and our contract wouldn't let them without good reason."

Mark gave a large folder to Kevin. "Leave what you're doing today. I want you both to have a look at these figures, and come back after lunch with a projected cash flow for the next twelve months. I also want a list of any areas where we can save money. They don't have their own in-house Accountant, the Office Manager carries out the duties of bookkeeper and will provide you with any further information. Her telephone number is in the folder."

"A female Office Manager in Newcastle? Is Newcastle becoming politically correct?" Kevin expected it to be a 'Boys' only' club.

"Her name is Emma, so I can't see it being otherwise."

Peter was trying to visualise the cash flow statement, but needed more information before he could start. "How are we going to fund the new business?"

"We'll pay their bills centrally, and give them a float for petty cash."

"Most of the accountants at the forum we went to in London said that they let their branches run as independent businesses. It's supposed to improve morale and production. But if we do that we'll need to pay this month's wages, and their own suppliers."

"OK, give me two cash flow statements, one where we pay their expenses at the end of each month, and one where we provide initial funding, let them run their business as normal, and pay them at standard cost for their deliveries to us."

Kevin didn't like this answer, and more questions from Peter would result in even more work.

"Come on Dad, if we don't start soon, we'll be working all night!"

Kevin gave the folder to Peter, and went off to get himself another cup of coffee. When Kevin returned two hours later Peter had drawn up the two cash flow statements.

"How's it going Dad?"

"They're both done. It's pretty simple really. There aren't many areas of expenditure, mainly raw materials, wages and facilities costs. We are the only customer, so all of their income comes from us. I've obtained the years' planned deliveries from Burridges, and multiplied them by the contracted cost. When you take out the Directors' salaries and dividend payments which no longer apply, the company should make a nice little profit."

Kevin looked down at the cash flow statements and Burridges' Profit and Loss statement on Peter's desk

"What about the depreciation payments?"

Peter sighed inwardly. After all these years, Kevin still didn't understand the difference between cash and non-cash costs.

"They're not included in the cash flow statement. We haven't been asked to draw up a revised Profit and Loss statement, so we can ignore depreciation."

"Have you found any areas where we can save money?"

"We will save money by centralising most of the admin work, and by compiling the Accounts ourselves. Our Company board will devise the business strategy, and give direction to the middle-management, so there is no need to pay for Senior Management in Newcastle, or shareholders' dividends. The wages bill seems high compared to the size of the workforce, but we can look into that later."

Kevin took the paperwork from Peter. "Let's go and tell Mark the good news."

As expected, Mark was pleased with reports, and optimistic that the purchase of Burridges would be a step forward in the growth that he had planned for the company when he became the FD.

"I want you both to visit Burridges later this week, and go through their admin and bookkeeping procedures. After that, have a look at how they carry out their business. If you drive up after lunch on Wednesday, you can spend all day Thursday with Emma, and report back here on Friday morning. When the new positions are announced you two will be given company cars, so you may as well borrow mine for the trip to Newcastle."

Kevin was about to complain that it was very short notice, and there wasn't enough time to get everything done, but was struck dumb when the company car was offered. Peter would do the work anyway, and he could get time to check out Emma.

The following evening, Peter turned up for the first read-through of the play. Although he arrived early, the club was already half-full. It was more than three years since he'd been in Aladdin, but his memory from those rehearsals was that most of the cast always turned up fashionably late. He hadn't been there for the auditions, when everyone is eager to get the good parts, or in this case, one of the few female parts on offer. Peter recognised a number of those present from when he was in Aladdin and greeted them quietly. There were only three parts for females in the cast; one of them was a well-to-do lady who was the cricket team captain's wife, another was a teenage bimbo, and the other was an attractive but large and domineering woman. There were quite a few females already there, trying for the three parts, but Peter was not a threat to them, and male actors were a scarce commodity, so they were happy to see him. Peter looked around the room for Susan and Dawn, and was surprised that they weren't there yet. Dawn appeared from backstage and called them through to the main changing room. She quite fancied the part of the cricket team captain's wife, but the play was a particular favourite of hers, and she took the opportunity to direct it.

The main changing room had been re-arranged. The sofa and the easy chairs had been pushed back, and a group of chairs were set up in a semi-circle. Susan was already in the changing room, and had set up a small bar of cans of beer and coke, and boxes of wine. Peter tried to think of something witty to break the ice with Susan, and looked at the sofa. "Don't I have to take my turn on the casting coach?" Dawn stared at Peter as if she'd been stung, but Peter looked oblivious to any other meaning to his comment, so she decided to treat his comment with the innocence that it was offered, and proceeded with the audition.

"*Outside Edge* is a comedy about a village cricket club in two acts. The first act is before a game, and the second act is during the game. The action takes place in front of, and inside the club house, with the game taking place off-stage. Please sit down, and pick up your scripts, as there is a lot to get through."

Peter wanted to sit next to Susan, but only those reading for parts in the cast were seated in the large semi-circle of chairs around Dawn. On each chair was a copy of the script and a description of each character. Peter looked at the descriptions, and noticed the description of Kevin. Kevin was small, enthusiastic and easily dominated. Peter didn't like the character's name, but the size and temperament shouldn't be a problem.

The read-through was hectic, and lasted for what seemed to be hours. They all read through pre-selected parts of the script, whilst Dawn listened and took notes. Peter found his role very funny and he read it with the right amount of pathos and enthusiasm. He was worried that he wouldn't get the chance to speak to Susan. They finally took a break to have a beer or coke, whilst Dawn read through her notes, making additions. Susan helped with the small bar for the cast, and he managed to have a quick chat with her when she had served everyone. Dawn went round quickly talking to the prospective cast, and they were soon dragged back to the read-through. Dawn sat everyone back down, and went through her notes, matching characters to actors. She offered Peter the part of Kevin, which he quickly accepted. He was concerned that the lady playing his wife was much taller than he was and. although pretty, was very well built, and not the sort of girl that he would marry in real life. He hoped that it wouldn't deter Susan.

Dawn gave a copy of the script to all those chosen for parts in the play. "Rehearsals start next Tuesday, we'll have a complete read-through. This play is scheduled to be performed in eight week's time. I want everyone to be word

84

perfect within three weeks. You won't be able to get into character if you're still reading from your script."

Peter tried to speak with Susan, but she was busy tidying away the bar, so he made a quiet exit, happy in the fact that he would be spending some time with her during the next eight weeks.

Wednesday lunchtime, as planned, Kevin and Peter had a quick meeting with Mark then made their way to the frozen North, to run the rule over the setup at Burridges. Kevin played rock CDs all the way up, and chain-smoked with the driver's window open. He made no attempt to open up a conversation with Peter, spending most of his time singing out of tune with the music. They reached the pre-booked Bed and Breakfast in time to take their bags to their room, and then headed out for a bag of fish and chips and a few beers. Peter would have preferred a proper sit-down meal, but Kevin over-ruled this.

"I'm not wasting my time waiting for some food to be served, when there's beer and women waiting for us. Where's your sense of adventure?"

After two pints of beer each, all paid for by Peter, Peter needed to get back to his room to avoid arriving at Burridges in the morning with a raging hangover.

"There's some paperwork that Mark gave me that I need to read up on before tomorrow's meeting with Emma."

"Don't be such a ker-nob, the bar is filling up, and there's lots of women arriving."

"If I drink any more, I'll have such a bad hangover, that you'll have to do all of the work, and write up the report." Kevin thought this over, and decided that it would be better all round if Peter did the work tomorrow, so allowed him to leave without further argument.

Peter walked back to the B&B to clear his head, and took out the folder containing the details of Burridges' Income and Expenditure. He wrote down a few calculations based on the figures and added some more points to the list of questions that he'd already drawn up. He gave them a final read through, then picked up his script for the play, and started to learn his lines. Kevin must have heard by now that he was taking part in the play, but he'd made no mention of it, or asked any questions about Susan.

He was woken up by the sound of Kevin clumping back just after closing time, accompanied by the sound of girlish giggling. Peter could never understand what females saw in Kevin, but he was never short of their company. He hoped that Kevin wouldn't spend the whole of the following day chatting up Emma, and preventing him from getting the answers to his questions.

The following morning, Peter was up bright and early, washed and shaved and ready for breakfast. He was clothed in his most conservative clothes with black platform shoes, and a dark suit. He knocked on Kevin's door, and after the third try finally heard some signs of life on the other side of the door.

"Fuck off, you ker-nob, it's too early."

"It's eight o'clock."

"That's not my fault."

"We need to get to breakfast now, or we we'll be late getting to Burridges."

"Bring me back a bacon sarnie, something's just come up that I need to attend to." The same girlish giggling as the night before came from the room. "You'd better make it two sarnies, but take your time." Peter shook his head in disbelief as he went on his own to the dining room.

By the time Peter got back from breakfast, Kevin was up and dressed, and ready to leave. His female companion walked with them to the car. Her clothes were wrinkled, her make-up was smudged from the night before, and she smelt of really cheap perfume. 'A bit classy by Kevin's standards', Peter thought to himself, and then hurriedly added 'except for Susan'. A smiling Kevin dropped her off at a bus stop, with a swift "see you around", and then drove to Burridges.

"Have you arranged to see her again then?"

"Not likely. I wouldn't run away if I saw her again, but it's usually easier to keep it to one-night stands."

"Don't you love any of them?"

"Love? I love all of them. Life is short and love is always over in the morning."

They were met at the main entrance by a man younger than Peter and Kevin, with a beer belly and a bald head.

"Hello, Mr Stevens and Mr Stevenson I presume."

"All depends on who wants to know." Kevin was in a good mood from his horizontal exploits, and smiled at the man.

"I'm Emma."

"Yeah, and I'm the Queen of Sheba."

"No. It's true. I'm Emma."

A look of uncertainty appeared on Kevin's face. The females that he had met during the previous night were nothing like this one.

"My surname's Dale, hence the name Emma."

"Oh, right." Kevin smiled in recognition of the explanation. He remembered the T.V. programmes that Susan used to watch whilst he played computer games, so he was well aware of how the name came about. Peter was still in the dark, but he didn't want to show his ignorance if Kevin understood.

"The office is this way," Emma opened the entrance door and ushered them down the corridor. The main office was small, but large enough to provide enough working space for Emma and a real female. "This is Chris; she assists me in the running of the office,"

Chris was much more like the females that Kevin met the previous night. She offered them a cup of coffee, which was swiftly accepted by Kevin.

Peter opened his file and looked at the list of questions that he'd prepared.

"How are your duties shared out?"

Emma was the office manager, so Chris looked at him to take the lead on the answers.

"Both of us can carry out all of the duties required, in case one of us is ill or on holiday."

"What about signing the cheques to pay the bills?"

"We send the cheques off every Friday. Either of us writes the cheques, and a member of the board signs them."

"Who's going to sign them now that there's no senior management here?"

"We thought you would tell us that sir."

Peter made a quick note and carried on. "Who works out the payroll?"

"We have details of what everyone earns. Each department head sends in attendance reports each week. We work out the tax and National Insurance deductions, and the staff are paid by Bank transfer at the end of each month."

"Who writes up the Company accounts?"

"We have an accountant who comes in at the end of each financial year. He writes up our Profit and Loss statement and our Balance Sheet for the year, and compiles our Tax return. He also wrote up a report for the board with some performance ratios, and something called Rocky. "

"That's Return on Capital Employed. It shows the investors the level of profit that the business is making compared with the money invested in shares and assets, so that they know whether it's worthwhile carrying on with the business or selling their shares and investing the money in something more profitable."

"The last time that the Accountant was here, the figure was a negative."

"It would be negative if you were making a loss. How do you know if you're making a profit during the year?"

"We get Bank statements each month. We reconcile the statement to the cheque book, take off any cheques that haven't been cashed, and we're usually OK if the balance isn't too much lower than the month before."

"Is that usually the case?"

"Not recently."

"Do you have anyone to carry out any performance analyses during the year?"

"No."

This wasn't the answer that Peter expected, so he had to change tack.

"Have you ever been asked to carry out any performance analyses?"

"No."

"Do you know how to do them?"

"No sir, why should we. It's not part of our duties." Emma was getting a bit pissed off with the interrogation, and Peter picked up on it straight away.

"It's not a problem. It's quite easy, but really needs to be done, to warn the senior management early if there are any problems with the business. We can do them for the first month, but we expect you to do them from then."

"But we don't know what to do."

"I'll write up a spreadsheet on the computer with all of the calculations, all you'll have to do is put in the figures each month and send us the results."

Kevin was bored already and took his cigarettes out. Chris tugged at Emma's sleeve and nodded towards Kevin. Emma looked at Kevin, looked back at Chris and gestured outside.

"We don't smoke in the office sir. We don't smoke in any of the working areas."

"Where's the smoking area?"

Chris picked up her bag and walked towards the door. "Follow me sir, I'll show you."

Kevin was quite impressed with being called sir, and was thinking how he might be able to make it to his advantage.

Peter wrote up a few notes in his file whilst Chris picked up her bag and went outside with Kevin.

"Why do you keep calling me sir?"

"We called the previous chairman and Board members Mr Burridge or sir, and after the takeover, Mr Lambert. It's easier to call you sir than Mr Stevenson."

"Well, you don't have to, we're not members of the board. My name's Peter, and my colleague's name is Kevin. Are you OK with being called Emma?"

"I've been called Emma since school. Everyone calls me it now, I'm used to it."

Peter looked at the computer in the office. A screen-saver of Alan Shearer in a Newcastle shirt wavered across the front of the monitor.

"Do you only have the one computer?"

"We were lucky to get this one. The owners thought that it would be a waste of money, and that we would spend all of our time playing games on it. We use it for work all of the time, it saves hours when we do the pay run. The only problem with it is that we only have two phones in here, and when we dial up to the internet, it takes away one of the phone lines."

"All right. Look, I'll set up the layout for the Profit and Loss statement and Variance Analysis formulae on your computer. You only need to enter the figures into them each month, and they will automatically calculate the answers."

Peter wrote up the formulae, took out the report of the previous month's figures and entered them into the relevant formula, along with the expected performance figures that he calculated the previous night. The printer in the office coughed to life, as it produced the numerous reports, as Kevin and Chris returned from their extended fag break in time for Peter's explanation of the variance reports.

"This variance calculation shows you the production against the forecast production. Last month's production was better than expected. This one shows the cost of raw materials used in production, against the forecast cost. The actual cost is a little bit lower than expected, which is also good. This one shows actual staff costs against the expected staff cost, which is higher than expected. You need to do this after the end of each month to keep an eye on your performance. At the moment the business is very efficient according to these ratios, but that's because you no longer pay the salaries to the previous owners. You'll need to keep an eye on them, and provide reasons for any of the variances that are larger than normal, either positive or negative."

Emma took in what Peter had showed him, and the importance of carrying out the work.

"Did the previous owners get reports like this before they took over?"

"Yes they did. They had to increase their prices to you by five percent when they took over the company to be able to pay their salaries, and make a profit. But I've not seen any reports like these since then. They were running out of money quickly when they sold up."

Peter wrote some more notes in his file and turned over to a new page.

"I sent you an e-mail yesterday morning to check your address, did you get it OK?"

"Yes. We don't usually get letters via the computer."

"I think that you'll notice a large increase now that we're working together."

Peter spent the rest of the morning looking at the bookkeeping methods, and the filing system, whilst Kevin pretended to read the variance reports. After lunch Peter and Kevin had a tour around the factory, and Peter noted how the raw materials flowed from the store to the production lines, and how the finished goods were moved into the despatch building and made ready for being transported to Oxford. There was plenty of spare room on the site to expand or re-arrange the buildings.

Kevin was much more talkative on the way back home from the visit, and actually showed some interest in the implications of the takeover, instead of listening to noisy CDs.

"Why did the previous owners need to compile accounts if they owned the company?"

"The business is a Limited Company, so they had to do so by law."

"Why would they do that if they had to spend time and money writing up the company accounts?"

"A Limited Company has limited liabilities, so if the Company goes bust that means the payments of any money owed would be limited to the value of the shares that they hold. The owners wouldn't have to sell their own assets such as their house or cars to pay the Creditors."

"Oh yeah. We learnt that in our CIMA studies didn't we, along with that variance analysis stuff."

"We were taught those on AAT, but we went into much more detail for CIMA."

"I didn't take much notice of them when we were studying. I never thought that we'd ever use them in real life, but we use them all of the time. It's my thirtieth birthday in a couple of month's time."

Peter was thrown by the swift change of subject, but his memory took him back to the presentation in London three years earlier.

"Can you remember what the Fraud Awareness presenter said in London?"

"What – If I see you again I'll kill you"

"No, at the age of thirty if you're still single, you either have a drinking problem, or you prefer the company of boys in bed than girls."

"Best I go to the pub then Dad, unless you fancy another trip to Blackpool to celebrate."

"I don't think that my liver would survive."

"We need to do something. We've been promoted, and we need to let everyone know, and the best way is to do it in style. It would also get them on our side if we treated them to a few drinks."

Peter knew who would end up paying, so had to try to kill the idea before it got too big.

"I don't have the time, I'm busy doing a play."

"That'll be finished before my birthday."

So Kevin had heard about the play. No doubt he'd also heard that he'd been in touch with Susan as well. Peter was surprised that Kevin hadn't spoke about it.

"There's a lot going on at the moment. I expect there'll be a retirement do for the FD, and Mark will also want to celebrate his promotion as well as ours, so it would make sense if the company rolled them all into one massive shindig."

"OK then, two piss-ups. One for work, and one for my birthday."

Peter wanted to get Kevin away from the thought of going out to celebrate Kevin's birthday, because he would end up ill and short of money.

"I think I'll start writing up my report for Mark."

"Aren't you giving him a typed report?"

"Of course, but if I draft it now, it'll take me less time tonight to type it up."

"OK, make sure I get a copy before we go to see Mark tomorrow, so that I can read through it and add my comments." With that, the CD player sprang to life, and the sweet tones of Motorhead started their assault on Peter's ears.

The following morning Kevin came into work relatively early, and caught Peter before he had the chance to go to Mark with his report on Burridges. The Executive Summary at the start was longer than the whole report that Kevin would have produced, and the detailed report painted a glowing picture on the future of their new part of the business, backed up by the reports from the day before. Kevin took all of the copies and walked round to Mark's office, with Peter trailing behind him.

As expected, the first rehearsal consisted of a read-through of the play, and Dawn pointed out how certain phrases should be spoken. Peter was still shy with the cast members, and got over this by putting on voices of famous people when he read his lines. Dawn was mildly upset with the distraction, but had to admit that he was very good, and it was amusing. Peter felt a warm glow when he looked over at Susan and saw that she was smiling at him.

As in everything that he did, Peter was word perfect within two weeks, so during the breaks in rehearsals, whilst the rest of the cast were trying to learn their lines during their time off-stage, Peter had the chance to talk to Susan. Dawn still felt guilty about Kevin, so she was delighted that Susan had found someone nice showing an interest in her. Peter was still terribly shy with Susan, and she found him quite hard work to talk to. Susan had spent the previous three years staying at home watching the soaps on television, frightened that her next romance would end as badly as the last one. In all of the time that she had known Peter, Susan had never thought romantically of him, and was surprised that, as the rehearsals progressed, she was starting to feel jealous during the kissing scene between Peter and his on-stage wife. Susan realised that she could do a lot worse than Peter, and started to show more of an interest during their conversations. As usual, it was Susan leading the discussion.

"What's it like in the finance office at your work these days?"

"About the same. The FD's retired, and Mark has been promoted to take over from him. I do the work that Mark used to do. Where are you working now?"

"I work in a beauty salon in town."

"What, as a model."

"Don't be silly. No, I've always been interested in make-up, so I decided to make it my job as well. I've been going to college for the last two years to learn more. Eventually, I'd like to run my own salon." Peter smiled appreciatively at Susan's change of employment, and her future plans, but couldn't think of anything to add to the conversation, so Susan had another try.

"What do you do in your spare time?"

"I don't get much spare time. I spend most of my time working."

"You must do something more than work, surely?"

"I go to the pub on Fridays sometimes with Rob from work, you remember Rob from work don't you?" Susan nodded, not wanting to stop Peter's flow now he'd started. "We usually end up talking about work anyway. He used to talk about football, but he seems to have lost interest since Oxford United were relegated from the first division."

"Don't you have any hobbies?"

"I like going to the theatre and the cinema, but it's not as good when there's no-one to go with."

"I love going to the theatre." Susan smiled at the thought that they had something in common.

"Did you ever go to the theatre with Kevin?"

The smile left Susan's face even quicker than it had arrived. "I'd prefer it if you never spoke his name in front of me."

Peter stood open-mouthed as Susan stormed off. He was shocked at her reaction to the mention of Kevin's name. He had no idea that she felt so strongly about him, especially after all this time. Luckily, the rehearsals were almost finished for the night, but he went home feeling distraught.

Not wanting to give up his chance with Susan after he'd waited for so long, he managed to book two seats at the theatre for Friday of the following week. Due to the short notice, the seats weren't as good as he'd wanted, but he needed to get back into her good books.

The director of the play should always be the first person to arrive at rehearsals. As Susan travelled in with Dawn, Peter knew that Susan would be there early. The director always spent the first twenty minutes looking at the progress on the set design, the costume department and the properties, such as all of the cricket gear, whilst the cast turned up fashionably late and caught up with the latest gossip, or frantically read through their lines. Peter had no idea how he could apologise to Susan, so he didn't. Instead, he made sure that he arrived on time and he bought her a Gin and Tonic, which seemed to please her. He took his chance whilst she was in a good mood and took the theatre tickets out of his pocket.
"I managed to get two tickets for the Playhouse next Friday. Would you like to join me?"
"Buy me another G and T and I might think about it."
Peter still couldn't understand girls, and his face dropped at the thought of being blown out.
"Don't be silly, I'd love to go to the theatre with you."
"Oh, great, marvellous, fantastic."
"You can still buy me a G and T."
Peter was so happy, he would have bought her a bottle. What he didn't realise then, was that she'd have drunk all of it that evening quite easily.

Peter put his whole body into the rehearsal that evening, and Dawn was hugely impressed with his acting. The opening night was getting close, so there were more than the usual cast members at the rehearsals, and all of the back-stage team stopped what they were doing when he made his entrance early in the first act, and watched his performance as he took command of the stage, which came to life with his presence, and they all clapped at the end of the scene.

Peter returned home in great spirits and looked through his wardrobe and selected his clothes for his Friday night date. Although his clothes all looked the same, he wanted to make sure that they were clean and ironed. He thought that he looked cool and colourful when he picked Susan up the following week. His cream coloured platform shoes were hidden beneath his Oxford Bags, which he'd bought to replace the 21 inch flared trousers that he could no longer buy. The safety pins used to temporarily repair the trouser hems were clearly in view. He was really proud of his blue velvet jacket, despite the loose stitches on his right armpit, and he felt that the yellow shirt and red tie were a perfectly balanced colour match.

Susan was impressed when he opened the car door for her, especially as it was in full view of her parents. He drove her to the Westgate car park, and they walked to the Playhouse hand-in hand.

"Would you like a drink before we take our seats?"

"G and T please. Are you going to book drinks for the interval as well?"

He went to the Playhouse bar and bought a G and T for Susan and a small coke for himself, and also paid for the interval drinks. He would have preferred an ice cream at the interval, but wanted to keep her happy. The bell rang three times, and they walked hand-in-hand to their seats. Susan had started to work out how she would change his dress sense, and spoke to Peter as they sat down.

"Do you still live with your parents Peter?"

"I've never considered the need to move out. My mother's a good cook, and we live close to work. The money that I pay to them for keep helps supplement their pensions."

"They must have retired early."

"No, they were quite old when I was born."

"What about girlfriends?"

"I've had a few, but they all seemed to have the same shortcoming." Peter finally had the chance to use one of the conversations he'd practised for years.

"What was that?"

"None of them were you."

Susan cuddled up closer to him, and kissed him on the cheek. Luckily the darkness in the theatre prevented Susan from seeing how red Peter's face had become.

Peter had a great time at the theatre, and Susan gave him a quick kiss on the lips when he dropped her home that evening. The opening night for 'Outside Edge' was next Thursday, and the play was on for three nights, so he would be able to spend every evening of the week with her. The technical rehearsal, where they tested the lighting and sound effects was on Monday. It would be pretty straight forward, but Peter was interested in how they would make the sound of the cricket game in progress off-stage, and the heavy rainfall that stops the game at the end of the play. Tuesday night was the dress rehearsal, with Wednesday as the second dress rehearsal, if it was needed, and Peter hoped that it would be. Susan stood next to Peter for the dress rehearsal, and kissed him for luck prior to going on. Peter was wearing flat cricket shoes, and Susan noticed that she didn't have to stretch upwards to kiss him. She made a mental note of this and added it to her ideas on his future change of wardrobe.

The opening night went better than Dawn could have wished for. Peter's parents and work colleagues, except for Kevin, turned up on the opening night, and clapped and whistled at the end of the play. Friday night went just as well, apart from the team captain forgetting his lines when Peter came on stage with a blister on his 'spinning' finger, but Peter managed to cover for him, by adding the captain's lines to his own. No-one in the audience noticed, because they didn't have the words in front of them, and the dialogue flowed quite normally. But it was too good to last, and on Saturday, everyone in the cast had a stomach bug, and had trouble moving too quickly without having spillage flying out from both ends. It was a very subdued final performance, with limited on-stage movement. Linda, the girl playing Peter's on-stage wife was the worst affected, and Susan had a difficult job with her make-up, adding some life and colour to her face, and making it look

97

realistic. In the first act, Linda had to pick Peter up and hug him. Peter noticed the pained expression on her face as she struggled not to cough in her rompers at the effort. During the second act, the rest of the cast were jealous, as in the script, the young bimbo ran off in tears and locked herself in the toilets. Half way through the second act, just as the bimbo was due to re-appear, Linda walked offstage and stood in the wings, out of sight of the audience but in full view of the whole cast, and started throwing up into a fire bucket. Peter knew Linda's words as well as he knew his own for the scene, and was prepared to step in with Linda's line when the bimbo appeared, but on her re-entrance and her line, "I've just come from East Molesley." Linda walked back onto the stage, and wiping her mouth with her sleeve answered, "I don't blame you."

They all struggled through to the end of the play, and despite the lack of movement on stage, the dialogue was funny enough to keep the audience happy, and they clapped heartily at the end of the performance. However, the closing night party was a very subdued affair, with longer queues for the toilet than the bar. Peter could only manage the fizziness of one coke without incurring Montezuma's revenge, so said his goodbyes to Susan, the cast and back-stage crew before crawling off home early.

Peter turned up for work the following Monday morning feeling as bad as the time that he came back from Blackpool. This time, however, there were no incriminating photographs. Mark was now the FD, and Peter had moved into Mark's old office with Kevin, who, as expected, had taken up all the space apart from a small area around Peter's computer. The increase in work from the new business had resulted in Peter working late every night, and there was no way that he would be able to take time out to appear in any more plays for the foreseeable future. However, the ice had been broken with Susan, and he could now carry on his long wished for romance on the nights that she wasn't busy helping with the plays and pantomimes.

SIX

Peter usually worked late on Fridays. Everyone else had gone home for the weekend, so he could take advantage of the peace and quiet, and get on with his work without the normal distractions. Even though he was now going out with Susan, he found it a hard habit to break. He was surprised when his phone rang, and even more surprised when he heard Kevin's voice. Kevin's visits to the Newcastle branch had reduced to once a month, and coincided with the compilation of the monthly accounts. Peter was surprised that Kevin did this without his usual complaints.

"We've just done the Profit and Loss statement for the month, and we've made a loss."

"Have you completed the performance ratios?"

"Emma's checked the figures twice. The Raw Materials and Staff costs variances are both negative."

"E-mail me the Profit and Loss statement and the performance ratios. I also need to look at the breakdown of expenditure, especially staff costs. If you send them to me now, I'll look at them over the weekend, and get back to you first thing on Monday morning."

By the time the e-mail arrived, Peter was already running late. He printed off the details, put the paperwork into his briefcase, and rushed home. He was taking Susan out for a meal that evening, and had to make sure that he picked her up on time, or she would keep on about his time-keeping all night long.

Half way through the meal Susan plonked her cutlery onto her plate as noisily as she could, sighed deeply and stared at Peter.

"You haven't listened to a word I've said. I might as well go home."

Peter blanched at the thought of Susan leaving him. "I'm sorry, there's a problem at work."

"Since when has your work been more important than me?"

"Never, it's just that we're starting to lose money at the Newcastle factory, and it could have a large effect on the company."

"You spend too much time at work as it is. I would have hoped that you could pay some attention to me when you take me out instead of worrying about the Company. We've been going out for three years now, have you lost interest in me?"

"Good God no." Peter was panic-stricken, expecting Susan to finish with him in her next sentence.

"Well it feels like that to me. My friends go away for the weekend. You still live with your parents, so you can't ask me to stay there. All of the girls that I went to school with are either married or engaged. Some have even been married and are divorced. How do you think that makes me feel?"

"I don't know what you mean."

"Have you never thought about proposing to me?"

"All the time. But I'm frightened that, if I proposed to you, and you turned me down, you wouldn't go out with me any more."

"What makes you think that I would turn you down?"

"I just couldn't take the chance. You're too important to me to lose."

"Try me, I'm sure that you won't be disappointed."

"I always thought that when I proposed to you, I would go down on one knee."

"Not in here you won't!"

"I don't know what you want me to do?"

"For God's sake Peter. Just ask me!"

The problems with the Newcastle branch disappeared into thin air, and Peter was now fully focused on Susan.

"Susan, will you marry me please?"

"Of course I will."

Peter never thought that he would propose like this, and was overjoyed at the outcome.

"You earn quite a lot of money now, don't you?" It was a statement more than a question.

"I suppose so."

"Don't you think that it's about time that you bought your own home? You don't expect me to live with your parents do you?"

"Certainly not. It's just easier for me to live at home. It allows me to spend more time at work, and when I eventually get home, my dinner is always ready for me."

"So when are you going to move out?"

"I'll start looking tomorrow. Would you like to help me?"

"Do you think that I would let you choose my future home without me? What else do you have planned for tomorrow?"

Peter's face went blank. Had he forgotten something? Was it important? Susan smiled at him, so it wasn't bad news.

"Aren't you going to buy me an engagement ring?"

"Anything you want. Money is not an object."

"I've already chosen my engagement ring; we can pick it up tomorrow whilst we're visiting the Estate Agents. When are you going to ask my father for his permission?"

Peter moved back into panic mode. What would her father say? Did he think that Peter was good enough for his precious daughter?

"When do you want me to ask him?"

"My parents are at home tonight. We could go inside when you drop me off from here, and ask them then."

The meal had gone cold, and Peter wanted to get out of the restaurant to clear his head. It was a lot for him to take in after the attack on his senses.

"Can we go now, and get it over with?"

"I've lost my appetite too, but I could do with another G and T before I meet my parents."

Peter called the waiter over.

"Is there something wrong with your meal sir?" The waiter looked surprised. Peter and Susan were regular customers, and had always finished their meals before.

"The meal was as good as it always is, thank you, we just have to leave." Peter found himself smiling for no apparent reason. "Could you please bring me a large gin and tonic first, and then the bill?"

Peter was still smiling when they walked hand-in-hand into her parents' living room. Although it was Friday night, Geoffrey and Dawn were reading, with an operatic CD playing loudly. Brahms and Liszt had long gone past their boisterous phase, and lay where they were, wagging their tails at the new arrivals. Jaeger jumped at Susan's companion, his stumpy tail moving vigorously. This friend of Susan was much nicer than

101

the last grumpy one, and was always ready to play games, and take him for walks. Dawn looked up from her book.
"You're back early."
"We have something to tell you Mummy."
Geoffrey sat up in his chair, instantly expecting the worst.
"Peter's asked me to marry him."
Geoffrey smile matched Peter's. He liked Peter, and had been hoping for this for some time.
"I think there's a bottle of Moet in the fridge for occasions such as this." He eased himself out of his chair, turned down the volume on the CD player, and went out to the kitchen.

All of the excitement had left Peter completely worn out, and he flopped into an arm chair as he tried to regain his senses. He also lost his self control and a long and silent but very smelly fart erupted into the room. He'd managed until now to protect Susan from his flatulence problem, so her first instinct was to blame Jaeger. Peter was relieved to have a scapegoat to cover for his poisoning of the atmosphere, and as dogs think that farts as are funny as young boys do, Jaeger appeared happy to take the blame, and sat next to Peter, wagging his tail throughout the mild castigation and embarrassed laughter.

Geoffrey returned with the champagne and four glasses, to the sight of the three occupants fanning their noses, and pointing towards the dog. When the smell had reduced to a tolerable level, the discussion returned to the imminent wedding.
Dawn was really happy with Susan's news, and her feeling of guilt towards Susan regarding her part in the break-up of Susan and Kevin finally disappeared.
"Have you set a date yet?"
"We haven't even thought about it. I would prefer a summer wedding, with everyone outside in the sunshine, but that would mean waiting a whole year. The photographs always look so gloomy in the winter, and I don't want to wait that long."
"You'll need some time to find a new home for yourselves, and it takes a long time to arrange a good wedding." Dawn was always the practical type, and didn't want her friends raising

comments about a rushed marriage. "Spring is a lovely time to get married."

Peter's usual Friday night feeling of exhaustion made him look at his watch. "I'm sorry, but I'll have to leave now, or my parents will be asleep by the time that I get home, and I'd like to tell them the good news."
Susan stared at Peter. "I hope that you're not going to tell your parents without me."
"Well, it's late, and I'll be too tired to drive us home, tell them the news, bring you back here, and then drive back home again." Despite his fatigue, Peter never once contemplated asking Geoffrey and Dawn whether he could stay the night, even though he was now engaged to Susan, and would have been far too embarrassed to ask such a thing.
"Then come and pick me up early tomorrow morning, and we'll tell them then."
"O K, but I still have to leave."
Dawn picked up the half-empty Champagne bottle. "You can't leave yet, we haven't finished the bottle."
"I can't have any more, or I'll be over the limit."
Susan walked with Peter to the front door, and gave him a big kiss goodnight.
"I love you Susan, I always have. This is the best day of my life."

As usual, Peter did what he was told. He picked Susan up early the following morning and took her to tell his parents of their proposed nuptials. His parents were both overjoyed, and Peter's mother gave Susan a huge hug.
"Well, I can't pretend that it's a surprise." Apparently Peter was the only person expecting Susan to say no. "I can't understand why it's taken you so long."
Peter's mother was more practical than his father. "Where do you intend to live?"
Susan smiled. "We're going to the Estate Agents this morning."
"Houses in Oxford are expensive for first time buyers, you know."

"I have enough saved up for a large deposit, and the mortgage payments won't mean the complete demise of my social life." Peter's father smiled at the recollection of his statement many years before. "We could easily give you some cash to increase your deposit."

Peter's parents lived on their pension, and Peter didn't want any sacrifices on his behalf. "Certainly not. You keep your money in the Building Society earning you interest."

"We took our money out when they started having the banking and credit-crunch problems. I didn't want the Building Society going bust, and us having nothing left of our savings."

"What have you done with it?"

"It's in a tin box hidden underneath the Christmas tree in the attic, along with our other important papers, including copies of our wills. If we were burgled, they wouldn't be able to find it. You need to know about it, in case anything happens to us."

"Such as?" Peter was getting worried. Is there something that he should know?

"Anything really. We could be run over by a bus just as easily as the next person."

"You should put your savings somewhere where it's earning you money."

"We're happier with the peace of mind thank you. Although we would be happy if you took it for part of the down-payment for your house, and paid us back when you could afford to."

"I wouldn't dream of taking your life savings. You never know when you'll need them."

"They will come to you when we die anyway, so it's not a problem."

Susan was getting embarrassed, and changed the subject back to the wedding. "We were thinking of having a Spring wedding."

"I think that we can hang on that long. Just don't make us wait too long for grandchildren."

Susan was now mortified at the new topic of conversation, and wanted to get to the business of looking at houses before her face went any redder. "We really need to be going. Peter's going to buy me an engagement ring after we've been to the

104

Estate Agents, so we have to get to the shops before they're closed."

Peter drove into town and Peter and Susan walked down Cornmarket Street looking in the Estate Agents windows, when Susan came to an abrupt stop.
"This house is beautiful, and it's close to Mummy and Daddy as well."
Peter looked at the price. It was far more than he expected to pay, but he had to admit, it was a nice house in a good area. House prices had been rising since the slump during the early nineties, and Peter regarded houses as a sound investment. It would be difficult to make the mortgage payments, but apart from the occasional meal and trip to the theatre, his social life was already quite dead.
The young man in the suit took his feet from off of his desk as Peter and Susan entered the air-conditioned office.
"We would like to look at the house on Banbury Road please."
"Houses in Banbury Road are very expensive. Do you already own a property?"
"No."
"Why do think that you can afford this house?"
Despite his high wage, in line with his elevated position in the company, Peter was embarrassed by the raised eyebrows from the spotty youth when he pointed out the house that he was interested in.
"I have a large amount saved in cash for the deposit, and a very well paid job."
As well as putting the young man in his place, Peter also wanted to show Susan how successful he was.
"It's my duty to warn people that their house will be re-possessed if they fail to meet their mortgage payments, and the more expensive houses are usually purchased by older people, who already have a house to sell for their deposit, and have had a longer time to build up a large enough nest egg to assist them if they fall ill or lose their jobs. It would be a better idea if you bought a cheaper house to begin with, and wait until you have increased your savings to enable you to purchase a more expensive house like this one. Have you

thought about putting your savings into shares? You get a much larger return for your money than a deposit account."
Bloody cheek. Peter was a Management Accountant, and earned twice as much as these people, and he's being told what he should do with his own money.
"I have a large amount invested in shares as well, thank you. I'm not here to discuss investments with an Estate Agent. Could you arrange a viewing of the house please?"
The young man, suitably admonished, picked up the details of the house, and phoned the current owner. He looked over to Peter, "How about three o'clock this afternoon?"
Susan squeezed Peter's hand in delight, and his head swam with joy when he saw Susan's smile. It was worth twice as much as the asking price for the house just to get this reaction from her, and he responded a resounding "yes".
Susan took Peter's hand and pulled him towards the jewellers, and pointed out the ring that she had chosen some time ago, in the hope and expectation that Peter would finally get the message and propose to her. "This ring is lovely, and it'll look so much better when we view the house if I'm wearing an engagement ring."

Peter had been earning good money with nothing to spend it on for longer than he cared to remember, so the price, which would have put most people off, was a mere drop in the ocean of his savings. He usually paid cash for his purchases, but he wouldn't dare walk around town with this much in his pockets. His flexible friend appeared, the jeweller made the phone call to check Peter's credit, and the transaction was completed. Susan walked out with a shiny diamond on her ring finger.
"Have you finished spending yet, or did you have something planned for tonight?"
"I haven't booked the theatre tonight, or a place for dinner yet."
"That's lucky, that means we're free to book into a hotel for the night."
They'd stayed in a hotel when they went away for a week's holiday last summer, but Susan had never allowed him to book a local hotel before.
"Is there anywhere in particular where you'd like to stay?"

"The Bear in Woodstock. We could walk around Blenheim Palace gardens tomorrow. I think that it would be a really romantic thing to do."

Peter made the call to the hotel, and booked a double room with dinner and breakfast. "Did you want to have lunch in the Randolph today as well?"

"No, I think we should go home and have lunch with Mummy and Daddy. I'm sure that they would like that. I can have a G and T as well. That should set me up for the viewing of the house."

Although it was only a few minutes walk to the house from Susan's parents, Peter wanted to drive there, to show off his company car. An elderly woman answered the door, and invited them inside. Susan fell in love with the house as soon as she set foot inside it, and Peter was impressed with its elegance.

"I lived here for forty years with my husband, but now he's no longer with us, and my children have moved out, I don't need such a large house. I have a house in Eastbourne where we used to stay during the summer. I'm going to move there as soon as this house is sold. Let me show you round."

The upstairs were as tidy and stylish as those below, and Peter wanted to buy the house there and then, before anyone else could see it.

"Have you shown many other people around yet?"

The old woman looked at Peter. He was about the same age as her husband when they moved in, and looked as happy as they were. "I've only just put the house on the market. I was surprised to receive the phone call this morning."

"It really is a lovely house. We would like to make an offer, but it would leave us short of money."

"When you go back to the Estate Agents, tell the spotty little Herbert that you would like to offer ten thousand pounds less than the asking price."

"They won't accept that."

"That's not their decision to make, and I'll tell him that when he phones me later. I have plenty of money, and would love this house to go to a nice young couple like you two. If you two are as happy in this house as we were, I would be really pleased."

Peter and Susan left the house hand-in-hand, and Peter drove them back to Susan's parents' house to discuss their new home.

"Oh Mummy, it's really lovely, and it's only a few minutes' walk from here"

Geoffrey looked at the Estate Agents flier, and tapped the price with his pipe. "It's a lot of money to pay for a first home."

"It would be if I was young, had no savings and didn't have a well-paid job." Peter was surprised that he was having to defend his financial position for the third time that day, especially to Geoffrey.

"I knew the man who used to live there. He used to work in the City. He had a very well-paid job, but spent all of his time working himself into an early grave. You can spend all your time making money Peter, just make sure that you stay around long enough to enjoy it." When Geoffrey was Peter's age, sixty five years old was ancient, now that he was over fifty, sixty five was no age at all.

Dawn looked at Geoffrey, "I'm surprised to hear that from someone who spends as much time at work as you do."

"How many gravestones have you seen with the words, 'I wish I'd spent more time at the office'?"

Susan tried to lighten the tone of the conversation, "The lady selling the house told us that she would accept ten thousand pounds below the asking price."

Geoffrey was still looking at Peter. "It's still a lot of money?"

"It'll be difficult at first, but I can pay a large deposit, and I don't expect to have too many problems making the monthly payments. I'm going to give up my company car, and receive an extra payment of a few thousand pounds a year instead. It will mean that I'll pay less money in tax as well, as the value of the company car included in my taxable income. We'll have to do without getting a new car every year, but we can buy a cheaper car, and keep it for a few years until the mortgage payments become more manageable."

"We can give you help with the deposit if you like."

"That's really good of you, but I'm sure we'll be fine."

"I don't want you having to go without. You're only young once, there's a whole World out there to see, and it's best to see it whilst you're still young and healthy enough to appreciate it."

Dawn and Susan were again surprised at Geoffrey's speech. True, they'd been to lots of places on holiday, but he'd always seemed just as happy to stay at home with the dogs.

"Ooh Daddy, does that mean that you're going to pay to send us somewhere exotic for our honeymoon?" Susan gave her father a large hug.

"Only if you promise to come back happy." Geoffrey smiled down at his daughter.

"We can have an expensive honeymoon instead of a posh wedding."

It was finally Dawn's turn to have her say. "If you think that my only daughter's going to have a cheap wedding, you can think again. My friends will never let me forget it."

Peter didn't like the way that the conversation was moving away from the main topic. They'd be talking about babies next, unless he could stop them! "Right, it's agreed then. I need to go back to the Estate Agents to tell them our offer."

Geoffrey looked at Dawn. "If you're sure that's what you both want, you can phone your offer from here. Then we can start making plans for dinner."

Peter blushed, and didn't know how to tell him his arrangements for the night, especially what he had planned for Susan. Susan moved next to Peter and held his hand.

"We're going to Woodstock for the night tonight Daddy. I wanted to walk around Blenheim Palace tomorrow, and look at the gardens, so we're booked into a hotel. As soon as Peter's phoned the Estate Agents, we need to get ready to leave."

"You'd better phone in your offer now then." Although Susan had lived with that useless oik a few years ago, he had never felt in danger of losing her to another man before, and didn't want his emotions to show.

The weekend went past like a whirlwind, if whirlwinds could be that pleasant. When he eventually arrived back at his parent's house on Sunday, Peter checked his briefcase in preparation for the week ahead, and found the paperwork that Kevin had sent him. Although he was concerned about it when Kevin phoned him on what felt like ages ago, other factors had taken his focus away from his work for the first time in his life. He took out the paperwork and reviewed the details. Production was as expected, but the costs were much higher than budgeted for. The recent loss of value of the pound had magnified the large increase in the cost of raw materials from overseas. The largest expenditure was incurred on staff wages, as he had expected, but he was surprised at the amount of overtime being paid to the production staff. He looked through his notes from his first visit to Newcastle, and added the regularity of bill payments to his new comments. He would need to report this problem to the FD first thing in the morning, this was something that needed to be resolved quickly. Peter never thought that it was odd that he called Mark the FD after years of referring to him by his first name, and hoped that he would be called 'The FD' if ever he had the honour of holding the post.

Peter took his notes and the reports into the office first thing the following morning and phoned the FD's P.A. requesting a quick meeting regarding a problem with the Newcastle branch. He was told to come straight down.
"What's so important first thing on Monday?" Mark was concerned. Peter was invariably right about these things.
"They made a loss in the Newcastle branch last month."
"Which areas caused the problem?"
"The main problem was a large rise in the Raw Material price. The low pound made it worse."
"Do they have any ways of reducing the loss?"
"Not really. We're looking into reducing the staff costs, but wouldn't want any redundancies. It would be bad for morale, and our reputation. This increase in the price of Raw Materials will affect our rivals just the same as us. They will have to increase their prices sooner or later, so we could raise ours in line with them, and increase the standard cost that we credit to the Newcastle branch."

He hoped that the FD would buy the plan, but when Peter looked at his face he knew that it would never happen.

"Our competitors will try to absorb some of the increase as well, so Kevin will need to find some way of saving money at Newcastle."

"He's phoning me in a few minutes, what should I tell him?"

"Tell him that, if he can't find any savings, we'll have to make some staff cuts."

"He won't be very happy with that."

"If you're so concerned, why are you looking so pleased with yourself?"

Despite being tired from a busy weekend, and the problems in Newcastle, Peter couldn't disguise the huge smile he'd had since he woke up on Saturday morning. "Susan and I got engaged on Friday, and I had an offer for a house in Banbury Road accepted."

"It's about time too. She'll be good for you."

Peter walked slowly back to his office, trying to think of how he would pass this message onto Kevin, without causing alarm. Peter made a few notes what to say before he phoned the Newcastle branch office with the bad news. As usual, the phone was answered by Emma.

"Is Kevin in yet?"

"Kevin and Chris aren't in yet, can I take a message for him?"

"Kevin and Chris?"

"He stays in her flat when he comes here for the weekend." Emma sounded more than a little pissed off with this arrangement, and Peter remembered the way that he looked at Chris during Peter and Kevin's first visit.

"Your figures are correct, and the main factor is the rise in raw materials. The problem was amplified by the low value of the pound."

"Surely we can ask the Company to absorb the extra costs, as they're not our fault"

"I've spoken to the FD. Head office will have to accept some of the increase, but some savings will have to be made elsewhere to compensate."

"How are we going to make any more savings? We run quite a tight ship up here, and have had to for some time to keep our production costs as low as we have."

"You're also paying far too much overtime to the Production Department."

"We've always paid overtime to the Production Department."

"Tell Kevin to phone me as soon as he gets back."

He looked at the overtime figures whilst he waited for the phone to ring. The overtime was only paid to the production team. The production targets were always met, and usually exceeded, but paying overtime rates to achieve this was not good business. He finally gave up waiting for Kevin, and phoned him.

"Is Kevin there yet?"

"He's just having a cigarette outside. He should be back in by now. Hang on, I'll get him for you."

Peter could hear Emma walk to the door, followed by raised voices at the doorway.

"Give me a chance to take my coat off, you ker-nob!"

Although the young females in Newcastle went out in short skirts and no jacket, Kevin had bought himself a long blue raincoat to keep out the cold and the rain, which he never seemed to be without, even in the summer. Peter heard Kevin stomp over and pick up the phone.

"What's the verdict?"

"The FD has agreed to increase the standard costs that we pay the Newcastle branch, but wants savings at your end."

"How are we going to do that here?"

"Whenever the board have to reduce costs, the first area they look at are the staff costs, and the easiest way to reduce staff costs is by laying people off."

"They're not going to be very pleased with that up here. If I tell them that, I'll get lynched."

"I've looked at the overtime payments to the Production team. If we stop those, I think that should keep him happy."

"They've always had overtime in Production."

"It's one or the other, unless you can see any other alternative?"

112

"What other alternatives are there?"

"You could try to find savings elsewhere, unless you can find a way to increase turnover."

"How the hell am I going to do that?"

"Speak to the workforce and get their ideas on how they can improve some of the processes and make changes in the way they carry out their work that will result in lower costs and reducing waste."

"How are they supposed to know that? I thought that was our job?"

"They're the people who do the work, if you explain that reducing costs could save their jobs they'll come up with some good ideas, or identify some bottlenecks."

"What?"

"Ask them to report any areas where production sometimes stops whilst they're waiting for a previous task to be completed. How often are you paying bills from your suppliers?"

"Every week, why?"

"Tell the suppliers that you're changing your procedures, and you will only pay bills at the end of each month, unless you are given a discount."

"They won't agree to that."

"Some companies sell off their debts or pay other companies to collect the amounts due to them to keep their cash coming in. Ask them for a discount, you might be surprised."

"That's not going to happen is it?"

"Then you need a way to convince the Production team that the payment of overtime is no longer available, as it's putting their jobs at risk. Why do you pay so much overtime to them anyway?"

Peter heard a clump as the phone hit the table, and then a muffled discussion taking place in the office.

"Emma says that the Production team have to prepare the finished goods for despatch."

"Why can't someone else do it?"

"How the fuck would I know?"

"The Production team are usually busy most of the time. Why not rearrange the duties, and get the guys from the Raw Materials store and Maintenance to do it."
"That's the way it's always been done here."

Kevin's response reminded Peter of a story that the CIMA instructor told them whilst they were looking at Business Culture. "Can you remember the story of the four monkeys?"
"What the fuck are you talking about now?" Kevin knew that Peter was cleverer than he was, but sometimes he was on Planet Gaga.

"Four monkeys were put into a cage containing four stools, and they each sat on a stool. In the middle of the cage there was a banana suspended on a string from the roof, and a step ladder was placed underneath the banana. One of the monkeys notices the banana and starts to climb the step ladder, and all of the other monkeys were drenched with ice cold water. The monkey that tried to get the banana was taken out of the cage, and replaced with a new one. They were all sat back on the stools. When the new monkey starts to climb the step ladder to get the banana, they were all drenched with ice cold water again. One of the original monkeys was taken out of the cage, and replaced with a new monkey. When the new monkey tries to climb the step ladder to get the banana, all of the other monkeys jumped on him and stopped him. Another one of the original monkeys was replaced with a new monkey and the same happened again, until all of the monkeys that had been soaked had been replaced. When the new monkey tries to climb the step ladder to get the banana, he was attacked by the other three. When he asked why he was being attacked, one of the other monkeys said "I don't know, that's the way it's always been done around here"."

"E-mail that to me, and I'll call a meeting and read it out to them. I'll still need to convince the Production team that they have to give up their overtime."

"Remind them that the business has almost gone bust twice in the last few years. Tell them that Head Office wants to lay people off, and this is the only alternative. That way it'll make Head Office the bad guys, and you the good guy saving their jobs."

"OK, e-mail your other ideas about making savings, and I'll talk about them at the meeting."

Kevin phoned Peter back later that afternoon. He was in a much better mood than earlier. "The meeting went really well. I didn't use the monkey story in case they thought that I was referring to them as monkeys, but they were impressed with the fact that I wanted to save their jobs instead of just making a profit for the company."

"The FD said that he would only get rid of a few of them."

"They didn't know that. I told them that their company had already had to be sold twice in the last three years as it was losing money, and if we didn't make changes now, and stop overtime payments, then it would go bust. They understood that, because there's a few businesses here on the brink of moving overseas where the labour is cheaper. I'm knocking off now. I've more than earned my pay today, and there's a certain member of staff here who wants to show her appreciation to me for saving her job."

"Aren't you coming down to Oxford tonight? We have a meeting with the FD tomorrow."

"I need to stay here to see if the Production team have thought of any ways to make savings, or if they have identified any bottle tops."

"Bottlenecks."

"Yeah, those too. See you Wednesday."

Despite Peter's new house containing many of the features that she had envisaged in her dream home, Susan did not feel the same excitement that she'd gone through when she'd moved into Kevin's small terraced house eight years previously, but that was a move of independence into the unknown. Jaeger moved into the new house with Susan, and showed enough enthusiasm for the both of them, tearing from

115

room to room, sniffing every nook and cranny, and only just managing to overcome the urge to pee in each of them. He made up for this in the large garden at the rear of the house, but was still frantically wagging his tail when he re-appeared in the kitchen. Susan wasted no time in inviting her parents to dinner, something that she had never done whilst living with Kevin. Susan had only cooked ready meals from Marks and Sparks since she had moved in, and Peter had distressing memories of the last time that Susan had cooked a proper meal for him at Kevin's house, and hoped that her culinary skills had improved.

"I've found this recipe called 'Portuguese Cod'; it's cod steak cooked in tomato soup."

Peter tried his hardest not to pull a face, but it sounded worse than the 'Spanish Pork' that she'd cooked for his visit when she was living with Kevin.

"Do you have something against the Iberian Peninsula?"

"Is he one of those chefs on television?"

"Something like that." Peter was becoming concerned that Susan was not as clever as he'd originally thought.

Dawn and Geoffrey arrived politely on time bearing house-warming gifts. Susan guessed the contents of the oblong shaped boxes, despite the large sheaves of wrapping paper covering them. Susan ripped of the paper to expose two 'Le Creuset' cooking pots.

Geoffrey was pleased with Dawn's generosity with his money.

"We used to have one of these. I haven't seen it for ages."

Dawn went bright red when she remembered where she'd left it. "I've left something in the car, I'll be back in a minute." Her face had returned to its normal pink when she returned five minutes later.

The meal greatly exceeded expectations, mainly because all Susan had to do was put all of the ingredients into a pot, and put the pot into the oven. Peter kept his eye on the clock, and regularly checked the food in the pot just to make sure that the meal was still bubbling gently, and hadn't dried up. He prepared and cooked the accompanying vegetables, telling Susan that she should act as host, and keep the sherry flowing, whilst she gave them a guided tour of the house. He didn't tell her that the sherry was to anaesthetise their guests in case the meal was as bad as he thought that it would be. Susan had made a fruit salad for dessert, with shop bought ice cream, which was a safe and tasty choice. Peter reconsidered his assessment of Susan's intellect, she knew that tomato was a fruit, but she was clever enough not to put it in the fruit salad.

After dinner, Susan piled the dishes into the dishwasher, and they moved into the sitting room. Almost immediately, Peter had the inevitable urge to break wind. Feeling safe that the dog would act as his scapegoat, he lifted his leg slightly and the room was filled with an almost unbearable stench. Susan returned to the room with the after dinner drinks with the dog, who'd followed her into the kitchen in the hope that there would be some left-over food for his bowl. She had problems holding onto the tray of drinks, as she walked into the wall of disgusting odour, and quickly placed the tray onto the coffee table, and sprayed some perfume into the air to mask the smell. Everyone looked at the dog, who had been out of the room at the time that the crime was committed, and Peter blushed, revealing him as the offender. He tried to think of a witty apology to ease the tension. "Sorry about that, the dog's flatulence must be contagious."

The initial glasses of sherry and the Gin and Tonics imbibed later that evening reduced the memory of the fart, and at the end of the evening Susan felt proud of Peter. Whilst Susan and her mother spent the evening talking about the wedding, he held an articulate conversation with her father on business and the state of the country, and didn't try to shag her mother.

The wedding was all arranged for the following Easter, and the honeymoon flights and hotel in South Africa had already been booked and paid for by Dawn, as usual, with Geoffrey's money. Kevin had made regular comments regarding Peter's loss of freedom, he didn't mention Susan by name, but never missed the opportunity to call her his cast-off, much to Peter's dismay. Weeks turned into months faster than Peter expected, and after wishing that the time would pass quicker so that he could spend Christmas in his own home with Susan, the New Year had arrived, and they were back at work. Kevin had spent the festive period with Chris in Newcastle, but was still out chasing females on his return to Oxford, and had spent the night before his return to work entertaining a young blonde that he'd met in a pub in the Jericho part of Oxford.

"Where's your list of people you want to invite to the wedding?" Susan wanted to send the invitations out with plenty of notice, and was becoming frustrated at the lack of names forthcoming

The only person that Peter could consider as a friend was Rob from work, and he only had a handful of relatives to invite to the wedding. The majority of Susan's friends were the ones that she shared with her mother from amateur dramatics, so most of the guests at the wedding would be friends of Dawn and Geoffrey.

"There's only my parents, and my uncle and aunt from my family, and Rob, Kevin and the FD from work"

As usual, Susan blanched at the mention of Kevin's name. "If Kevin's at the wedding, then you can be sure that I won't be!"

"But they're the only people that I know well enough to invite."

"It's up to you. Kevin or me."

"OK then, my parents, my uncle and aunt, Rob and the FD."

"You're senior management, so you should invite the Chairman and the other board members."

"But I hardly ever mix with them outside work."

"It'll be good for your profile. What about the other people who work in Accounts?"

"I don't mix with them at all outside work."

"You should invite them. They'll think much better of you. Mummy's inviting all of her friends, and it will look strange if there are no guests of the groom present."

Peter knew better than to argue with Susan once she'd set her mind to doing something.

"OK, I'll give you their details."

"Who's going to be the best man?"

"The only person that I know well enough is Rob."

"Have you asked him?"

"Not yet."

Susan sighed, "He's not going to volunteer is he? I suggest that you ask him tomorrow at work."

"What am I going to say to Kevin?"

"Tell him that I don't want him at the wedding."

"What excuse shall I give why you don't want him there?"

"Don't worry about excuses, he'll know why."

Rob was delighted to be asked to be Peter's best man. Peter's standing in the company was well established, and Rob hoped that he could accompany Peter in his rise through the ranks. Kevin showed no surprise when Peter told him that he was not invited to the wedding.

"That doesn't let you off of the stag night, Dad. That is going to be a night to remember, you just leave the organisation to me."

"Oh no, I don't want a big party, I would be happy with a meal and a trip to the theatre."

"No chance. This will be a pub crawl to end all pub crawls, ending up at the Jericho Arms, I'm sure to get a late night there."

Peter was scared that he would end up with no trousers, chained to a lamppost, or worse still, drugged and put on a plane to Outer Mongolia, but could not see any way of changing Kevin's plans.

Kevin was not the only person who had plans affecting Peter's life, which he discovered on his return from work much later that evening.

"Get upstairs, and take your clothes off. I have a surprise for you." Although they had only just moved in together, Susan wasn't usually this spontaneous when it came to 'getting upstairs and taking your clothes off' activities. Another thing that Peter had discovered early in life was that it was always better if he did as he was told. Some people were born leaders, and he was definitely a born follower. He was soon upstairs in his pants and socks.

119

Susan took out numerous bags from the side of the bed and emptied the contents onto the duvet. "I've decided that you need a change of image, and a change of wardrobe."

Peter looked at the wardrobe in the bedroom and scratched his head. It was the same one that Susan bought when they moved in.

"You need new clothes befitting a Management Accountant, who is a member of the Company's senior management team. I've also bought you three pairs of flat sensible shoes."

Peter looked at the dark suits, and crisp shirts with small collars, and ties with no colourful patterns. "Where are my old clothes?"

"I've sent them to Blue Peter. They had an appeal for clothes for the poor in the Third World. As they're twenty years behind the rest of the world of fashion, your clothes should still be popular over there."

"What about my shoes?"

"Those as well. They've all gone in the post today. Try the clothes on, and let me see how good you look."

The shirts, trousers and shoes all fitted Peter, and Susan smiled in appreciation of her choices. "It cost me a lot of money, but it was well spent. My credit card is spent to the limit, so I'll need you to write a cheque for my bank account so that I can pay it off."

The irony of Peter paying a lot of money for something he didn't want was lost on Susan, as she was now treating his money as available for her to spend as she saw fit. The reflection in the bedroom mirror was not compatible with the person who was looking at it.

"That's much better, you look like a proper accountant."

Peter felt more like a proper twat, and doubted that he would ever like his new 'fashionable' look. The worst part was the flat-heeled shoes that would result in him being much shorter than everyone else again. He tried his best to put on a brave face to keep Susan happy. He also realised that he would be unable to replace the old clothes that he had almost worn to death. The shoes had been re-soled and heeled on numerous occasions, and each time the shoe mender had commented upon their antique value, and asked him if he'd thought of taking them to the *Antiques Roadshow*. He hung the new clothes in the wardrobe, whilst Susan went down to the kitchen to celebrate her new-look man by cooking a meal that would be as dull as the clothes that she had just bought. He then put the clothes that he'd worn to work into one of the bags that had contained the new clothes, and hid the bag in the attic, before Susan had the chance to send those to the Third World as well.

SEVEN

Peter's father had once explained to Peter why time appears to go faster as you get older. "The older you get, the smaller a percentage a year is compared with the years that you've lived already."

Peter thought that this was rubbish, but couldn't think of a better explanation why he'd just celebrated Christmas, and he was now getting dressed for his stag night. Despite the rain shower, he walked into town to ensure that he arrived with a clear head, and also to delay the commencement of his drinking that evening. He had promised both himself and Susan that he would stay sober and wouldn't do anything stupid, but things often happened that he had no control over whatsoever. There was quite a crowd waiting for him in the Glock, not only from work, but course members from his CIMA studies, and Emma and the branch manager from Newcastle. Kevin had already arranged a kitty for the drinks, and had collected £10 from everyone, and had earlier arranged a whip round to purchase gifts for Peter that were hidden underneath Kevin's raincoat. The crowd was already in good spirits, especially Kevin, as he controlled the kitty, and hadn't contributed himself. He also expected to be able to help himself to some of the money left over at the end of the night. A large cheer greeted Peter on his arrival, and Kevin moved his raincoat to reveal the 'gifts'. He attached 'L' plates to Peter's chest and back, taped a fully inflated blow-up doll to his side, along with a bag of oysters. He also hung a large bunch of cherries from Peter's neck, "Just in case you finally lose yours, Dad!"

A voice from the crowd shouted above the cheering, "What's the significance of the blow-up doll?"

Kevin turned towards the audience, "He'll need that if he wants to get his end away on a regular basis. The oysters are to help his performance in bed, but you can't always trust them. I had a dozen oysters once and only ten of them worked."

A pint of lager was thrust into Peter's hand, which he took a sip from, and then put down onto a table. Rob brought him a pint of coke, and swapped it for the lager, and the FD came and shook his hand.

"I'm really pleased for you, Peter; she'll be the making of you. When I was young, the stag night was held the night before the wedding, not a week before."

Peter noticed for the first time that the FD was no longer a young man, the remaining hair combed over the top of his head was white, instead of the dark brown colour when Peter had started work. If Peter had looked in the mirror, he would have noticed that he was also no longer in the throes of youth, although his low intake of alcohol had resulted in a thinner waistline compared with Kevin.

Peter had managed to stay on soft drinks throughout the evening by putting any glasses of lager that he was given down onto the table next to him, which were then swapped for coke by Rob and Emma. Kevin had noticed this, and switched to plan B, which involved putting large vodkas into Peter's coke, and after three hours and four different pubs, the room started to swim around Peter. Rob took the blow-up doll and the L plates off of Peter's clothing and put them onto a seat in the pub. Peter was trying to tell everyone that he was the happiest and luckiest man in the World, but the words were barely audible. Rob supported him to the closest Taxi rank, to get him home before his condition became worse. The fresh air took the bones out of Peter's legs, and Rob had to take a firm grip to stop him from falling into the road. "You're my bess fren, I love you."

Rob leant Peter against the first taxi in the row, and he slipped down the car onto the pavement. "Banbury Road please."

The taxi driver looked at Peter, and shook his head. "He's not coming in here, I'll have to spend the rest of the night cleaning up the car. He'd be better off if you walk him home, it's only a few minute's walk."

Rob picked Peter back up and put his arm around Peter's waist. "Come on Peter, best foot forward, we're off to see Susan."

At the mention of Susan's name, a small light flickered in Peter's glazed eyes, and he struggled to put one foot in front of the other. The fresh air and exercise had no effect upon improving Peter's condition, and the few minute's walk was stretched to forty five. They stopped half way for a piss, and Peter swayed from side to side washing both pairs of shoes.

"It was always me she loved you know, if Kevin hadn't got her drunk on her birthday we'd have been married year's ago."

"Be quiet, Peter, you'll get us locked up."

"But it's true I tell you, it was always me, not him, he's a bastard!"

They finally arrived at a dark empty house. Susan was out on her hen-party, so Rob went through Peter's pockets until he found the house keys to let them in. Jaeger usually barked all night when he was left at home on his own, so on the rare evenings that Peter and Susan went out, he would stay the night with Geoffrey and Dawn. Rob sat Peter on a chair in the kitchen, and searched, unsuccessfully, for a beer. Half an hour later Susan returned to find Rob watching over a fast-asleep Peter.

"Me and Emma tried to keep him on cokes, but I think Kevin slipped a few vodkas into his drinks."

"I knew he'd do something like that, he always was a bastard. Leave Peter with me, I'll look after him if you want to get back to the others."

As expected, Rob caught up with the stag-less stag party in the Jericho Arms just before eleven o'clock. The crowd was beginning to thin out, but there were still some of them ready and able to carry on drinking for a further few hours, now that the stupidity of the pub closing time rules had been changed from the bad days of either having to find a pub prepared for an illegal 'lock-in', or spending good drinking money to get into a night club where they paid over the odds for their drinks, and couldn't hear themselves speak. The majority of Friday night drinkers would usually return home with money in their pocket, instead of in the tills of the pubs, where it truly belonged.

Kevin had deflated the blow-up doll, to take away with him, and was stood at the bar with his arm around a tarty young blonde, much to the disgust of Emma. Although it was getting late, Kevin was still playing to the gallery.

"When Susan lived with me, I bought some flavoured condoms from the bogs in here. I took them home, and showed them to her. The normal ones had pictures of different types of fruit on the wrapper, but one of them had question marks on it. "What do the question marks mean?" she asked me. Well, I tell her, I put it on my cock, and you put it in your mouth and tell me what flavour it's supposed to be. So she says "OK, if I have to, but only with the lights off." So I turn the light off and she goes down on me, and says, "I'm not sure, is it cheese and onion?" Hang on, I says, I haven't put it on yet!"

Emma greeted Rob on his re-appearance with a pint. "I really can't understand what Chris sees in him, you know. He's a real bastard."
The consensus on Kevin's personality was unanimous.
"How's Peter?"
"He'll survive, but will have a headache for the rest of the weekend."

'Headache' was a vast understatement when describing Peter's state of health the following day. Luckily for him, Susan's dictionary contained the word 'sympathy' so she allowed him to stay on the living room sofa whilst she carried out the Saturday shopping. He still didn't feel like eating when she returned from her parent's house, and barely managed to show some enthusiasm when he won £10 on the lottery that evening.
"I wish it had been more."
"But you're well off. You have a good job, with a good salary. What would you do with it, if you won a million?"
"Go and live somewhere else, where I wouldn't have to do everyone else's work for no gratitude or reward."
"Why don't you start your own business then?"
"I spend too much time at work already. If I ran my own business, I'd always be working, and I'd have no time to spend with you."
"But I thought that you loved your job."
"It's interesting enough, and very well paid, but I'd rather spend my time with you and the dog, and in a few years' time,

with our children. It would be really great if I had enough money so that I didn't have to spend so much time working."
"How many children would you like?"
"Hundreds."
"How do you know that? You're an only child the same as I am?"
"I don't want my children to be as lonely as I was before I met you." Even in his wrecked state, Peter managed to say just the right things.

Although Peter was still under the weather on Monday morning, he still made it in to work. He very rarely took a day off sick, as he was usually only ill during his holidays. If he felt a cold arriving, he drank a cup of Geoffrey's guaranteed cure 'Hot toddy', which consisted of Whisky, lemon juice, hot water and honey, or as Peter called it, much to the disgust of Susan, 'bee puke'. Although Peter rarely drank alcohol at home, apart from the occasional glass of wine, he always kept a bottle of 'medicinal' whisky in the drinks cabinet.

Peter still had a permanent smile on his face, and the sense of humour he had as a boy when he wasn't being bullied had returned. On Saturday he was bright and bubbly, but his nerves were becoming frayed as Rob was getting him ready for the wedding.
"Are you sure you've got the rings?"
"Yes Peter, for the umpteenth time, I'm sure that I've got the rings."
Geoffrey gave Peter a glass of sherry to calm his nerves.
"I'm not sure that's a good idea. It only takes a couple of these and I'm drunk."
"Well I need one myself to calm my nerves." Geoffrey could no longer stand the female pandemonium at his house, and had walked down to Peter's house to escape it. Peter looked at the clock for the tenth time in the same number of minutes, not wanting to be late.
"Shouldn't you be with Dawn and Susan?"
"I'll make sure that I'm back there in good time for the taxi, until then, I'm staying well out of the way. There's an hour yet

until we have to leave for the church, isn't there anything that you can do to keep your mind occupied, instead of getting yourself worked up?"

Peter put his hand into his trouser pocket, and pulled out his 'to do' list, smiled, went to the telephone and dialled a number.

"Can I add my wife to my Credit Card account please?"

"Could I have your name and account details please sir?"

Peter answered numerous questions as they were asked.

"How long have you been married, Mr Stevenson?"

"I'm getting married in about an hour." Of all the answers he'd just provided, this one pleased Peter the most.

"You're very calm if I may say so."

"Thank you."

"Your wife will receive her card in five days time, with the instructions on how to register the card. Good luck."

"Thank you. Goodbye." Peter was unsure whether the girl on the phone was wishing him good luck for his wedding, or good luck on giving Susan access to his credit card account. His smile was firmly back in place as he ticked the task off of his list.

The rest of the afternoon was a blur. Susan looked lovely, despite not losing as much weight as she'd planned in her New Year's resolution, so the wedding dress was a tight fit, and her mother and the bridesmaids had a long fight to zip it up. Peter remembered to say the correct words in the right order, a large improvement on the rehearsal with the vicar three days earlier, and Rob really did have the rings. Rob was surprised that most of the guests were the same age as Geoffrey and Dawn, and they all had posh accents. He was worried that his best man speech would be too down-market for them, but it went down really well, especially the part when he explained to all those gathered that Susan was now a one-man woman, and everyone who had keys to her house should return them. Peter was stunned when all the men in the room left their seats, walked to the top table and gave a door key to Susan, but laughed out loud when he realised that it was a joke (wasn't it?).

The evening function was a great success, except for the array of old men dancing to the modern disco, until, at long last, Peter finally was back home with his new bride all to himself. He had wondered whether sex with Susan would be different now that they were married, as he cuddled up to her in bed.

"Where's your Durex?"

"We're married now, I thought that we wouldn't need one."

"I'm not ready to start a family just yet Peter. I have my career to think of."

"You're no closer to getting your Beauty Salon than when we started going out together. I thought that you wanted children?"

"Of course I do, lots of them, but we need to wait until we can afford the mortgage without my wages."

Peter opened the drawer in his bedside cabinet trying not to show his unhappiness to Susan that sex with his new wife was no different to sex with his fiancée. He would soon discover that, although it was no different, it was much less frequent.

The following day they flew out to South Africa on their honeymoon. The disappointment of the previous night was long forgotten, and his sense of humour was reinstated. Susan tried to read her magazine on the flight, but was far too excited to concentrate. Luckily she found no reference to the dangerous spiders in Africa, which would probably have made her change her mind about going there. She was terrified enough of the British version that ate flies and spun webs, these African ones were poisonous and could be twice as large.

"I really can't believe we're going to South Africa for our honeymoon. It's what I always dreamed of."

"I thought that you wanted to go to Paris."

"Only because Mummy went to Paris for her honeymoon. She said that the weather would be much better in South Africa in March, and we could go to Paris for a long weekend when the weather was warmer."

"Are you expecting to spend much time out of bed this week then, Mrs Stevenson?"

Susan blushed at Peter's question and changed the subject. "Why is it called a honeymoon?"

Peter vaguely remembered reading something in a book about strange names for things, and honeymoon was one of the strangest names for what actually happened.

"In biblical times, the father of the bride would supply the newly married couple a month's supply of mead to ensure fertility and happiness. The mead was made from honey, and each moon lasts for one month, hence the name honeymoon."

"That's a strange wedding gift."

"There probably wasn't much call for toast racks or Debenhams' vouchers in those days."

"You're making it up."

"I'm not," Peter tried has best to disguise his smile.

"Well, how do people know that's what happened?"

"They probably had pictures of all of the drink in the wedding photos."

"Oh, OK." Susan tried to read her magazine again, but looked up after a few minutes. "They didn't have cameras in those days."

"Perhaps the bride wrote it in her diary, and an archaeologist dug it up and read it."

The ten days spent with Susan in South Africa was the best time of Peter's life. He woke up smiling and grew increasingly happier as the day progressed. Although Susan thought that she was getting out of bed early for someone on holiday, Peter had been up much earlier, and returned from his breakfast with a selection of cake and fruit, and made a pot of *Rooibos* tea to wake her up with, before climbing back into bed for a spot of early-morning honeymoon nookie. Susan tried her best not to compare Peter's performance in bed with Kevin's, but there was something missing that she didn't know how to explain to Peter without upsetting him. She just smiled at him warmly as he joined her back in bed. Peter was her sunshine in the morning, but not the fireworks at the end of the day that she dreamt her husband would be.

South Africa was even more fascinating than Peter ever expected. Although Peter had teased Susan about the biblical bride keeping a diary of the events, he found himself doing exactly that. Susan helped Peter with his share of wine at the visit to the vineyards, and swallowed most of it instead of spitting it out after tasting it. Peter made a lewd comment about the merits of swallowing instead of spitting, and Susan wouldn't speak to him for an hour, when she realised what he was talking about. Later that day they visited the Cheetah enclosure. Their guide explained to them that cheetahs would not attack anything bigger than themselves, and they were quite safe to enter the enclosure and walk amongst them. Susan's intake of wine gave her enough Dutch courage to want to join the large cats, and Peter felt uncomfortably obliged to accompany her. After a few minutes, Peter had to agree with the guide, and the cheetahs took no notice of them whatsoever, as they walked within stroking distance of the large cats. The cheetahs lay down around them as if asleep, until a small child walking outside the enclosure stumbled and fell over. The cats sprang into action and flew at the bars dividing them and their prey. Shocked at the swift display of violence, Susan and Peter made their way quickly to the exit of the enclosure.

They were both amazed at the many different types of wild animals that they came really close to during their bus tour around the Kruger National park, and surprised at how tall the giraffes were. Susan had seen the giraffes at Longleat many years earlier, with Kevin, but had not been allowed to get this close to them. On their return from the tour Peter and Susan had a quick shower and went to the dining room to have an early drink, and miss the rush for dinner. They had become quite adventurous with the menus provided, and particularly liked the Wildebeest they'd chosen for their main course.

After dinner Peter and Susan walked hand in hand to the small bar to try the local Gin and Tonic. They thought that they were alone, until they noticed another customer at the far end of the bar. He was a tall, good looking, but very old, man, and, although it was empty, he was sitting alone in the shadowy part of the bar. Susan was attracted by his distinctly upper class English accent when he responded to their greeting, and Peter asked him if he would care to join them for a drink.

"Please come and join me, I don't like sitting in the light."

"Are you here on holiday?" Peter's usual shyness with people that he didn't know was overcome by his curiosity aroused by the old man.

"No, I've lived here for years."

Susan liked him instantly; there was something charming about his about his old-style demeanour. "I could live here for the rest of my life, it would be lovely to live in peace and tranquillity, and leave behind the hustle and bustle of modern-day life. If I had to escape, this is the place where I would hide."

The old man warmed to the young couple, and enjoyed the chance to speak with someone normal for a change, instead of the intolerable American tourists.

"I've met quite a few people who have tried to escape to live here, hiding from casino owners or loan sharks that they owe money to, or from jealous husbands looking for revenge."

"Or people on the run from the law." Susan was always trying to bring in 'every-day' stories from her magazines, but the man smarted as if the comment was a little closer to home than she'd meant. "It's not possible to live in a place like this unless you have a new identity and money to set you up and survive on, and people on the run, as you call them, usually have to leave home at short notice, so they don't have time to arrange that."

"You sound like you speak from experience."

"Not really, it was just better for me to start a new life somewhere else for personal reasons, and this is the best place I've found so far." They carried on talking for half an hour about South Africa, until the bar suddenly filled up with customers from the dining room. The man put his head down, muttered a quick "sorry, I don't like crowds", and made a swift exit through the back door.

131

The following day, Peter and Susan went for a ride on an elephant. Once again, they were surprised at the huge size of the animals. The man in the elephant park looked at Peter and Susan and walked away muttering to himself. Susan couldn't understand what, if anything, they had done wrong. "Where's he going now?"

"He's probably gone to find an elephant big enough to carry you."

Although Kevin had made numerous sarcastic comments regarding Susan's weight, this was the first time that Peter had dared to allude to the fact that she might be a little on the plump side. Luckily, Susan was too excited about her trip aboard such a large beast, and the comment didn't really register with her, and she was soon looking at the World from a greater height as the elephant strolled around the park.

The ten days went far too quickly, and before they knew it, Peter and Susan were back in Oxford, having dinner with Geoffrey and Dawn, regaling them with tales of their time away. Peter was back at work the following Monday, and noticed that Susan was correct in her statement that the Accounts' staff treated him with more deference now that he was a married man.

Peter had heard somewhere that, if you put a pea in a bottle every time that you had sex in the first year of marriage, it would take much longer to empty the bottle if you took a pea out every time that you had sex in the following years. After two years of marriage, the hypothetical bottle still contained almost as many of the hypothetical peas that he'd put in there during the first six months of marriage.

"Don't you think that it's about time that we started a family?"

"You still don't earn enough to support us without my wages, especially if we have another mouth to feed."

"But you'll have maternity pay."

"It's nowhere near enough, the mortgage still takes up most of our income."

Peter always put up a good case when he was negotiating his pay rise with the Managing Director, especially as his future life as a father depended upon a higher wage, but although his work resulted in lower costs, and a more efficient business, the company hadn't progressed as much as he'd hoped since the purchase of Burridges. Kevin was always trying to get the FD to agree to further acquisitions to expand the business at the FD's meetings, but Peter had always talked the FD out of making decisions that Peter thought would be too risky, or would lose company money.

Emma usually phoned him with an update every Friday, so Peter was surprised by a phone call first thing on Monday morning.

"I heard something interesting yesterday."

"Newcastle have re-signed Kevin Keegan as their main striker?"

"I said interesting, not impossible. The company that my dad works for has had an offer from a Supermarket chain for its land."

"Why is that interesting?"

"The company is like ours, and still has a large customer base. They just aren't profitable anymore, and their losses are going to get worse, not better."

Peter was ahead of Emma already. He sat up straight in his chair, his mind racing with the new possibility.

"Do we have enough room at our site to accommodate this extra business and their machinery?"

"We'd have to construct another Production building, and double the size of the store room, but there's plenty of space."

"How many people know this?"

"No-one yet, apart from the board and the Supermarket chain. The company haven't told the workforce anything, as they're still considering the offer, but they are almost certain to accept it."

"How does your father know about it?"

"He's the Production Manager. They had a senior management meeting on Friday to discuss whether they should accept the offer or not."

"And do you think that the company would sell its machinery and customers to us?"

133

"If they think that they could make some more money out of the deal to make it worth their while, I think that they would jump at it. If it looks like most of their workforce will be guaranteed jobs with us, it would greatly reduce their redundancy payments, and make them look better."

"Why do you think that we should take on their business if they're making a loss?"

"Because it would be the same as when you took over our company."

"What did Kevin say about this?"

"I haven't spoken to Kevin for a couple of weeks. He doesn't visit us as much as he used to. We manage quite well up here without his assistance. His main reason to come here now is to see Chris, but she's worried about the way that he treats her."

Kevin's weekly visits had quickly changed to every other week, and then to monthly to check the Accounts and the performance reports. "He still stays at Chris's house during his visits, but hardly speaks to her when he's back in Oxford."

"I need to speak to the FD about this, and I'll get back to you for contact details within the company. I'll phone you later this morning. Thanks for the information."

"Yeah, speak to you later."

Peter called the FD's P.A. and booked a meeting with him for nine thirty. He typed up a quick report and waited for Kevin's usually disruptive Monday morning entrance. He had just finished the report, and was printing off three copies, when Kevin came galumphing in, and threw his blue raincoat onto the table. Although he was sceptical when they tried to buy Burridges for the first time, Kevin was now very keen to buy other businesses, and was continually telling Peter this.

"Your wish has finally come true."

"Kylie Minogue's phoned, wanting me to be the father of her children?"

"No, there's a good possibility that we may be able to expand the company. We're having a meeting with the FD in ten minutes." He gave Kevin a copy of the report, but Kevin threw it onto his desk, and went off to get himself a coffee.

"You'd better come with me to the coffee machine and brief me on the way."

Ten minutes later, Peter, Kevin and the cup of coffee were in the FD's office. Peter briefed the FD with the information from Emma, with the occasional interruption from Kevin.

"I've told you loads of times that we need to increase our business base."

"Yes, Kevin, but this idea looks like it might actually work for us."

The FD put the report on the table and stared at Peter.

"We've discussed numerous ideas for expansion over the last five years, what makes this one so special?"

"All of the other ideas were either too risky, or had nothing to do with our core business. This is an extension of what we're doing already, and we're doing it really well."

"Will the local Council approve the construction of extra buildings at our premises?"

"They're already pleased that we've managed to employ a large number of people where the jobs could have quite easily gone overseas, they will get slaughtered if they turn down the possibility to keep more jobs in the area."

"How do you know it will be profitable?"

"I won't know that until I look at the figures. It just feels right."

"When can you provide me with a report that I can take to the board for agreement? I'll need a long-term viability report plus a forecast Return on Capital employed, a cash flow statement, and a payback calculation"

"Friday. I need to talk with the Company MD first to see if they will agree to us looking at their books, and taking over their customer base. Then I need their MD to talk to the customers to get their agreement for us to take over the contracts. I also need to speak to the Council to push the extension through quickly if the board approves the idea, so that we can commence production as soon as they close down."

"Let me know how things are going by lunchtime. When do you plan to go to Newcastle?"

Kevin was feeling badly left out, and needed to get himself back into the discussion.

"If their MD seems up for it, I'll leave this afternoon. I'm overdue a visit there. Are you coming with me Peter?"

"Is there anything here that Rob can't handle?"

Once again, Kevin was the first to respond to the FD. "I'll have my mobile on, so he can phone me if there are any problems." Their work over the years had been made much easier by the introduction of the electronic spreadsheets, the internet, and e-mails, and was further enhanced by the mobile phones that kept the workers in constant touch. A few years earlier, Peter had never considered the need for a phone that he could take with him everywhere, now he wouldn't dream of leaving the house without it.

Four hours later, Kevin was speeding up the M1 to Newcastle. His taste in music hadn't changed, but his hearing had deteriorated, so it was even louder than ever.

"You still married then, Dad?"

"Yes, we've just celebrated our second wedding anniversary."

"Has she learnt to cook yet?"

"Not really. She tries new recipes now and again, but we're mainly living on ready meals from Marks and Sparks that she just puts in the oven."

"It's a lot easier to get a takeaway. I usually get an Indian or a Chinese on Friday night, and I warm up the leftovers to eat on Saturday."

"You'll get food poisoning if you do that!"

"Not me, I've got the constitution of an ox. Didn't she mind you going to Newcastle for three days?"

"I told her that it was for the benefit of the Company, and our future. She understands that."

"Does she understand that Newcastle is like Las Vegas?"

"How can Newcastle be like Las Vegas?"

"They're the only two cities in the World where you can pay for sex using chips." Kevin thought that this was hilarious, but the humour was lost on Peter.

"Susan knows that if this venture is a success, it will result in a pay rise."

"Are you sure that she's not just glad to see the back of you for a few days?"

"Why should she?"

"Are you getting your end away every night still?"

Peter declined to answer.

"I thought not. You should have taken the blow up doll that I bought for your stag night."

"What happened to it?"

"It's at home, somewhere. Do you want me to drop it round your house? It might buck her ideas up a bit, if she sees that she's got competition." Kevin thought that this was also hilarious. Peter declined to answer again.

"You should get a woman like Chris. She never says no."

"You don't see her often enough for her to get tired of it."

"There's a lot to be said for regular periods of work-enforced absences. It works for the women in Oxford as well."

"What? You have a girlfriend in Oxford as well as Chris?"

"Not a specific one, there's usually someone that I meet in the pub whose willing to come back and stay the night. Did you expect me to live like a monk whilst I'm down here?"

"Does Chris know?"

"I haven't asked her."

"Does she see anyone when you're not there?"

"She wouldn't fucking dare!"

"Oh, it's OK for you, but not for her then?"

"Too fucking right."

It was Kevin's turn to be quiet. He turned the CD player up louder, and drove even faster than the speed limit than he was already. They arrived at Chris's house in record time.

"Hurry up and get the bags out of the boot, Dad. I want to have a few beers before I give her a good seeing to."

Peter carried the bags into the house, and was greeted by Chris. He'd spoken to her on a regular basis, but had only met her a few times.

"Are you sure it's OK to stay at your house for a few days?"

"Of course it is. It'll probably save Kevin spending hours in your hotel room, working with you on the report, and the financial statements."

Did she really think that Kevin helped Peter with his work? She would find out otherwise in the next three days.

The following days went as well as Peter hoped. Peter spent most of the time talking to their FD, their Management Accountant, and the finance team, going through their accounts. It was quite obvious that the company would carry on losing money for the foreseeable future, unless there was a drastic change in their circumstances. The obvious option was for them to cease business and sell their land to the highest bidder, in this case the Superstore. The business that Peter was looking to buy out was much bigger than Burridge's was when they purchased it, but it was nothing that Peter and the Production team couldn't manage. The large reduction in management salaries and facilities costs would make the new branch highly profitable. Peter also highlighted the savings that the company would make by not having to make redundancy payments, and informed the board back in Oxford of how his comments had been accepted, resulting in the board picking up the assets and customer base for next to nothing.

The acquisition of the company and the building of the new production area were completed in a few months, to the great relief and benefit of all involved. Another benefit to the Company of the new acquisition was that they now had an Accountant in their Newcastle office. Kevin was relieved that he would no longer have to make his trip up to the frozen north at the end of each month, unfortunately, Chris was less than pleased with the change of arrangements. When the visits changed to a few days each month, Chris had considered telling Kevin that she wasn't prepared to spend her life on her own, and was about to tell him that they should stop seeing one-another, but something had happened during his last visit which had changed everything, and she needed to speak to Kevin about it, preferably face to face. She had sent him e-mails, and left messages on his phone for him to contact her, but they had been ignored, so Chris had booked herself on the Friday morning bus to Oxford, and ventured southwards. Although she'd never stayed at Kevin's house, she knew Kevin's address from the numerous greetings cards and unanswered letters that she had sent to him over the years, but when the taxi arrived at her destination, the house was dark and empty, and Kevin had already left for the pub. Chris phoned Kevin's mobile yet again, but as usual her call went straight through to his voicemail. She frantically searched through her address book, and found Peter's mobile phone number. The display on Peter's mobile showed the identity of the caller.

"Hello Chris, you're working late."

"I'm not working today. I'm in Oxford."

"Why didn't you tell us that you were visiting? We'd have shown you around the Company."

"I'm here to see Kevin, but he's not at home, and he's not answering my phone-calls either. Do you know where he is?"

"He could be in one of three or four different pubs. Why don't you come to our house, and I'll try to get in touch with him." Peter gave her his address, and she arrived in the taxi, in tears, soon afterwards.

Kevin carried on with his usual random Friday night pub crawl, the noise in the bars was always too loud to allow him to hear the numerous calls on his mobile.

"If you like, I can phone the pubs and ask them to get Kevin to the phone, but he'll probably be drunk by now, and not make much sense."

Chris started crying again. "I just don't know what to do. I never should have got involved with him in the first place. I've wasted six years of my life with him, and now that I've decided to finish with him, I get pregnant."

Susan felt relieved that she was no longer part of Kevin's life, and understood Chris's despair.

"There's nothing you can do tonight. We have plenty of room for you to stay here, and Peter can drive you round to Kevin's house in the morning."

"No, I can't impose any more. You've done too much already."

"Don't be silly. We'd be glad to have someone staying with us for a change. Peter's always saying that this house is too big for two people."

"I meant that it's too big for the two of us, so we should start a family."

Unfortunately, Chris burst into tears at the mention of children, and Susan glared at Peter for his lack of sensitivity. "Why don't you settle yourself here for the night and have a gin and tonic?"

Chris looked up at Susan in shock. "I don't want to get rid of the child. I just need to tell Kevin about it."

"Well I'm sure that we can make you some tea or cocoa." Susan nodded at Peter, and moved her head in the direction of the kitchen.

"No thank you. I've had enough to drink. I think that I'll go to bed and hopefully I'll feel better in the morning, when I speak to Kevin."

Peter was always up early on Saturdays to take the dog for a walk, and Chris was up and ready to leave on his return. The drive to Kevin's house was in complete silence, neither of them knowing what to say, Chris not knowing whether she should be apologising for her predicament, or Peter somehow feeling obliged to apologise for Kevin. Peter banged on Kevin's door until it was answered by a very dishevelled Kevin, with a half-dressed young blonde stood behind him in the doorway. Chris burst into tears yet again at the sight of Kevin's companion. She had always expected that he spent his time in Oxford with other girls, but didn't want to see it for herself.

"What are you doing here?"

"I've been trying to speak to you for days. Why haven't you answered my calls?"

"I've been busy. Why can't you wait until I visit Newcastle?"

"Because I need to talk to you urgently."

"What about?"

"It's private."

"Don't mind this lot. What do you want to talk to me about?"

Chris took a deep breath, and looked Kevin straight in the eye, "I'm pregnant."

"And?"

"I thought that you should know?"

"Why?"

"Because you're the father."

140

"How do you know it's mine?"

"Of course it's yours. Who else could it be?"

"I don't know what you get up to in Newcastle when I'm not there."

Chris was stunned speechless by the accusation, and stood open-mouthed.

"Look, I don't intend going to Newcastle anymore. We have someone there now to complete and analyse the reports, so why don't we just call it a day."

"But I'm pregnant."

"You're not the first girl who has tried to get me to marry them by telling me that. It won't work."

"What makes you think that I want to marry you?"

"Why are you here then?"

"I thought that I should tell you to your face."

"Well, you've done that. Is there anything else you want?"

"No, nothing at all." Chris turned away from Kevin in disgust, and walked back to the car. "Could you take me to the bus station please Peter?" Peter and Chris sat in the car, once again in silence, as he drove her to the bus station to catch a bus back home.

Peter arrived back home still appalled at Kevin's behaviour. Susan could see that he didn't want to discuss the matter, but felt that she needed to know what happened.

"What did Kevin say?"

"Kevin had a girl with him who'd obviously spent the night there. He told Chris that the child could be anyone's, and said that he didn't want to see her again."

"That poor girl. One day he'll get what's coming to him."

"I doubt it. He leads a charmed life."

Susan had noticed that Peter had become more and more short-tempered over the last year or so, and she was beginning to get worried that he didn't love her any more. She had never seen him so happy as when they were in South Africa on their honeymoon, so she decided that a holiday away together would cheer him up. She didn't want to return to the times of living with someone as short-fused as Kevin. Susan had a pleased look on her face when Peter arrived home from work that night.

"I've booked a winter holiday in the sun," she smiled.

"What about the dog?"

"He'll stay with my parents for the week. It's funny; the brochure said that the Bed and Breakfast allowed pets. I don't know how they expect us to get Jaeger there; I'm sure he'll be fine with my parents."

'I wish you'd stay with your parents for the week and left me and the dog alone!' Peter thought to himself.

"You don't seem very pleased. I thought that you would be happy that we're going away for Christmas. We haven't had a proper holiday for years, and when I saw the pictures in the brochure, I couldn't resist it. The long sandy beaches, the mountains."

Beaches and mountains? "Where are we going?"

"The Outer Hebrides." The smile re-appeared.

"What?? Do you know where the Outer Hebrides are?"

"I don't care where they are. The pictures looked lovely, and we deserve a holiday."

Peter went upstairs to his office, returning swiftly with a road map of Britain. Susan's smile changed to a frown, and then to a look of shock as he pointed to an area in the sea to the north-west of Scotland.

"The Outer Hebrides are cold and wet in December, and VERY windy. If you want to go sun-bathing on the beach you'll need a wet suit and a sleeping bag."

"I thought that you'd be pleased?" she showed him the pictures. "It looks lovely."

142

Peter looked at the pictures of the desolate countryside. It did look lovely. The dog would enjoy himself, and the peace and quiet would probably do him some good as well, away from the turmoil, frustrations and arguments in the office. His tone mellowed.

"What have you booked?"

"I've booked a B and B for a week in a place called Benbecula, I can't find any details of flights from Heathrow or Gatwick, so I haven't booked them yet, and there were no details of hire cars."

"Have you spoken to your parents about having the dog?"

"Give me a chance, I've only just booked the B and B."

"If you really want to go there, it would probably be easier to drive up to Scotland and catch the ferry over". He showed Susan the map again. "Look, it says here that the ferry that goes from Oban can take about seven hours, but the ferry from Skye takes less than two hours. As you get seasick in the bath, we'd be better off sailing from Skye. It's a long way to drive, especially as we're only going away for a week, but we can stop overnight at Loch Lomond. We could take the dog as well, I'm sure he'd enjoy it as much as us."

"We won't need a ferry if we're going to Skye. I read somewhere that they've built a bridge."

"The bridge is from the mainland to Skye, not to the Outer Hebrides."

"But that must be a long way surely. I remember singing the song at school about Prince Charles rowing over the sea to Skye."

"That was Bonnie Prince Charlie escaping the English by rowing from the Outer Hebrides to Skye, not from the Scottish mainland to Skye." Sometimes he wondered whether she'd learnt anything at school.

"I knew you'd be happy. I'll book the ferry tomorrow." The smile was firmly back on her face, as she skipped to the kitchen to burn dinner.

A few days later Susan had the same pleased look on her face when Peter arrived home.

"The ferry out is booked for the Friday before Christmas."

"What time does it leave?"

"Twenty minutes to ten, we have to be there by nine at the latest."

Peter was surprised that the ferry left so late at night.

"We'll have to leave here early in the morning to catch that, and hope that there's no problem with the traffic on the way up."

Susan looked confused. "No, the ferry leaves at twenty to ten in the morning, not at night."

"We won't be able to catch that. The Finance Director's meeting is on the day before. I told you that I had to go to that. I even put it on the calendar on the fridge."

"We can drive there on Thursday night after the meeting, and arrive in the morning."

"I'll be far too tired to drive through the night."

"We'll share the driving. It'll be much quicker, as there will be no traffic."

"There's a good reason that there will be no traffic. No-one in their right mind would drive through the Scottish highlands in the middle of the night during winter. It's far too dangerous, and if it snows, the road will be blocked, and we'll be stuck in the freezing cold until the snowplough comes along the following morning."

"You're just trying to under mind me, like you always do."

Peter ignored her version of the English language. "Well, I booked this ferry because that gets us there for the day that we are booked into the B and B, and that's the one I want to catch." Susan stormed off upstairs.

Peter heard the bedroom door slam, and realised that she would not surface again until the following morning. Double bonus! He would be able to watch the football on television, and would get a take-away instead of the usual burnt offerings for dinner. The dog was already waiting at the front door, frantically wagging his tail as Peter put on his coat to take him out for a walk.

The day that they left to go on holiday went from bad to worse, and ended even worse than he could have ever imagined. The Finance Director's meeting dragged on far longer even than he expected. The acquisition of the new production company had been a huge success, and Kevin brought this up at the end of the meeting.

"It's well over five years since we made our last acquisition, and we need to keep expanding to stay ahead of our competitors."

Peter agreed with Kevin's comments about having to continuously improve and expand, but there were many different ways to skin a cat, and you had to check each company thoroughly.

"We have to be careful of acquiring other businesses to expand. If we make the wrong choice, we could lose our competitive advantage."

"There shouldn't be a problem making some mistakes, as long as the overall total is positive. You have to take some risks in business, if our competitors are successful with opportunities that we reject because they're risky, they will be the ones with the advantage over us."

Peter was surprised to notice that, after all these years, Kevin was starting to get an appreciation of what he was supposed to be doing, and was concerned by the lucid argument against him; an argument which he would usually dismiss with hardly any effort. Peter tried to end this discussion quickly, as he had to leave as early as possible for his holiday.

"Our successful acquisitions have allowed us to reduce our overall prices, resulting in an increase in sales, and a corresponding increase in market share and profitability. If we start taking too many risks, we would jeopardise our position."

"We've made poor decisions when releasing new models."

"Those decisions were made by the production department for the Management Board's approval. Our work affects the funding of the company, and the price of the goods, not what the company produces."

"I know that, what I'm saying is that if the production company are allowed to take risks, then so should we."

Mark sat in silence listening to the argument, waiting until the discussion had provided him with enough information so that he was able to make his decision. At the moment it could go either way. Peter had usually won these arguments by now, and looked at Mark for his nod of agreement, but it was not forthcoming. He tried another tack.

"The two acquisitions that we've made have been such a success because of the work carried out to check all of the aspects involved. If you find another opportunity, I'll check it out, and let you know whether we should proceed or not."

"I've done that already; lots of times, but by the time you've completed your report, the businesses have been bought by one of our competitors, or ceased trading."

"But some of these businesses purchased by our competitors have flopped."

"They wouldn't have if we'd have taken them on and managed them. I think that we should start actively looking for new acquisitions."

"We're already doing that."

"Not actively. We've only ever made two large acquisitions, the first one we missed the first time around, and the second one was just lucky. We should increase the areas of business that we expand into, instead of just focussing on businesses the same as ours. We have plenty of cash in the bank; we need to start making it work for us."

"There's lots of ways that we can use our bank balance to benefit the Company that would be better for us than buying up unprofitable businesses."

"No there aren't, all we ever do is increase the dividends to our shareholders. We're just giving our money away."

Peter was panic stricken. Kevin had obviously planned for this meeting, and Peter's mind had been elsewhere, worrying about his drive to the Outer Hebrides, allowing him to be ambushed. He had to think on his feet to win the argument.

"We could start by buying back the shares of shareholders not connected to the Company. They usually cause trouble at the AGM, and by buying their shares, the Company would pay out much less in dividends every year, and the Management Board and the Senior Management shareholders will benefit by the future increase in share price and larger dividends."

"But that won't result in expanding the Company."

"I know that, I was just explaining another option that we could use the cash in the bank. Now that we have so much cash, a good way of using the balance is to make it available for Investment Bankers to invest during non-working hours. The cash would be available to us the following morning, and they would pay us a good dividend for the use of the cash, which we could use for the benefit of the Company."

"How?"

"We could reduce our selling prices even more, resulting in an increase in sales, and profitability."

"But that would take much longer to get results than by buying other businesses to add to the Company."

"Of course it would take longer, if your acquisitions were all successful, but if we used my methods there would be no risks involved."

"Okay then, why don't we close down our factories here, and have the work done overseas, where the workers are much cheaper?"

"We can't do that! All of our workers depend upon us for their living."

"It's not as if we'd be the first to do it."

"But it's not the way we do our business."

"Perhaps it's about time we joined the twenty-first century. We're sitting on property that's worth millions. We could really expand with that amount of funding."

Peter looked decidedly shocked by the idea of laying off all of the workforce.

"Hey, don't look so worried. I don't intend for our jobs to go as well. We'll still run the company from here; it's only the workers that will be based overseas."

Mark was still undecided about Kevin's idea on acquisitions, and the heated discussion had made him much more tired than usual. "Look, it's getting late, and there's too much involved in this discussion for me to make a decision tonight. We need to get together after Christmas to continue the argument. Have a good time over Christmas, you deserve a rest. I'll see you in the New Year."

Kevin picked up his papers and left straight away, but Peter stayed with Mark, whose face had gone white.

"Are you OK?"

"Yes, I'm fine. It's been a busy time since my summer holidays, I just need a rest."

Peter could see that it was more than just tiredness. He brought Mark a cup of tea and sat with him, until some colour came back into his face. Mark broke the silence, "Kevin's right about the acquisitions."

"I know he is. The problem is, if we rush things through, we'll buy businesses without properly checking them out, with money that we don't have. This could result in the Company paying interest on the loans that we'll have to take out to purchase the businesses, whilst making a loss on them. If that happens too often, the whole company could go under!"

"He's frustrated that all of the possible business purchases that he's found have been rejected."

"If he found a viable business, or one with potential, I'd support him, but he hasn't. I hope that you don't agree with his idea of laying off the workforce and selling the land?"

The FD changed the topic, as that was what made him feel ill in the first place. "Are you doing anything special this Christmas?"

"Not really, just catching up on lost sleep, and watching some television programmes that I've recorded." Peter hadn't told anyone at work that he and Susan were going to the Outer Hebrides, mainly because he thought that it was a stupid idea, and he was too embarrassed to tell them.

"Good night then. Have a good Christmas."

Peter rushed home to a reception almost as frosty as the one waiting for him in the Scottish Highlands. Susan had made a chilli for dinner so that he could eat and then clear the plates away quickly, for them to leave as early as possible. The chilli was more overcooked than normal, and after packing the car in record time, he had to rush down his food, resulting in Peter embarking on a long journey not only struggling against the dilemma of having to concentrate on his driving despite his expected tiredness, but also fighting against indigestion and the overpowering need to break wind on a regular basis, to prevent his intestines from exploding. There was only so many farts that he could blame on the dog, and he was getting

148

sick of the smell of the cheap perfume that Susan was spraying in the car to mask the odour from his SBDs. Despite the proximity to Christmas, Susan was correct about the traffic, and they made swift progress onto the M6 and further North. Peter stopped at Charnock Richard so that both he and the dog could relieve their bladders, and to let out numerous loud farts that he had just managed to hold in for the last few miles. The sound echoed across the deserted parking area as Susan appeared with two cups of coffee to fight off the impending exhaustion.

By the time he reached the M8 he was struggling to keep awake at the wheel, but had noticed that, by regularly squeezing the spot he had found on the back of his neck, the short surge of pain brought his senses back on line. This worked for almost half an hour, until the increased pressure resulted in an initial spurt as the spot erupted, that just missed the dog, followed by a trail of pus rolling down his back. It was now too sore to touch. By the time that they reached the filling station at Dumbarton it was no longer safe for him to continue. He got out of the car and walked around for a few minutes. The cold and the flakes of snow falling onto his face revived him a little, but not enough for him to be able to drive through the windy road alongside Loch Lomond and over the highlands.

"I need to sleep for an hour" he stuttered, stifling a succession of yawns.

"I said that I would help with the driving. You sleep in the passenger seat, and I'll drive until you're rested."

Although he acknowledged that Susan had offered to drive when the trip had been arranged, Peter never expected that this proposition would be required to be fulfilled. Although they had made better time than expected, he was worried that they could be held up on the roads over the mountains, and could not take a chance on sleeping in the stationary car for an hour. His dilemma was that Susan's driving was, if anything, worse than her cooking, and the roads would become more and more difficult from now on. The snowfall was still quite light, and had not yet really started to settle. He

149

consulted his book of the road. It would take them about an hour to reach Crianlarich, and the Green Welly shop, where the road started to go uphill at an unnatural rate.

"I'll sleep until Crianlarich, and take over for the road through the highlands. Just keep the speed down, and let me know if the snow gets any heavier."

Susan ejected the Beatles CD that Peter had been listening to, to help to keep himself awake, and chose Simon and Garfunkel's Greatest Hits. She had learnt how to choose her favourite tracks, and to replay the current CD, on the car's CD player, so that she wouldn't need to take her hands from the wheel to change the CD for another one. Peter was asleep before they reached the traffic lights at the next bend.

His dream of driving the Dodgem car at the fair subsided, as the punches from Susan brought him awake. He tried to swallow the plastic taste from his mouth as he came to his senses.

"The snow is getting heavier, and starting to settle." She sounded worried.

The car started to slip a little in the snow.

"Just take your feet away from the pedals."

Peter tried to sound calm, but Susan decided to disregard his advice and brake as hard as possible. The car took on a new life and skidded on the snow. It flew to the left of the road and charged up the steep bank on the side of the road until it could no longer go upwards, and flopped upside-down on the verge. In a surreal episode, the passenger window shattered inwards, covering Peter with small sharp pieces of glass, cutting his face. The engine stopped, and the acid drained from the upturned battery. Peter felt that his life was running at half speed, as the sound of 'Mrs Robinson' came slower and slower out of the speakers as the battery power reduced.

Fully awake now, Peter found himself hanging upside down by his seat belt. The passenger door would not open, so he cleared the window area of the remaining glass with his elbow, unclipped the seat belt, and pulled himself out through the window onto the road. Shaking off the shards of glass from his clothing, he shuffled round to the back of the car to check that the dog was OK. Susan's foot was trapped in the car, with her right boot wedged between the brake and clutch pedals. She unzipped the boot, wriggled out through the passenger window and stood gawping at the wreck of the car. Peter stood at the back of the car with the dog, trying to think of a reason why his life was so shit.

"My boot is stuck in the car, can you find me another one?" Peter found the pair of wellies at the back of the car and flung one at her. Luckily it was a right wellie, but it still looked stupid when she put it on.

"The ignition is still on."

Peter crawled back into the car, turned off the ignition, and retrieved the stuck boot. Mrs Robinson had juddered to a halt, but the sound of silence was broken by a car appearing in the distance. He was half way out of the car, as the new arrival slowed, then picked up speed again and disappeared into the darkness. Peter sighed in disbelief, and then went back into the car to get the breakdown company's details from the glove compartment

Peter took out his mobile phone to phone the recovery services, but his luck was still below the 'shit' level, and there was no signal on his phone. They had just dug out warm coats when another car appeared and stopped next to them.

"Need a hand?" the driver asked, for want of anything better to ask.

"Could you take me to the closest phone box please? I need to phone the recovery service, and there's no signal here."

"No problem, we're only a few miles from Crianlarich."

Peter swore under his breath. In a few more minutes, he would have been back in the driving seat.

"Right, everyone in the car, and I'll take you to the phone box." Susan shook her head. "My clothes are in the car. I don't want anyone stealing them."

Not wanting to waste time questioning her logic, Peter thought it more productive to just go and do what needed to be done. Crianlarich was closer than he expected, and oddly enough, there was no queue of people waiting at the phone box, or waiting to request assistance at this time of night. They were back within fifteen minutes.

"The closest recovery garage is in Glasgow. They won't be here for about two hours."

"We're in no hurry, get in the car and we'll wait until the recovery arrives."

Peter looked at the driver. Although it was about two o clock in the morning, and freezing cold, he really wanted to be left on his own with his misery.

"You may as well get in. I'm not leaving until the recovery vehicle arrives anyway".

Peter wanted to be left alone with his sorrow, but Susan looked at the car, and then at the snow covered bleakness that surrounded her. As far as she was concerned, it was a no-brainer, it's going to stay cold and wet for the foreseeable future, and his car is warm and dry. She pushed the dog into the car, and climbed in, reluctantly followed by Peter.

"A car went straight past us, just before you stopped." Susan usually waited until being formally introduced to people before speaking to them, but the crash must have shook her out of her shell.

"Perhaps they thought that you had set up the crash, so that you could steal their car," the driver's wife suggested.

"I think that it would be a bit extreme for your husband to crash a good car, on the off-chance that you might steal something better in a remote area of Scotland." The driver could find no creditable excuse for the other car driver's actions. "He was probably over the limit, and didn't want to get involved, in case he was caught."

"I was driving our car, not my husband," Susan thought that Peter was already pissed off enough without him being blamed for the crash. "There was nothing I could do, the car skidded on the snow and went off the road."

'You could have listened to me, and taken your feet away from the pedals', Peter thought to himself.

Luckily his severe flatulence had now abated, and Peter stared silently out of the window at the falling snow, whilst he waited for the recovery vehicle, until falling back to sleep. The hiss of the air brakes made him jump awake from his fitful sleep, and he looked out of the window hoping that it had all been a dream, but the headlights from the recovery vehicle shone onto the wreck of his car. Peter thanked the car driver profusely, and left to speak to the driver of the recovery vehicle.

The garage confirmed that the car was a write-off, and gave Peter the paperwork to sign so they could dispose of it. The garage also gave him the number of a local hire car company. Susan phoned Caledonian Macbrayne to inform them that they would not be on the ferry that morning, and asked if it was possible for them to squeeze the car and them on the ferry for the following morning. Susan thought that it was odd that, despite it being the last weekend sailing before Christmas, there was enough room to fit them on. Peter still hadn't washed the blood off of his face, in the hope that it would remind Susan of her part in the accident, and to make her feel as miserable as he did. He only offered the occasional grunt in response to Susan's questions and remarks. The replacement car was delivered to the garage, and although he had only slept fitfully during the slow drive back to Glasgow, the bleak sunlight and the breakfast at the Little Chef at Dumbarton gave him enough of a pick-me-up to ensure that Susan did not have the chance to crash this car on the second attempt to reach Skye. The journey to Skye was much less interesting than the first try. They booked into a B and B in Portree for the night, which was only a few miles from the ferry terminal. As they booked in, the woman in the B and B showed more interest in the dried blood on Peter's face than at the dog sniffing at her crotch.

A handful of cars were waiting at the jetty at Uig the following morning, and were quickly loaded onto the ferry. Although the sea journey lasted less than two hours, Peter felt that they were going up and down more than across the water towards their destination. Susan spent the entire journey on the open deck, throwing up over the side, despite taking two Stugeron tablets. When they finally reached the jetty at Lochmaddy, the sea tossed the boat around like a discarded stick. It took the boat-hand three attempts to get the large rope around the post to haul the ferry tightly into place in the mooring. Susan made her way very gingerly, to the car deck, but by the time she finally reached the car, the drivers were still waiting to be allowed onto terra firma. As he drove off of the ferry, Peter noticed that there were many more cars waiting to get onto the ferry than the few leaving it. He was astonished by the collective expression of relief on the faces of those looking at the newly-arrived ferry, enabling them to escape the Islands, and wondered whether his earlier thoughts that it could not get any worse may well have been horribly mistaken.

Not surprisingly, the fact that he had caught the ferry that he originally wanted to, instead of the one the day before, did not improve Peter's feeling of despair.

The colour of Susan's face had receded by a couple of shades of green, but she was still unable to move without being sick, and could only whisper the words "slow down" every time that he went over 30 m.p.h. As the road was single track, he spent ages in the passing spaces to allow the regular build-up of cars to overtake him. He stopped at a small shop at Clachan, a few miles from the jetty, and asked for a bottle of water, but he could not make the shopkeeper understand that you could actually buy water in a bottle. He ended up buying two small bottles of lemonade. Susan had already got out of the car, but she was so wasted that she only managed to keep herself from falling over by leaning against the side of the car. She drank the contents of the first bottle, hardly pausing for breath, and it came back out as quickly as it had gone down. She took her time sipping the second bottle, and when they reached the B and B, over an hour later, she had improved to a light shade of grey, but still looked awful. As soon as Peter had unloaded the car, she went to bed to try to recover.

Peter was starving. He'd not eaten since breakfast, as the café on the boat was closed due to the bad weather making it too dangerous to prepare any food. He found the owner of the B and B in the kitchen. She introduced herself as Morag in the soft, singing voice that he would become accustomed to during his brief stay on the islands.

"We have to work on the croft, so breakfast finishes at half past eight. Tea will be at seven o'clock. We'll let you know what it is at breakfast."

"How many choices are there for dinner?" Peter understood what 'tea' was, but hadn't called it by that name since he was a child.

"The usual two."

He looked at Morag, expecting further explanation. Fish or meat? Meat or vegetarian?

"Take it or leave it." Morag laughed. "I'm sure with all of the fresh air, you'll eat whatever is put in front of you."

She gave Peter a handful of candles. "You'll be needing these, no doubt."

He had heard of Eskimos eating candles, but didn't think that it was also the custom here. Morag observed the confused look on Peter's face. "You'll need some light when we have the power cuts."

"Oh yes, of course." The thought of eating the candles reminded Peter of his hunger. "Where is the closest fish and chip shop?"

"You can buy a piece of fish at Neily's, but we make our own chips here from potatoes."

"No, a shop that sells cooked fish and chips."

"A shop that sells cooked fish and chips? Well now, and who would be wanting that?"

Was she taking the piss?

"What about McDonalds?"

"Oh, there's plenty of those about. They still don't get on with the Campbells."

Peter gave up on the conversation, badly beaten. He put on his wellies and coat, and helped the dog into the back of the car. He had passed a small shop a few miles before reaching the B and B, and drove there, to see if they sold any English food. Parking outside the shop, he noticed the name 'Neil' above the entrance. Hoping that 'Neily' sold more than just pieces of fish, he went inside. He didn't like the look of the

Scotch pies, so he bought some crisps and biscuits. He then parked by the beach next to the airport. Although it was only three o'clock, it was too dark to let the dog roam free, so he walked the dog on the extendible lead along the edge of the tide, eating the crisps, whilst fighting to keep his footing against the gale force wind, whistling around him.

Peter arrived back in pitch dark, and stumbled through the gloom to their bedroom. The torch from the glove compartment managed to light the way, but he still got his feet tangled up with the dog on the way up the stairs, and he dropped the bag containing the biscuits. He really needed a cup of tea to accompany the now broken biscuits, but the power cut had taken away the option. He shone the torch towards the bed, and Susan stirred, and sat up. The grey-green colour had drained from her face, and her sunken eyes stared back at him.

"What time is it?" she croaked.
"About half past three."
"Why did you let me sleep all night?"
"I didn't. It's three thirty in the afternoon."
"Why is it so dark?"
"There's a power cut."
"But why is it so dark outside at half past three in the afternoon?"
"Because we're so far north it gets dark really early."
"It's hard to tell the night time from the day."
He lit one of the candles that Morag was in no doubt that he would need, and put it on the bedside cabinet. A flickering light illuminated the small bedroom.
"Oh good. At least we won't have to watch the T.V. in the dark."
"There won't be any T.V. if the power is off, will there." He wanted to put her latest show of stupidity down to her not feeling well, but he knew deep inside, that wasn't the case.

Luckily, the power cut did not last too long, and tea was ready at seven o'clock, as promised. Lamb chops and heaps of potatoes and vegetables, followed by Apple pie and custard.

Morag was also right about the food. Peter finished his with no problem whatsoever, and Susan even found the strength to eat a small amount before going back up to bed. She would have probably eaten more, but after initially being worried about scratching the pattern from her plate with her knife, she noticed that the pattern did not match that of Peter's plate, and then realised that the 'pattern' was actually the residue of food left from previous meals.

"Have you got anything planned whilst you're on the Islands?" Morag asked Peter, after he'd eaten his tea.

"Just catching up on lost sleep, reading a few books, and walking the dog," he replied. "Will there be any entertainment on anywhere during Christmas and the New Year?"

"If you're looking for entertainment, you shouldn't have come to the Outer Hebrides, and you would have been better off staying in a hotel than a B and B. You'll not have the problems from the power cuts in a hotel. They have a generator, you know."

"My wife booked the holiday. I'm surprised that there are any B and Bs open during Christmas."

"Och, we don't bother with Christmas any more, and we only make a few pounds from the croft."

"I was just trying to find something to do tomorrow. Hopefully Susan will be fully recovered by then."

"The Dark Island hotel has a carvery every Sunday lunchtime, and live music in the bar on Sunday night. It's only a few miles down the road."

"I thought that the bars were closed on Sundays?"

"That changed some years ago. People still moan about it, but it doesn't stop them from going out drinking in public."

It was still dark the following morning when the dog nudged Peter with his nose, wanting to go out. It was too dark and windy to take the dog for a run out, so Peter just walked him down the road on the long lead, promising him that he would let him wander round on his own when it got lighter. He went back and woke Susan up for breakfast, and had a shave whilst she was contemplating whether to join the ranks of the living just yet.

"There's live music in the hotel bar just down the road tonight, and a carvery this lunchtime."

"I hope their plates are cleaner than the ones here." Susan, as usual, had woken up full of the joys of Spring.

"I'm going to take the dog for a walk along the beach after breakfast. Did you want to join us?"

"What's the weather like?"

"Windy."

"How windy?"

"Very."

"Maybe tomorrow."

Who said that the art of conversation was dead!

Susan inspected her breakfast plate, but didn't comment on the strange patterns. She felt much better after her night's sleep, and had spent a day without throwing up, so her appetite had returned, and it would take more than a few engrained marks on her plate to put her off this time.

When it was finally light enough to see outside, Peter put on his wellies and coat and helped the dog in the back of the car, whilst Susan sat in the room reading a magazine. He parked up next to the airport beach again, and let the dog off of the lead. Jaeger was now a very old dog, and no longer rushed around like he used to. Despite the *Cartrofen* injections and the *Metacam* on his food to alleviate the pain from his arthritis, Peter had to walk slowly to stop himself from getting too far ahead. The dog still enjoyed his walks, but his main interests now were investigating the various smells, and finding different places to wee. Peter was surprised how much larger the beach was now that the tide was out. The dog did a 'rattler' on the sand, and Peter checked his pockets for a bag to pick it up with. The empty crisp bag from yesterday was much too small, so he scraped a hole in the sand with his boot, and buried the evidence. He knew it wasn't the done thing to do, but it was better than leaving it exposed, or taking it home in his pocket. The beach was deserted, but he doubted that he would be so lucky next time.

Whilst the dog was checking out the strange smelling sea weed, which sprouted vertically from the sand, Peter climbed up the bank to get a view of the airport, wondering how many flights they would have to such a remote area. The runway, as expected, was empty, but much larger than he had thought that it would be. 'Perhaps the islands attract the jet set, and I'll be drinking in the local bar with David and Victoria Beckham, whilst we listen to the live music?' He didn't believe it for a second, and went back down to catch up with the dog. He took advantage of the solitude to carry out his favourite 'secret' pastime of imitating Kevin. He had done this so often that he was so convincing that even the dog was sometimes worried that the grumpy bastard had returned.

That evening, they ventured out to the hotel. Jaeger was left behind, which was no bad thing, as the seaweed that he'd eaten on the beach was causing him to produce strong and repulsive smells. Although Peter had encountered no signs of life during his walks with the dog, the bar was quite crowded. They sat in the corner away from the area that had been set up for the 'live music' to try to protect their ear drums from the expected onslaught. He had been to a few music pubs in his time, but the layout was a bit different to what he was used to. Instead of the drum kit and numerous amplifiers, speaker stacks and microphone stands, there was a bar stool and a small amp and speaker. 'Oh God, please not a whole night of *Donald Where's Yer Troosers*'.

Peter went to the bar and bought himself a pint of beer, and a large G & T for Susan.
"What sort of music do you have tonight?"
"Och, we have both types of music here, Country AND Western." The crowd around the bar laughed as if it was the funniest thing that the girl behind the bar had ever said, and was surprised that Peter did not join in with their hilarity. Was it possible that no-one in the Outer Hebrides had seen '*The Blues Brothers*', and as far as they were concerned, it was an original statement? The bar started to fill up even more than he'd thought possible. Except for the village next to the

159

airport, he'd only seen a few houses dotted here and there on the island, and he thought that most of their inhabitants had beaten a hasty retreat on the last ferry out. As if on cue, a tall man with a beard appeared, plugged his guitar in, and started to play a Johnny Cash song. The noise of the conversations around Peter increased to overcome the noise of the singer, and this competition carried on for about half an hour, until the singer stopped for a break, and a quick pint, or two

An old man came to the small table where they were sitting. "Mind if I join you? I usually sit here on a Sunday, as it's the furthest away from the noise. I didn't expect to find a seat when I arrived, the car park's full up. My name's Doug." This was the first person to talk to them who didn't have the local accent. Actually, he didn't have an accent at all. He had put his glass of whisky on the table already and sat down with his back towards the singer.
"Are you here on holiday?" Peter asked.
"God no, I've lived here for donkey's years."
"We're only here for a short holiday. My wife Susan thought she'd booked us somewhere on a tropical island."
"Easy mistake to make," Susan warmed to him immediately. "Did you fly over?"
"No, we caught the ferry from Uig. It was horrendous. I spent the entire journey being sick over the side."
"You were lucky that the ferry made it over, they're often cancelled at this time of year due to the weather. You can fly over from Glasgow, but I'm too used to the Hebridean way of life to chance anything like that. The plane stops half-way to take on more wood."
For once, Susan understood that this was a joke, and laughed out loud. "Why are you living here?"
"I was stationed here with the Army, and my wife and I just took to the place. You get used to it after a while, you know, the first twenty years are the worst. Did you put your clocks back when you arrived?"
Peter and Susan both looked puzzled.
"You must have noticed the time difference. You should have put your clocks back by thirty years."

"I haven't really been out much," Susan replied, "I've only just recovered from the ferry journey."

"Is there much work here?" Peter asked. It was good to have someone to talk to after Susan's illness-enforced silence.

"A lot of the local people work for the Army. The Army brings their soldiers here to carry out live firings with their missiles. It doesn't really matter that the missiles land in the sea, much better than taking out a block of flats. The hotel bar is usually full of soldiers, during their off-duty time when they're here training, but there's no missile firing over the Christmas period. Most of the soldiers posted here permanently, and the civilian staff from the mainland have also escaped back home to avoid the gales and the power cuts." Doug paused whilst he had a large gulp of his whisky. "The Army also have a big problem getting used to the locals. They're a bit manâna."

"What does that mean?" Susan asked.

"It means 'tomorrow'. The locals can't understand that things need doing quickly, not when they get around to it. It's just their way of life. A man who lives down the road from me had his house catch fire, so he phoned the fire station. They're all volunteers here. We don't usually need a fire engine, as the wind and the rain will normally extinguish the fire quite quickly. Unfortunately, it was one of the odd dry days, so he was quite worried."

"Quick, quick, my house is on fire."

"Och, what's yer hurry."

"My house is burning."

"Well, we'll get there as quickly as we can, but it won't be for a while though."

"But my house is burning down!"

"Och well, at least you'll be warm while yer waiting." Doug had sang the words in a good imitation of the local accent.

Susan laughed fully for the first time in ages. Doug, inspired by the attention, was on a roll.

"Their mentality is probably down to the dark winters that we have here. They call Benbecula the Dark Island, you know. You've probably noticed that it gets dark at about half past two, and doesn't get light again until about March. But the summers can be really nice."

"Is it hot up here in summer then?"

"Not really hot, but it stays light almost all of the time, and when the wind drops it can be quite pleasant, apart from the midges."

"Is there much to do up here in the summer?"

"You would have been much better coming here during the summer months. There are two mountains just South of us here, that you could climb within a day, and there's plenty of fishing, both in the lochs, and in the sea, as long as the Army aren't firing their missiles."

"Is there much wildlife?" Susan rarely went out walking, but she always seemed to be interested in the local wildlife, which she probably got from her Open University course that the dog helped her with many years ago.

"There's not many birds around, apart from the ground-nesters, or the seabirds that nest in the cliffs. Mind you, there's no trees for them to nest in anyway. An idiot brought some hedgehogs over from the mainland, and their numbers have multiplied by a large extent. As the birds are ground-nesters, the hedgehogs eat their eggs, so their numbers are decreasing in line with the increase in the number of hedgehogs. I've been fishing in the sea and seen numerous seals, dolphins, whales and basking sharks."

"How did you know they were basking sharks?" Susan asked, quite innocently.

"They were drinking Pimms, and had parasols." Susan was really getting used to Doug's sense of humour, and was having more fun than she'd had in years.

"Some friends and I sailed over to the Monarch Isles, to the west of here a few summers ago, to go fishing for a few days. When we opened the box of Army rations that we'd been given, all it contained was tins of Mock Turtle soup."

"Mock Turtle?" Susan was confused again. "I've never heard of a Mock Turtle before. What does it taste like?"

"Chicken."

The reply came out just before the guitar started its twanging noise again, and try as they could, it was difficult to keep up this level of conversation against the noise of the singer, and the heated discussions around them. Peter used this time to

162

get a round in, including a large whisky and water for Doug, whilst Susan tapped her foot along with the music, trying to work out whether the current song was Country or Western. At the next break, their conversation started up again, where it left off.

"Will there be much going on during Christmas and the New Year?" Although Susan didn't go out much, Peter was keen to sample some more of the Hebridean night-life.

"There will be nothing open on Christmas day, but New Year's Eve will be quite lively in here. Are you staying in the hotel?"

"No, Susan booked us into a B and B just down the road."

"There's not many B and Bs that stay open during Christmas and the New Year. You'll be staying at Morag's then?"

"Hers was the only B and B that I could find in the brochure. The hotels were much more expensive."

"Have you noticed the strange patterns on the crockery?"

"Straight away. I hope I don't get food poisoning, I've only just got over my sea-sickness, and we're going home on Friday."

"I wouldn't worry too much, I can't remember hearing of anyone dying, well not this year anyway."

"Are there any special celebrations held on the Islands?"

"Most of the Army goes back to the mainland for Christmas, so the biggest celebration we have is Bonfire Night." Doug had problems disguising the smile that had appeared on his lips, as he could see Susan being drawn into another of his stories.

"Bonfire Night? Really?" Susan had never really thought of it as anything special.

"Oh yes, it's a really big celebration up here. The trouble is that the weather isn't always too good in November."

"Oh that's a shame, what do they do with the bonfire and the firework display if it's too wet and windy?"

"They hold it in the gymnasium." There was no reaction from Susan as she failed to see the idiocy of his comment, but he still carried on. "We have games as well as the fireworks. The local favourite is bobbing for chips."

"Really. From a bucket of water?"

"No, from the deep-fat fryer!"

Susan squealed with delight at the silliness of the idea. The crowd had expanded closer to their table, and the locals turned and looked at her. Doug ignored them, and carried on his conversation

"We usually have an open house on Boxing Day morning, any time after ten o'clock. We'd be pleased if you came round for some brunch and a few drinks."

"I'd love to, but I don't want to leave the dog on his own for too long. He gets lonely."

"Bring him along, my dog would love to have someone English to talk to. Would you like another drink?"

Doug's glass had miraculously emptied, whilst Peter's beer glass was still half full.

He looked over to Susan to see if she wanted another gin, but she had her 'I've been out for long enough, and want to get back to check on the dog' look on her face. The locals were starting to get quite noisy around her, and she much preferred the quiet life.

"Oh no thank you. I don't usually drink beer, and never more than two pints, even at Christmas. I can't have anymore, or I'll be over the drink-drive limit. It doesn't seem to worry this lot though. How are they going to get home if they've had too much to drink?"

Doug laughed at this comment. "There's not many policemen around on the islands. They'll all drive home from here without a second thought. They'll be far too pissed to walk."

Once again the twanging of the guitar broke up the conversation. It was louder than before, and the beer seemed to have started to take its effect on the singer's playing. Doug wrote down directions to his house, and Peter and Susan shouted their goodbyes over the noise and went outside into the current gale.

The rest of the week flew by. Susan was fully recovered, and although she preferred to stay in the room rather than fight against the wind whilst Peter took the dog out for his walk in the morning, she sat with him in the car as they drove around the islands, looking at the sights, and the waves frothing against the deserted beaches around the island, but there was no sign of basking sharks, or even discarded Pimms glasses. Peter bought Susan a pretty necklace from the Hebridean

Jewellery shop for her Christmas present, and expected her to show some appreciation in bed.

"Not here, I'm sure that Morag will hear us. I'll make it up to you when we get back home."

The birthday, anniversary and Christmas shag had now been reduced to birthdays and anniversaries only!

The visit to Doug's house was one of the highlights of their holiday. Brunch consisted of kedgeree and the full English breakfast, all laid out in 'Hostess' trays in the dining room. One of the trays was labelled 'Mock Turtle', Susan lifted the lid to find a latticed pastry shell containing sausages protruding from each corner, to represent the turtle's legs, with a head poking out at the front, and a smaller sausage at the back for its tail. It looked a bit like a turtle, but didn't taste of chicken. Doug was his usual entertaining self, and they promised to keep in touch.

The weather seemed to quiet down on the morning that they left. The sea was calm enough for Peter to get a decent lunch inside him on the ferry, but he couldn't trust himself to have any beans for obvious reasons, and Susan went the entire journey without throwing up once.

The ferry left just before midday and arrived at Uig on time, unfortunately the Highlands of Scotland had just received a huge fall of snow, and the roads were beginning to close. The road at Glencoe was already closed, but that shouldn't be a problem, as they could go down the West coast road towards Oban, and then go East towards Crianlarich. The hire car had to be delivered back to the office in Glasgow. There was no time limit for the return of the hire car, if the office was closed, all they had to do was fill it up with fuel, park the car outside the office, and put the keys through the letter-box. The problem was that they had to get to the airport to pick up the hire car that they'd arranged to drive back home, and that office closed at nine o'clock. Although the route by-passing Glencoe would take longer than expected, there was plenty of time to spare. It was only after they left Fort William that Peter started to get worried. The wind had really picked up, and the road to Oban, next to the coast, was closed due to the waves crashing over it. Peter turned around and headed for Inverness, hoping that the A9 would remain open long enough for them to reach Glasgow. By the time that they reached Stirling, it was touch and go whether they would reach the Airport in time. The road was deserted so he jumped the traffic lights on the dual carriageway just outside Glasgow. As usual, when you don't want a policeman, he'll be sure to arrive, and the flashing lights and siren brought him to a standstill a little further up the road. Peter looked over at Susan. The last thing he wanted was for her to say something to upset the police.

"Just keep quiet, and let me do the talking."

Peter wound down his window as the policeman reached the car.

"Do you know what speed you were travelling at, when we pulled you over?"

"Yes officer. Fifty miles per hour." Surely he was being pulled over for jumping the red light; he hadn't been speeding.

"This is a thirty miles per hour speed limit area."

"But it's a dual carriageway, how can the speed limit be only thirty?"

"Did you not see the road signs?"

"No," now Peter was confused, and time was getting short. "The last speed sign that I saw was for fifty miles per hour." Peter looked down the road in frustration, and just in front of him was a speed sign, covered in snow. "I'm sorry, but the road sign is covered with snow. I was going fifty, because that was the limit on the last sign that I saw. I didn't expect the speed limit to be lower than that on a dual carriageway."

It was now the policeman's turn to be confused.

"OK, but keep your speed down. The speed limit will go up when you reach the M8."

The thirty mph speed limit would make it difficult to reach the airport on time. "How long will it take me to reach the airport from here?"

"It all depends on how fast you drive, doesn't it."

"Thank you officer, good night."

Peter pulled away before the policeman could bring up the point about jumping the red light, and was back up to fifty after the next few bends. He reached the hire car office just as it was closing, collected the car, and followed Susan to the other hire car office to hand back the first hire car. He felt refreshed from his holiday, and strong enough to do all of the driving home through the night. There were plenty of places on the M6 where he could stop for a coffee and grab a few hours' sleep if he needed to, so there was no need for Susan to drive. If possible, he didn't want to stop for any length of time.

Susan fell asleep as soon as they reached the M6, so Peter was left alone to his favourite day dream of when he became the FD after Mark retired, and how he would make Kevin suffer for all of the years of torment. He made good time as the traffic was really light, and the wind had died down, so he arrived home before the early morning's traffic became busy. Was his run of bad luck finally changing? He started to mentally prepare for the next meeting with the FD and Kevin, to ensure that the Company didn't go ahead with any risky acquisitions. Peter also thanked God that Kevin would never be the FD, and promised himself that he would fight the idea of moving the workforce overseas with the last breath in his body. He'd worked hard to get the Company to the current level of market share and high profitability, and he didn't want Kevin to ruin this.

NINE

Peter spent the next few days trying to catch up the sleep that he lost driving back home. He went round to wish his parents a belated 'Happy Christmas', and found his father ill in bed, and his mother really worried. She had always expected to be the first to go, as Peter's father was rarely ill, whereas she had felt exhausted for as long as she could remember.

"He's caught pneumonia. I told him to stay indoors when the weather was bad, but he never takes a blind bit of notice of what I say. He's eighty now, and still acts as if he's a spring chicken."

"Can I see him?"

"He'll be upset if you don't, but try not to tire him out."

Peter went upstairs and was shocked at the sight of the person laid out in the bed. His father had always seemed young and active, but the frail old man smiled as he slowly sat up when Peter entered the room.

"Hello son, how were the Outer Hebrides?"

"Cold, wet and windy."

"God knows why you went there during the winter."

"Susan thought that Benbecula was a tropical island."

Peter's father laughed and coughed in pain at the same time, and Peter cursed himself for not listening to his mother.

"How's work going? Are you the boss yet?"

"Not quite, you have to wait until someone dies before you can get promotion."

"How's Susan? Any sight of any grandkids yet?"

He must be tired, he usually waited for about five minutes into the conversation before he brought in the subject of children.

"Susan's waiting until she's set up her beauty salon, then she will take time out to bring you hordes of grandchildren."

"Well, don't leave it too late like we almost did. We'd given up hope when you finally came along. I want a few years of bouncing them on my knee."

Peter's mother appeared at the door, and shooed Peter out.

"Come on, you need your rest. Peter will be back tomorrow."

"See you tomorrow, son."

Peter and Susan toasted in the New Year with Geoffrey and Dawn, where he had to listen to Susan telling her parents how lovely it was in the Outer Hebrides, and how she would willingly move there to live when she retired.

"It's so peaceful and stress free, we made a good friend up there who told us that it's really beautiful in the summer."

Peter shook his head in disbelief. Susan had spent all of her time either sat in the car, back in the bedroom reading magazines, or watching television, when there wasn't a power cut. He enjoyed the walks, the open spaces and the pace of life, but would prefer somewhere less cold and windy.

He returned back to work on Monday, fully rested and, this time, prepared for the next round of arguments with Kevin about expanding the Company, but this paled into insignificance with the news he was about to be told.

Expecting the FD's P.A. to have a follow-up meeting arranged, he walked down to the FD's office to enquire what time he wanted to carry on his discussion with Peter and Kevin. He also wanted to discuss the Christmas break, and to wish him a happy New Year, even though neither of them treated the first of January as the 'New' Year. An Accountant's year starts in April, and runs through to the following March.

The P.A. looked up at Peter, and then at the office clock.

"He's not in yet."

"It must be his New Year's resolution to spend less time in the office."

"He's usually in by now, or phoned to say that he's been delayed for some reason. I'll give you a call when he arrives."

Peter walked back to his office, wishing the newly arrived office staff 'Happy New Year' as he passed them. He caught up on his phone messages and his e-mails prior to starting to gather the performance information for December. His Blackberry had been banned by Susan during the Christmas holiday, so his In-box was overflowing. The FD had sent out his meeting notes the day after their meeting, and covered the Details of the Agenda items and Action Points, but did not include the discussion regarding the proposed increase in Acquisitions of other businesses.

Kevin arrived late, as usual, in his usual, untidy and hung over state, and went immediately to the coffee machine. At last, the phone rang, but it was the MD's P.A. on the line, not the FD's. Peter and Kevin very rarely worked directly with James, the MD, but obviously knew him well, both on a work and social basis. Like Mark, who was referred to as the FD, James was the MD.

"Could you and Kevin please come down to the MD's office? He would like to speak to the both of you quite urgently."

"Kevin, the MD wants to speak to us urgently. I'm worried. The FD's not in yet."

"You always worried too much. He probably wants to discuss our bonus."

They were ushered into the MD's office.

"Sit down, please. Look, there's no easy way to say this, but the FD's had a heart attack this morning." Peter was distraught. Numerous concerned thoughts crossed his mind. 'Should I have stayed longer with him before Christmas instead of rushing off home? Have I put too much strain on him by arguing about the acquisitions?'

"Is he dead?" Kevin was never one to stand on ceremony.

"No Kevin, but he won't be well enough for work for a few months. We need to arrange cover for his work."

Kevin also never missed the chance to push himself forward in front of the bosses, even if it was Peter who would do the work. "We can cover for him for a few months. It'll be much easier than getting an outsider in on a temporary basis, and having to waste time showing him what to do."

The MD had already made this decision, and wanted to 'run it past' Kevin and Peter. "Yes, that's what the Management Board was thinking. Is there anything that you were working on with the FD that the Board needs to know about?"

"Did you get a copy of the Minutes and the Action Points from the FD's pre-Christmas meeting?" If Kevin had got in early enough, he would have been able to check his e-mails, and the recipients, before asking the question.

"Yes Kevin, it was the last e-mail that the FD sent to me before leaving for his Christmas holiday."

"The FD was very keen that we reviewed our policy on new acquisitions to enlarge the company, and became actively involved in new purchases."

"He might have been, Kevin, but we need to keep those sort of things on the back burner until he returns. You and Peter will be busy enough covering for his work."

Kevin turned to Peter. "Peter, you know you said that you would like to have your office to yourself."

"Yes."

"Well, if we're going to be busy, would it make sense for me to move out to give you more space?"

"Yes, it would."

"Ok, I'll move into the FD's office until he returns."

Peter was astounded how easily he'd been outmanoeuvred again by Kevin.

Peter was now visiting his father every day. Since he'd moved into his own house he'd convinced himself that he was too busy at work to keep in regular touch with his parents, and he would go months without even talking to his father on the phone. His mother would always answer the phone, or if his father did answer, he would quickly hand the phone over to his mother. Now Peter was beginning to regret his lack of contact. There were many things that Peter wanted to ask his father; he hardly knew anything about his grandparents, or what his father had done as a young man. He expected his father to be there for ever and thought that there was lots of time when he wasn't so busy that he could have these discussions, but he'd noticed that his father's condition was getting worse instead of better, and his father's lack of breath made it difficult for him to talk. Peter had never been a great conversationalist, so was having to make up for his lack of these skills to fill the empty spaces where they used to talk, as his father would always take the lead. Unfortunately, the only topic that he knew anything about was his work, which was boring to anyone who wasn't involved. He spoke a few words about Susan and her parents, and his father always liked to hear stories of Susan's cooking and what Jaeger used to get up to when he was a younger dog.

Peter's father grabbed hold of Peter's hand when he was about to leave. "I've always been proud of you. You've grown up to be a good person, and you're successful with a lovely wife and home. I couldn't have wished for a better son than you."

Peter left the room before he broke down in tears, met his mother in the kitchen and the flood opened. He had to support his mother as she collapsed into his arms.

"The doctor doesn't expect him to last the week. I don't know what I'll do."

"Does he know?"

"No-one's told him, but I think that he suspects it."

"What are you going to do?"

"I'm only holding on long enough to look after him until he goes."

"You can come and live with us afterwards."

"Don't be silly. The only way I'll leave here is in a box."

"Well, the offer's there. Susan would love to have you come and stay with us."

She pulled away from Peter and filled the kettle from the tap. "Do you want a cup of tea before you leave, I'm just about to make a pot?"

"No, I'd better get back, otherwise Susan will end up burning the dinner. I'll see you tomorrow."

Peter's father was dead when she came into the bedroom with his cup of tea. The cup fell onto the floor, and she stood motionless staring down at the only man she'd ever loved.

The following evening Peter noticed how spotlessly clean the house looked. His mother was in the kitchen with a cloth wiping the cupboards, and took no notice as he entered the room.

"How's Dad today?"

She looked up absent-mindedly at her son. "Not very well at all. He's not eaten anything all day."

172

Peter went upstairs and discovered the reason why. The broken cup had been picked up from the previous night, and the carpet was clean and dry. There were endless cups of cold tea in the bedroom. Peter went downstairs and called the Doctor, and sat watching his mother as she moved back into the living room to resume her cleaning that she'd been doing non-stop since her husband had died.

The sight of the Doctor made no impression on her until he grabbed her by the arm and spoke directly to her.
"Mrs Stevenson, your husband's dead. We need to take him away."
The small flicker in her eyes subsided, and she collapsed onto the living room floor. The Doctor checked her pulse and her shallow breathing, and looked sadly at Peter.
"She's exhausted. She must have been cleaning the house all day."
She was put on oxygen and rushed to hospital, but didn't last the night.

Peter was away from work for the next week sorting out the funeral and the house. He found scores of photographs of himself from a baby through childhood and highlights of his adult life, such as his wedding, his honeymoon, and his appearances on stage. There were all of the postcards that he'd sent them from his holidays. He found the tin box in the attic, inside it was an envelope containing £5,000 in a mixture of £10 and £20 notes. The box also contained more photographs of Peter, and all of his school reports. There was also the will, which left everything to Peter. Although they had hardly any savings, the house was now worth a small fortune.

He took the will home to show to Susan. "They've left everything to me."
"Of course they have. What did you expect?"
"I never really thought about it. I thought that my father would live for ever."
"What are you going to do with it?"

"We could pay off the mortgage. You could start your own Beauty Salon if you wanted to."
"Let's talk about it after the funeral."

When Peter finally returned to work his in-tray was overflowing. Kevin came down with a list of priorities, which was just about everything.
"Did they leave you much?"
"What?"
"Your parents. Did they leave you much?"
"Not really."
"What about the house? That must be worth a bit."
"Probably. I don't know what we're doing with it yet."
"I would. If I was you, it would have been up for sale last week."
"I've had other things to think about."
"I wish that I was as lucky as you."
"Why do you think I'm lucky?"
"Well, your parents were quite old. They would have been in a home before long, and you'd have had to sell the house to pay for them to be looked after. And when that money was gone, you'd be paying with your own money. You got off lightly."
"I'd rather have my parents than any money in the world."
"You can say that now, it would've been different if you'd have spent all of their money on their care, whilst they sat in a home, not knowing you from Adam."
"Can we get on with this work, I need to catch up."

The MD was absolutely correct on how busy Peter was for the following months. Peter needed something to take his mind off the loss of his parents, but he almost committed the mortal sin of forgetting his wedding anniversary. He just managed to book a table at the 'Head of the River', and bought Susan something shiny, and a large bunch of flowers. Whilst he was buying her a 'soppy' Anniversary card he noticed 'Dirty Dancing' in the DVD rack. For some reason, of which he had no understanding at all, Susan always watched the film when it made its rare appearance on television, so he thought that adding it to her growing list of presents would put him in her good books. Luckily, their anniversary was on a Saturday, so Susan had a lay-in whilst he took the dog for its morning walk. He moved the flowers, card and the presents into the front porch from their hiding place in the shed on his return from walking the dog, and shouted upstairs to Susan.

"Wakey, wakey, the postman's been."

It was far too early for the postman, but Susan understood his strange ritual. She took her morning Nurofens to help clear away the previous night's gin, threw on her dressing gown, and went downstairs to find the usual flowers and jewellery. They opened their presents in mock surprise, and Susan kissed Jaeger for the bag of sweets that he'd bought her from the paper shop that morning. Peter thanked Susan for his usual smart shirt and pair of cuff links, and wondered why it was that women always thought that it was acceptable to give items of clothing for presents, when they were a normal requirement. Maybe if he'd taken the bother to inform Susan what he really wanted, he would have received something different.

"I've booked a table for dinner this evening."

"I hope it's not too early, I don't want to miss *Britain's got Talent*."

Peter was one of the many men in the country that couldn't understand the fascination that the females had for *Britain's got Talent*, but had long since bothered to waste his time worrying about it. "No dear, the table's booked for eight o'clock, so you can watch most of it in the hour that you take whilst getting ready. We can record any part that's on after we leave."

"If we're not eating until eight o'clock, we won't be back until late."

"That's the time that we usually eat, when we eat out."

"I know, but it's our anniversary. I thought we were going to have an early night."

"I'm not going to bed straight after eating a large meal."

"It's a euphemism."

"What is?"

"Us having an early night."

"Oh, a euphemism. That's a big word for you. Is eating out a euphemism as well?"

"You're being disgusting now. Don't you want to have sex tonight?"

"Of course I do. It's our anniversary. We always have a euphemism on our anniversary. We used to have a euphemism at Christmas as well."

"That was different, we were in someone else's house, and they would have heard us. If you want to continue this argument, I can quite easily spend the night at my parents' house."

"And what will you tell them when they ask you why you're not spending your anniversary with your husband?"

"I'll tell them that you farted again, and the house is being fumigated."

"OK, you win, I'll go without desert, and we can get back relatively early." Peter still thought that it was funny that Susan mispronounced pudding 'desert', but was probably choosing the wrong time to remind her.

"I'm going shopping. If you want to have sex tonight, you'll need to change your attitude." Susan went upstairs to get dressed, unsure whether Peter was being nasty or sarcastic, as the holiday in the Outer Hebrides didn't have the same effect on his humour as the one in South Africa had. Peter was left wondering what went wrong with their anniversary morning that had started so promisingly. He picked up his cup of tea and newspaper, and the dog slowly followed him upstairs into his office.

Peter was still in his office when Susan returned from shopping. He was bringing even more work home these days. He'd stopped working to make himself a salad for lunch, and later to take the dog out, but had returned to his work both times, so Susan watched television downstairs, waiting for her parents to get back from the garden centre. Peter heard the phone ring, and was sure that Susan let it ring longer than she normally does before answering it, just to disrupt his work. He heard Susan say loudly, "marvellous, Mummy, we'll be round in a few minutes" obviously for his benefit, before hanging up.

176

Susan picked up the car keys, and shouted up to Peter in his office. "I'm just popping down to see Mummy and Daddy, are you coming with me?"

"I still have some work to do for Monday morning. I'll probably be in no fit state to do anything difficult tomorrow, so I need to get it done now."

"It won't take long, they just want to give us our Anniversary present."

"Can I finish what I'm doing, and walk down and meet you in twenty minutes?"

"OK, I'll have a sherry and a chat with them, whilst we're waiting for you, and you can drive back."

"Why are you driving there, it's only a few minutes walk?"

"Mummy told me that it's too heavy to carry that far."

"I'll see you in twenty minutes."

Peter watched Susan from his office window get into the car and pull out slowly across to the other side of the road to drive to her parents' house. A car came rushing around the bend before their house in the opposite direction to Susan, and started to break furiously. The screech of the brakes sounded their warning but the speeding car had nowhere to go, resulting in the large CRUMPFFF as it crashed into the driver's side of Peter's car, just in front of the driver's seat. Peter ran downstairs as fast as he could possibly go, worried that his last words with Susan had been in a stupid argument, and praying to God that Susan wasn't hurt. He opened the passenger door, realising that, although he'd been short-tempered with Susan lately, he still loved her with all of his heart, and if she was dead, he might as well be dead as well. Susan was stunned, and didn't really know what had happened. So Peter helped her over the gearstick and out of the car by the passenger door. Despite his air bag having deployed, pushing him back in his seat, the other driver was already out of his car.

"You stupid fat cow! Look what you've done to my car." Susan started to cry, but curiously, she sounded like a police siren. A police car pulled up next to the crash, and Peter was even more confused when a policeman and woman got out of their car and grabbed hold of the other car driver.

"I did look when I pulled out. The road was clear." Peter was unsure whether Susan was trying to get sympathy from him, the other driver or the police, but the policewoman answered her comments.

"We know that madam. We've been chasing him since he caused a crash in Cowley. We'll tell your insurance company that he was speeding, and that he was the cause of this accident."

Numerous photographs were taken of the accident, and the two cars were pushed to the side of the road. Later, for the second time in three months, a car that Susan had been driving was taken away to be scrapped.

Susan sat in the living room, still shaking from her ordeal. The accident had frightened her much more than the one in the Scottish Highlands, as she could see the car coming straight at her, and had no means of escape, whereas, in Scotland, everything was pitch black.

"I think I need a G and T to help calm my nerves. There's no way that I can go out to dinner tonight, could you cancel it please."

Peter returned with a gin and tonic for Susan and a medicinal whisky for himself. He felt his senses come back to life as the effect of the whisky flowed through his body, and the shock at the possibility of losing Susan left him. He put his arm around Susan, and looked into her eyes.

"Are you sure that you're OK? I thought for a moment that I'd lost you. I was heartbroken, I love you so much."

"But you've been so short with me lately."

"I'm really sorry about that, it's not you, I've been having such a terrible time at work, and I never should have taken it out on you." He held her for a few minutes until the practical side of Peter re-emerged.

"I should phone your mother, she'll be wondering where you are."

"Yes please."

Peter phoned and cancelled the table for their anniversary meal, and then broke the news of the crash as subtly as he could to Dawn.

178

"We saw the flashing lights from the police car, and expected that you were held up because of the crash, not that you were part of it. Are you both all right?"

"Susan's still in shock, and the car's written off, but apart from that, we're fine."

"Good. We'll come down to you, and bring your present."

Geoffrey and Dawn arrived a few minutes later, and Peter let them into the house. They immediately rushed to comfort their daughter, and to check that she was unharmed by her ordeal. Eventually, Geoffrey brought up the reason for Susan's journey in the car, which led to the car crash.

"Susan, do you feel well enough to walk out into the garden?"

"Yes, I think so."

"Good, there's something in the car that I need a hand with, if you wouldn't mind Peter."

Peter followed Geoffrey to the car, and in the boot was a large rectangular box, covered in 'Happy anniversary' wrapping paper.

"We should take this straight out into the garden, and unwrap it there." The package was surprisingly heavy for its size, and Geoffrey and Peter were breathing quite heavily by the time that it was stood in what Geoffrey considered to be an appropriate place. Dawn had turned the garden lights on, and she stood with Susan in the warmth of the conservatory watching their slow progress, until Geoffrey waved an invitation to join them in the garden. Dawn smiled in appreciation of the place found for the object, visualising its effect once the wrapping paper had been removed. "We chose this from the display in the garden centre ages ago, but it only arrived today. Come on Susan, do the honours."

Susan took off the wrapping paper and Peter helped her manoeuvre the object out of the cardboard box to reveal a very expensive-looking sundial. The sun had long ago disappeared for the day, so they would have to set up the sundial tomorrow. Peter picked up the wrapping paper and the cardboard, and put them in the recycle bin, his actions prompted the others to move back indoors.

179

"Are you going out for a meal this evening for you anniversary?"

"No Mummy, Peter booked a table at the 'Head of the River', but I don't feel well enough to go."

"Would you like to have dinner with us this evening?"

"No thank you, Mummy. It's a lovely offer, but I will probably have a Chinese take-away, and a quiet night in."

Geoffrey and Dawn could see that Susan was much better, kissed her on the cheek, and left.

"I actually am quite hungry now. I'll phone the Chinese and order a take-away meal to be delivered. Is there anything special that you fancy?"

"I never thought you'd ask. Shall we go upstairs or do it in the living room." Peter had quickly recovered from his soppy stage.

"Don't be smutty, you know that I meant Chinese."

"It was worth a try. You order what you feel like. There's a bottle of Mateus Rosé in the drinks cabinet, I'll put it in the fridge."

Susan picked up the phone and dialled the number of her favourite Chinese take-away restaurant. It wasn't one of the numbers set up in the phone's memory, but she phoned it often enough not to have to look it up. She also ordered the same things every time, but didn't realise this.

"Could I place an order for delivery please? I would like Sweet and Sour Chicken Hong Kong style, Beef and Ginger, House Special Fried Rice and some prawn crackers please. Could you deliver it to…"

"No ploblem Mrs Stevenson, we have your address. You not want Spwing roll tonight?"

"Oh yes please, I forgot that."

"Hokay, meal delivered in thirty minnit."

Peter made Susan another G and T whilst they waited, and put two plates in the oven to warm through. He was still feeling the effect of the large whisky, and apart from the expected glass or two of fizzy wine to toast their anniversary, thought it better if he didn't have too much to drink in case he fell asleep, and missed his anniversary euphemism, as well as the Christmas one.

The meal duly arrived, and Peter poured out a glass of wine for each of them, and served up the meal.

"I thought that I would watch the DVD that you bought for me. It's always been my favourite."

Peter washed the plates after they'd finished their meal, not minding that he was missing 'such a good film'. It was well past Susan's normal bedtime when the film finally finished, and she'd drunk even more than she usually did. She kissed Peter and thanked him for a lovely day; she'd conveniently forgotten about the car crash.

"I'm going to bed now. It would be a good idea if you followed me quickly before I fall asleep." As well as the whisky, Peter had drank two glasses of the wine, and was alarmed by how unsteady his legs were when he opened the conservatory door to let Jaeger out for his goodnight wee. He stood there in the cool breeze re-gathering his composure, to prepare himself for the forthcoming bedtime activities, whilst Jaeger had a sniff around the sundial, then urinated against it. The dog came back inside and curled up in his box. Peter covered him with his towel to keep him warm, and went upstairs to clean his teeth. The toothpaste rejuvenated Peter a little bit more, kicking off his clothes in the darkness, he climbed under the duvet.

Susan snuggled up against him. "Do you really still love me?"

"Of course I do."

Peter put his arms around Susan, and started to fondle her breasts.

"You'll need to hurry up a bit; it's been a long day."

Peter pulled open his bedside cabinet drawer only to find a gap where the condoms should be. "I can't find the Durex."

"Just hurry up and get on with it."

Not wanting to miss his chance, Peter did as he was told, which seemed to be enjoyed more than usual by the both of them.

Early the following morning, Mark woke up with unbearable burning pain pains in his chest. He elbowed his wife awake, and said the only word that he could manage at the time, "ambulance." Mark was rushed to hospital, and his wife waited outside the ward whilst his condition was stabilising, despite still being 'critical'. She was eventually allowed in to see him. She realised immediately that he was in a bad way, and she sat down next to him holding his hand, trying her very hardest to hold back the tears. He smiled weakly at her.

"How are you feeling?"

"Rough. I wish they could take this pain away." Mark was talking with great difficulty. "I need to speak with James ASAP." He had so many things he needed to resolve before he died, but didn't realise that it would be so soon. Mark's wife left the ward and went outside to phone the MD on her mobile.

"Hello James, it's Sarah. Mark's in the John Radcliffe, and he's not too good. He's asking for you."

"I'll be there as soon as I can."

The Sunday traffic was very light through the City, and the MD was sat with Mark whilst Sarah sat on the opposite side of the bed, holding her husband's hand. Mark spoke softly and slowly, and with great difficulty.

"It looks like I won't be coming back to work."

"Of course you will, you just need time to rest and get better."

"No, we both know that's not the case. What's the plan to replace me?"

"We always like to promote from within, it's always been our policy, and gives every employee a future to look forward to."

The MD was concerned with Mark's weakened condition and gave the stock, company policy answer, instead of the one he would use in normal conversation with such an old friend.

"I know that. Who have you got in mind?"

"Well, the only two people in the frame have to be Stevens and Stevenson. Who do you think would be best for the Company?"

Mark went quiet as he thought long and hard before giving his answer. He had thought this question over in his mind on a number of occasions over the years, as he knew that, eventually, he would have to retire from his post, but his views had changed over the last year or so. Peter, obviously, knew the Company's finances inside-out, and was, by far the better

182

Accountant of the two, but Kevin wanted to push the Company forward into the twenty first century. Mark shared Peter's concerns about the risks that Kevin would be willing to take, and the expected problems if the risks actually happened. In reality, there was only one real option.

"Stevens."

Mark made a huge effort to give his answer, and could not manage the third syllable. The pain in his chest became a raging torrent, as he tried to add "son" to his response, but it was the last thing he ever did before he died.

When she had regained her composure, Sarah left the room to phone the family and friends to inform them of the bad news. James stayed with her for support.

"Should I phone anyone from work?"

"No, don't bother just yet. I'll tell them all tomorrow morning."

"What about Peter and Kevin? Mark was like a father to them. He was always telling me stories about what they'd done, especially when they were younger." She wiped away her tears. "His favourite story was when Peter had his photograph taken with a lap dancer in Blackpool, when he'd had too much to drink. He always used to laugh about the time that Peter and Kevin booked into a house for the night in London, and the lady who owned the house was only wearing a short dressing gown, and Peter was so busy looking at her legs that he told Kevin the wrong number for the Burglar alarm, and Kevin almost got arrested."

James had always thought that Peter was the quieter, more reliable one of the two.

"I need to speak to Kevin and Peter in person about the new FD position, so I'll wait until I have them together, and do that first thing tomorrow morning at work."

Susan stayed in bed until lunchtime, due to a combination of too much gin, mixing her drinks, and the aftershock of the crash. The second batch of Nurofens had started to clear her banging headache, but she didn't lose the urge to throw up until she'd had a hot bath. The recollection from the previous day broke their way through the mist, first came the horror of the car crash, followed by the nice meal, and then she smiled at the unusually happy memory of Peter's performance in bed, one that she wouldn't mind a repeat run of.

Peter was up early, as usual, and had taken the dog with him when he picked up the Sunday papers, and his hangover had receded to the far corners of his head by the time he returned home. When Susan finally made it downstairs, the dog was ready to go out again.

"You should come with us, the fresh air will do you good."

"I think I must have eaten something that didn't agree with me last night."

"I ate exactly the same as you, but I feel fine now. You'll feel much better if you get outside in the fresh air."

Peter was really surprised when Susan went to the utility room and started to put on her coat. Jaeger limped towards them wagging his tail, carrying his lead in his mouth. He never needed to wear a lead when he was in the park, as his running away days were well and truly over, but Peter always put him on the lead when they were walking down the road. When he was a puppy Jaeger used to run for miles and miles around the park, but these days he could only manage a slow walk for about twenty minutes, spending most of his time sniffing around the trees and bushes, before staggering back home. This afternoon, the dog completed his usual walk, then, instead of heading towards home, turned back to another area which he used to run around. He spent over an hour visiting and sniffing all of the parts of the park that he'd ran around as a young dog, until, totally exhausted, he headed back home, where he flopped on his box.

Peter started to cook the Sunday dinner, whilst Susan drank a coffee and started, in her words, to feel a little bit better. By the time Susan had eaten dinner, and downed a couple of G and Ts, she was back to normal. She had almost finished her third when Peter returned from the kitchen after doing the washing up.

"Do you fancy an early night?"

"What? Two euphemisms in the same weekend?"

"Are you turning me down?"
"That would be a first."
Susan started to climb the stairs, and looked back at Peter.
"Are you waiting for a written invitation?" Peter quickly
followed her upstairs.

Peter didn't have the benefit from drinking whisky and wine
that had put the lead in his pencil, and kept it there longer than
usual, the night before, so the night was still quite young when
he separated himself from Susan, and lay in bed with his arms
around her. Although Susan had spent the best part of the
day in bed, she had no problem going back to sleep. Peter
went downstairs to make his lunch for work the next day, and
then let the dog out into the garden. The dog sniffed all
around the garden, until he came back to the sun dial. He
cocked his leg, gave the sun dial another wash, and went back
to his box. Peter stroked the dog's ears, and pulled his towel
over him. "Good night dog, see you in the morning." Peter
went upstairs to the bathroom, smiling at his reflexion in the
mirror as he cleaned his teeth. Twice in the same weekend!
That hadn't happened since their first year of marriage.

It was still dark when the dog stumbled up the stairs and
entered the bedroom. He went to Susan's side of the bed,
and licked her face before moving around to Peter.
"Hello boy, it's not time to get up yet." The dog licked Peter's
face again, so Peter got out of bed, and put on his dressing
gown. "Do you want to go out? Come on then."
The dog slowly followed Peter downstairs to the conservatory.
Peter had already opened the door to the garden by the time
the dog arrived, but he just stood in the doorway peering out
into the darkness. "Come on then, back in your box." Peter
covered Jaeger with his towel, and went back to bed for the
final few hours sleep, before having to get up for the start of
another week at work.

As usual, Peter was awake before the alarm went off, and
pressed the button to stop it from waking up Susan. He'd not
had that much to eat or drink the night before, but still spent

ages on the loo before venturing downstairs. The dog was normally up waiting for Peter as soon as he heard him go into the bathroom, but was still in his box. "Come on you lazy old fartbox, up you get." No movement. Peter went over to the box to wake up the dog without startling him, but he was stone cold. A feeling of deep despair went through him as he realised that the early morning visit was the dog's way of saying goodbye. It also explained the unusually long walk of the previous afternoon, where Jaeger was wishing farewell to the areas that he loved. Peter was already crying by the time he'd reached the bedroom to give Susan the devastating news.

"Susan, wake up."

"It's not time to get up yet."

"I know. You have to get up." He took a deep breath so that he could say the next sentence without bursting out crying. "Jaeger's dead."

Susan sat up immediately. "Nooooo, he can't be, are you sure he's not just sleeping?"

"I'm certain. What do you want me to do with him?" Although Jaeger had had a good innings, they had never discussed what they would do when he died.

"Can we bury him in the garden? He loved it there."

"Are you coming down to say goodbye to him, before I bury him?"

Peter went to the shed and took out the garden spade. He chose a spot at the bottom of the garden where Jaeger used to like to lay in the sun, and started digging, the tears flowing freely down his face. The dog that he was about to bury was the best friend that he'd ever had, and had provided Peter with his favourite, happy memories. He completed the task and went back indoors to find Susan curled up next to the dog, her body heaving in time with her sobs. He carried the dog, wrapped in his towel, and placed him in the grave. Susan followed him outside. They were still crying as he covered the dog's body with the displaced earth.

Susan found it difficult to speak between her sobs, "I'm not going in to work today."

"Of course you aren't. I'll stay here with you. Are you going to tell you parents?"

"I don't think that I can talk about it yet. Maybe later."

Peter made them both a cup of tea, but neither of them could eat or drink. They sat there in each other's arms until the phone rang. It was Kevin.

"Oy Dad, get your arse into work, the MD wants a word with everyone."

"I'm not coming in today, I don't feel well enough."

"Bollocks, you're never ill. Get in now you skiving bastard."

"No honestly Kevin, I'm not coming in."

"Look, it's important. The MD specifically asked where you were."

Peter sighed deeply. "OK, I'll be in in half an hour."

Peter untangled himself from Susan, and remembering that he no longer had a car, phoned for a taxi and then went upstairs, had a shower, and got dressed for work. "I'll come straight back when we've had the meeting."

Peter walked down to the FD's office as soon as he arrived, and the P.A. called the MD on the phone. The MD was there within seconds.

"Peter, I'm sorry to have to call you in, but it's bad news again, I'm afraid. I wanted to speak to you both, in person, before it became common knowledge."

"What's happened?"

"Mark died yesterday morning."

Peter sat down with a loud thump. His mouth went dry, and his eyes welled up again, unable to take any more grief in such a short space of time.

"He had another heart attack. He was rushed to hospital, but there was nothing they could do for him."

"He was still a young man by today's standard."

"He was due retirement, Peter, we had arranged a meeting with him to consider his replacement. Luckily, we had a few minutes to discuss it before he died. He asked for me in the hospital, and held on until I arrived."

Although Kevin knew about Mark's death, this part was definitely news to him, and he suddenly became interested in the conversation.

"What, he actually chose his successor?"

"Not really Kevin. He put forward his view, and I spoke to the board about it yesterday afternoon, and we have agreed with his choice."

Peter knew that he was the obvious choice, but didn't want to take over the job that he'd coveted for such a long time until the FD retired, not under these circumstances.

"The new FD is going to be Kevin. He takes over the duties immediately."

Kevin let out a very ill-mannered "Yessss," and grinned from ear to ear, despite the gravity of the situation. Peter could not believe what he was hearing, and grasped the chair for support.

"We need to tell the rest of the staff. You know how quickly these things get around, and they have to be informed before rumours and uncertainty starts to spread."

Peter stood up, and followed slowly behind the MD and a strutting, smug-faced Kevin, on their way to the Finance Department. Kevin called them all to order. "Listen in; the MD has something important to tell you."

Peter listened in disbelief as the news was conveyed to all those present. Some of them were also shocked when they discovered that Kevin was chosen to be the new FD, as they knew how hard Peter worked, and how good he was at his job, especially when compared with Kevin. The MD completed his message with the usual platitude, "I know that it's hard to carry on after losing such a good friend and colleague, but he would have wished you to work hard, and remain focussed on the hard work that he put into the Company."

As soon as the MD left, Kevin turned to Peter. "I think we need to talk about this in my office." Not waiting for Peter's agreement, Kevin turned away, and walked off, leaving the finance staff to talk amongst themselves. Peter followed slowly behind. "Come on Peter, keep up, I've got a Company to run."

Peter sat down in the FD's office, completely shell-shocked by the whole morning's events.

"I'm not surprised by the decision to make me FD. You've been holding back the Company for as long as I can remember. Well that's all going to change from now on, I'll push through as many opportunities to purchase new businesses as I can find from now on, and we can also start to move some of the production overseas."

"What's going to happen about your replacement? Are you going to promote Rob?"

"No fucking chance. He's too much like you; I'll never get anything done. No, I'll bring in my own man from outside the company, with the proviso that he supports my decisions, and shows how things can be done, instead of giving piss-poor reasons why they might be a little bit risky."

"I only report what will be good for the Company."

"No Peter, you only report what you THINK will be good for the Company. There's a big difference. We'll soon see that I've been right all these years. If you continue to oppose my ideas, then you'll be looking for a job in another Company."

Peter sat there, hanging on in quiet desperation. He needed to get away as quickly as possible; this was far too much for him to take in.

"I need to go home."

"Look Peter, I can understand that you're upset that I've been chosen for the FD's job, but you have to get over it and pull yourself together."

"It's not that. Jaeger died this morning, and Susan's at home crying her eyes out."

"Fucking good riddance. That dog was a useless pain in the arse, I'm surprised that no-one put it down years ago."

Peter didn't want to give Kevin any more satisfaction by breaking down in tears in front of him, and swiftly got up and left.

189

Peter arrived home to find Susan still in her dressing gown, looking at photographs of Jaeger in the large album that she'd started when he was a puppy. Her eyes were red from crying. "Have you had anything to eat yet?"

"I'm not hungry. Did you want anything?"

"Not really." Peter had an empty feeling of great loss and sadness when he thought of the affection that the dog had shown him, and the fun that they'd had together as constant companions. "Have you told your parents about the dog yet?"

"No, I'll tell them this evening."

Peter turned away, and started to make his way towards the stairs.

"Where are you going?"

"Upstairs, I need to check that my black suit and tie are OK"

"You don't intend having a funeral for Jaeger, surely?"

"No, Mark died yesterday. That's why I had to go into work."

"Mark your boss?"

"Yes, Mark the FD."

"What are they going to do about his replacement?"

"The board has already decided. Kevin is the new FD."

"But I thought that you said he was useless."

"He's worse than useless, he'll ruin the Company."

"So what are you going to do about it?"

"There's nothing that I can do about it, the decision's already been made."

"Why did they choose Kevin if he's so useless?"

"I really have no idea. I don't want to talk about it."

"You can't just accept their decision, you need to stand up for yourself, and tell the bosses what he's really like."

"If I do that, they'll just say that I'm bitter about their decision."

"Well, get a job with another Company, I'm sure there'll be lots of people who would jump at the chance of having you work for them."

"I don't want to work for another Company. I'd rather stop working altogether."

"There must be a way to show how bad Kevin is at his job. Can't you sabotage the Company, and make it look like it was his fault?"

"Quite easily, but he would just say that it was my fault, and get away with it, like he always does."

"Then make it impossible for him to blame you."

"How?"

"I don't know, you're the clever one. Think of something."

"Such as?"

"Well, why don't you disappear, and pretend that he's killed you?"

"That's the stupidest thing I've ever heard. It would mean that I would never see you again."

"Not if I disappeared with you."

"And how would I be killed so that Kevin gets the blame?" Susan thought for a minute, and then the light bulb came on above her head. "I know! You could get Kevin to take you on a canoeing trip, and let him get in front of you, and when he goes round a bend you can paddle to the side of the river, get out of the water, sink the canoe so that everyone thinks that he drowned you, and then hide somewhere until he's sentenced for your murder."

"That's an even stupider idea. Someone's already tried that, and he was found out and put in prison."

"That's because he didn't have a false identity, like that man in South Africa said you need. He just hid in his own house. Don't you know anyone who can get you a false identity?"

Peter remembered the discussion he'd had with Richard after the fraud presentation in London, whilst Kevin was entertaining his wife. "I do actually, but why should I do that?"

"So you can live somewhere else without being discovered."

"But I don't want to live somewhere else. I'm happy living here with you."

"I could join you as soon as he's in prison. No-one would suspect anything if I said that the memories here were too painful, and I needed to move away."

"Why would he want to kill me?"

"You could make it look like he's stolen lots of money from the Company, and you found out, so he killed you to stop you from telling anyone."

"You read too many magazines. Who's going to believe that?"

"Everybody. Why shouldn't they?"

"Because they would most probably think that I tried to frame Kevin out of spite after he was promoted instead of me. And why would they think that Kevin resorted to murder?"

"You need to make them believe he did."

"How am I going to do that? I'll have to provide reasons why Kevin had to steal a lot of money and when I've done that, I'll need to provide enough evidence to convince everyone that he actually stole from the Company as well."

Susan nodded her head agreeing with Peter's comments.

"When they see that, they will believe that he is capable of anything."

"That's just stupid; I'll never be able to do that."

"I'm sure that you could if you put your mind to it."

Peter went upstairs to check his black suit and tie, thinking about what Susan had said. He'd daydreamt for as long as he could remember all of the ways that he would get his revenge on Kevin when he became the new FD after Mark's retirement. The thought that Kevin would be the FD had never entered his head. Susan's idea could actually work; well, it might work in theory, but there was no way that he would have the nerve to do anything like it. He also needed a large amount of luck if all of the parts of the plan were to succeed. His decisions in life were based on sound judgements after thorough investigation of all of the risks. He'd never considered himself to be lucky, if it wasn't for bad luck, he'd have no luck at all.

Kevin made Peter's life even more unbearable during the next few days.

"Draft me a job advert for the new Accountant. I want it to be in the paper this Thursday. Just make sure that it attracts the right sort of applicant, you know, one that's not too cautious and won't hold the Company back."

"What about the duties they're to carry out."

"Make them the same as yours, I doubt if you'll be around for much longer. We want do-ers in the office from now on, not stoppers."

On his drive to work the next day, Kevin pulled out from the slip road in front of a car in the main road, causing the driver to brake. A police car in the main road just behind the other car, overtook Kevin, sounded his siren, and pulled in to the lay-by on the side of the road. Kevin pulled in behind him, wondering what the problem was. The policeman got out of his car and walked to the passenger side of Kevin's car.

"Do you always drive like that, sir?"

"Drive like what? What am I supposed to have done? I've only been driving a few minutes."

"I was in the car behind the one that you cut in front of."

"And?"

"When you pulled into the main carriage, he thought that he was going to run into the back of you, and had to brake sharply."

Kevin looked at the policeman's uniform. "You're a cuntstable aren't you?" He made the word sound the way he meant it to.

"What do you mean by that?"

"I would have thought that you'd have been at least a Detective Inspector. There's not many people that can see through metal, and read people's thoughts."

"I beg your pardon."

"Look Sonny, I'm busy. I'm the Financial Director of a large company, and I don't have the time to talk to you about what you think you saw, or what you think that other people think they saw. Now if you've quite finished, I have proper work to do. Why don't you put your super-powers to good use and arrest some real criminals, instead of pestering law-abiding citizens."

"You can't leave; I haven't finished with you yet."

"Unless you want me to put in a complaint of harassment to your Chief Constable, I think you'll find that you have finished. Goodbye."

Kevin flicked on his indicators and pulled out into the traffic, leaving the policeman staring at the car as it disappeared up the hill towards the City centre.

The following Monday, Kevin arrived at Peter's office not quite as late as usual, and this time accompanied by someone who looked vaguely familiar to Peter.

"Morning Dad, remember Steve, he studied CIMA with us?"

Oh yes, Peter remembered Steve alright! He was almost as poor in class as Kevin was, but unlike Kevin, he didn't have anyone to help him to cheat in his exams. Steve had failed his exams and was moved back to another class to re-take the course and his exams, more than once, until he finally passed.

"I met Steve in the pub on Saturday. Luckily, he's currently between jobs, which means he can start looking for new businesses to buy straight away. We just need to sort him out with Personnel, and he'll be right on the job. This will be your office Steve."

"I thought we agreed that this office wasn't big enough for two people."

"That's correct. Steve will work in here, and you'll move back to the main Finance office."

Peter was still seething when he returned home. He changed out of his suit, went into the kitchen and started to cook the dinner. Picking up the loaf of bread, he started his usual impersonation of Kevin that he used to relieve his feelings of stress.

"This loaf of bread is named after me; well, it says 'Thick Cut', but that's close enough."

Susan walked into the kitchen, white-faced.

"I thought that Kevin was in here."

"No, that was me."

"But you sounded just like him."

"I should do, I've been doing it long enough."

"Well I've never heard you do it before. If you can do that, we can use your impersonation of him to put our plan into action. Who else knows that you can do that?"

"No-one, but I will need to look like him as well."

"I can make you look like him quite easily, all I'd need is a false beard and a wig."

"And a pair of stilts."

"It's a shame you threw out all of your old shoes with the big heels."

Peter shook his head at Susan's strange memory, in which he was the one that got rid of his old clothes.

"I still have a pair of shoes with big heels, which would make me closer to his height, but he's much broader than I am."

"That's not a problem. When we have to make someone on stage look fatter or more muscular, we get them to wear extra pullovers, or wrap a towel around their waist, it's much cheaper than a fat-suit. It would be really easy in Kevin's case, because he's always wearing that old raincoat of his."

"How is that going to help with your plan?"

Susan looked at Peter in surprise. "What do you mean, my plan?"

"You're the one that said that I need to make it look like Kevin's killed me, so that he's put in prison."

"You also have to make it look like he's stolen money from the Company."

"Why should I do all that?"

"Because otherwise he wouldn't need to kill you. He's been a horrible bastard all of his life, and it's time for him to pay for it."

"I didn't realise that he upset you so much."

"He didn't." Susan walked out of the kitchen to gather her thoughts, as she was still too embarrassed to tell Peter about Kevin and her mother. This was her chance to finally get her own back on Kevin for what he'd done to her and her family, and there was no way that she'd let it go. She returned within a few minutes, on the premise that she wanted a drink.

"Make me a G and T please." She paused, and watched for Peter's reaction to her next statement. "Kevin didn't upset me that much, but he needs to pay for what he did to Chris in Newcastle. That poor girl is looking after his baby, and he doesn't even recognise it as his, or give her any money to look after it. And he's always treated you badly. It's time you did something about it."

"There's not a lot that I can do."

"I'm sure there is, we just need to sit down and draw up a plan of action."

"I tried to catch him out before, and he made me look stupid. This time it'll be really risky, it probably won't work, and I'll be the one in big trouble when we're found out."

"That's why we need to plan. After dinner, we need to draw up a list of what we have to do, and how we're going to do it."

Peter was worried that he was being pushed into something that he didn't want to do, and needed to stop Susan before her momentum built up so much that it got past the point of no return. He gave Susan her Gin and Tonic and ushered her out of the kitchen. "I need to concentrate on dinner now, or it'll be ruined. We'll talk about this later."

There was no respite after dinner. Once Susan had set her mind to what she wanted Peter to do, she was like a terrier with its teeth sunk in a problem, unable to let go. Susan had started her list of things to do whilst Peter did the washing up.

"OK, how are we going to make it look like Kevin's stolen money from the Company?"

Peter thought that it was better to look as if he was trying his best to help, so that he couldn't be blamed when she decided that it was a bad idea, and not to go through with it. "I could get someone to set up a false bank account in his name, draw up some false invoices, and have them paid into his account."

"Who's going to set up the false bank account?"

"The same person who will arrange the false documents for my new identity."

"How do you know that he'll do what you want?"

"I'll tell him that it'll get Kevin in trouble. That should work, he doesn't like Kevin either. I'll phone him tomorrow." Susan put her hand up to stop Peter and wrote a few words on the list and looked back at Peter.

"OK Peter, carry on."

"Why would he need to steal money? He's in a much better paid job than he could have ever imagined, and he'll have paid off most of his mortgage by now."

"Can't you make it look like he owes people money?"

"I can't make it look like he owes people money, he either does or he doesn't."

"Who would he owe money to then?"

"He bets a lot of money on the horses every weekend. He's not very good at that, so he probably owes his bookmaker money. He probably owes Chris money to pay for his child." Peter paused whilst Susan noted these points down on her list, before resuming his points. "You could tip off the Child Support Agency that he's not paying maintenance for his child in Newcastle, or better still, get Chris to report him. I know that she doesn't want anything to do with him, but I'm sure that you could convince her to get him to pay up."

"Good point. Hang on a sec." Susan wrote on the list again. When she looked up, Peter continued.

"But why would people think that he wanted to kill me?"

"Because you know that he's stolen money from the Company, and he'll lose everything if you tell anyone. Everyone knows what a terrible temper he has. You also need to fake your death, and leave enough evidence to make him look guilty without him finding out what you've done, and how you did it."

"I need to think about that. I'll let you know."

"Then, of course, we need to dispose of your body?"

Peter sighed. "Look, Susan, this isn't going to work is it? There are too many areas where it could go drastically wrong."

"No, they're only small problems. Speak to your friend who can set up the false bank account and identity tomorrow, and I'll talk to Chris about the CSA. I've written down the remaining problems that we need to resolve."

Although he thought that Susan would soon forget her idea of punishing Kevin, he still phoned Richard as he'd promised. He might as well do as she asked him to until she gave up the idea, so that she couldn't pin the blame on him for her idea not succeeding. He searched through his 'useful information' drawer in his office at home, and found the business card that Richard had given him at their meeting. Getting Richard to agree to help was far easier than he expected. "Hello,

Richard. It's Peter Stevenson, we spoke at one of your fraud presentations."

"You and a thousand others. How can I help you?"

"You probably won't remember me, but you'll remember my colleague Kevin. He turned up with the police and your wife at the post presentation get-together in London some years ago."

"That bastard cost me my marriage! What do you want?"

"I want to teach him a lesson. I need a new identity, with a bank account, credit card, passport, driving license, National Health record, and three bank accounts setting up to do it."

"And he'll get in trouble over this?"

"Oh yes, big trouble."

"It'll cost you."

"No, it'll cost him. That's what one of the other bank accounts will be set up for."

"No problem, I'll be pleased to help. What exactly do you want?"

Peter discussed the details with Richard, and how much it would all cost. "I want one of the other accounts, into which a large amount of the Company's money is paid into, to be found by the police, so that the Company gets most of their money back. If the person who set it up is discovered, I want him to tell the police that Kevin asked for it. I'll pay him extra for his trouble."

"I doubt if he'll accept that, he could go to prison."

"Only if he's caught, and if he does get caught I'm sure that the police will let him off if he gives evidence against Kevin. He'll be well paid for the small risk he's taking. I'll phone you back on Saturday, for you to confirm whether your friends agree to do it and when everything will be ready."

Chris was also happy to agree with Susan that Kevin should start to pay his way towards the upkeep for his son. "It's really difficult making ends meet. I'm always skint, and it costs more each year as my son gets older. I'll get in touch with the CSA and see what they say."

"Ask them about back payment for the years that he's missed."

"Don't worry, I will."

"I'll phone you back in a few days to find out what they said."

Peter kept his head down for the rest of the week, waiting to hear whether they could continue with the plan or not. Kevin took every opportunity to belittle him, giving him menial tasks, and reminding him to make sure that his office was left neat and tidy for when Steve moved in.

On Saturday Peter heard from Richard that the false ID and documents, and the bank accounts were being set up as requested. The more difficult areas of his identity would take longer to arrange, but the main parts would be ready in good time. Chris phoned Susan and told her that the CSA were going to get in touch with Kevin, and request that he makes a large donation for back payment, and then make regular maintenance payments.

"All we need to do now is to work out how he's going to kill you and dispose of the body. Any ideas?"

"Can't I just disappear? I'll have a new identity in two weeks, and some money paid by the Company into my new bank account to set me up."

"We've already discussed this. Kevin would just say that you set it all up, and disappeared with the money. We need to make it look like he killed you and hid your body somewhere."

"How are we going to do that without him knowing?"

"You could visit him at his house, and get him drunk, and then, whilst he's unconscious, make it look like he killed you there, and then took your body to the country and buried it."

"That won't work; it takes hours for him to get drunk."

"OK then, how are we going to make him unconscious?"

This time, a small light came on above Peter's head, and he scurried off upstairs to his office. Hidden at the bottom of his cabinet was the small bottle that Rob had given to him on their return from Blackpool all those years ago.

"This is what Kevin drugged me with when we were in Blackpool."

"What do you mean, Kevin drugged you in Blackpool?"

"He wanted to make me look stupid, by making me fall asleep in one of the bars. The bottle fell out of his pocket, and Rob gave it to me."

"How much did he use?"

"I don't know, I didn't see him do it, did I? There's three quarters of the bottle left, so I suppose he used a quarter of the bottle."

"How do you know it'll still work?"

"I don't, we'll have to try it out."

"But that's dangerous."

"If we're going to use it, we need to know whether it still works."

"How are you going to do that?"

Sometimes you had to spell everything out to Susan. "I'll go to bed, put a quarter of the bottle in some water, drink it and see what happens. You'll need to look after me in case there's any problems. I need to know if you can taste or smell it, whether it still works, and how long it puts me out for."

Peter was unconscious within fifteen minutes, and was out for six hours, until he finally started to show signs of life in front of a very relieved Susan. He also felt like shit, but managed a weak smile. "Well, that works then!" Susan ticked another problem off of her list.

Peter spent most of Sunday recovering from the effects of the drug. Susan still had a couple of areas left in her list to resolve.

"Have you thought how he kills you yet?"

"Yes, I have, but however he kills me, I will need to leave some evidence of the murder at his house."

"Can't you leave some of your blood on the carpet, or a tooth that he could have knocked out in a fight?"

"There wouldn't be much of a fight, he's much bigger and stronger than I am. He wouldn't need to beat me up or stab me, he could quite easily strangle me with his bare hands. That's how people would think that he'd killed me, especially with his temper. He might punch me a few times, but I wouldn't need to leave too much blood there, or a tooth."

Peter had visions of Kevin finding out what they were planning, and throttling the life out of him. They both went quiet, contemplating the consequences if it went wrong.

Susan broke the silence. "Right, we need to work out a reason for you being at Kevin's on the night that he supposedly kills you, and then we need to work out how he disposes of your body. Apart from that, everything else should work." Susan stared down at the list for inspiration.
"What if he buried you in his garden?"
"No, the police would need to be able to find a body when they dig it up."
"How about Shotover Park then?"
Even Peter's drug-addled brain knew that Susan's ideas were no good. "No, Shotover's too busy. He'd probably be seen trying to bury a body if he really did bury one, and even if he wasn't seen, a grave would be discovered too easily if it really existed."
"But there wouldn't actually be a body to bury would there?"
Peter shook his head. "No, but it would still have to look like he'd actually buried a body. Shotover's not the place. We need to think like Kevin. How would he get rid of a body? This is not the sort of thing that he does normally. And he would have to do it on the spur of the moment."
Despite still feeling sick when he moved, Peter went upstairs to his office, and returned with his Road Atlas. He opened the book at the Oxford page, searching for a suitable burial place. Susan pointed excitedly at Ditchley Park.
"Ditchley Park. It's close, and Kevin knows it quite well. We used to walk Jaeger there when he was a puppy. It's really quiet, so he wouldn't be seen, and it's huge. If someone buried a body there, it would never be found, unless they knew where to look."
"What would he use to dig the grave at such short notice?"
"There's a garden fork and spade in his shed. He never throws anything away, I'm sure that they're still there. Just make it look like he's used them. If he has thrown them out, you can use ours, and leave them in the boot of his car. No-one will know that they're not his."

Peter was beginning to get worried. When this idea started, he was sure that it would be forgotten within a few days, but now he wasn't too sure. He had greatly under-estimated the feminine' stubborn-need to right any perceived wrongs. He still had no idea what was really driving Susan on to get her revenge over Kevin, but he suspected that it was more than Kevin's ill-treatment of Chris.

"If we're going to do this, we have to make up our minds now." Susan looked at Peter. "What are you talking about? Of course we're going to do it."

"Are you sure you want to go ahead with it? It will cost us a lot of money if you change your mind."

"Why would it cost us a lot of money if I change my mind?"

"Because if your plan doesn't go ahead, we'll have to pay for the cost of setting up the new identity and bank accounts ourselves. If it does go ahead, I'll raise an invoice for the Company to put the money into a bank account to pay for them, and make it look like business costs for research that Kevin has authorised for payment. I'll tell my friend to make sure that he has withdrawn the cash before the Company finds out and cancels the payment. If we change our mind after the invoices have been sent in for payment, we could be found out, and I would be arrested for fraud. Not only would I be sent to prison, I would also not be able to work again, and we wouldn't be able to keep up the mortgage payments for the house. We could lose everything that we've worked for."

"OK then, tell your friend that we're on."

"I'll also need a car registered and insured in my new name to get me somewhere where I can lie low for a while. I won't be able to travel by plane or train on the day that I disappear, in case the police check the security cameras looking for me."

"You can buy a car with some of the money that you found in your parents loft. The rest will keep you going for a while."

Peter was shaking with a combination of excitement and fear all the way through the next week. He logged in as Kevin and set up the new Supplier accounts on the system, and then phoned the payments team, impersonating Kevin. As well as the voice, he also had to remember to speak in the same manner as Kevin, instead of using his normal "please" and "thank yous."

"Linda, there will be some bills to pay for new accounts this month. We are branching out, and will need to make some large outlays for the first month, which will need to be paid promptly to keep the new suppliers happy. I've already authorised them, so they need to be paid as soon as they are received."

"Yes Mr Stevens."

The finance staff had become afraid of Kevin's temper since he had been promoted to FD and much preferred to speak to Peter than Kevin when they had any questions regarding invoices, so Peter hoped that this would prevent Kevin finding out about these payments until it was too late.

The first two invoices, one to pay for Richard's work, and the other to pay into a bank account that Peter had arranged to move around until it was untraceable, were paid by the end of the week.

The following Monday, Steve started work for the Company, but hadn't realised how busy he would be, and how difficult the work was. Peter had to stay in his old office and show him what to do. Peter was happily absorbed at work with Steve in his old office, until Kevin came storming in. Peter's initial thought was that, somehow, he'd been found out, and was ready to run away when the chance arose, but it was something entirely different that had angered Kevin.

"That filthy money-grabbing cow. I'll fucking kill her when I get my hands on her."

"Who?"

"Chris, that's fucking who. She's reported me to the CSA, and they're going to be after me for thousands of pounds."

"So what are you going to do? Can't you appeal against them?"

"I doubt it. They only come for the good guys like me."

"So what are you going to do?"

"Fuck knows. I'll have to find a way to pay her off."

"You must have plenty of money. You're better paid than I am."

"I spend most of my money enjoying myself whilst I'm still young enough to enjoy it, not like you, who saves every penny to pay for your sad old age."

"What? You've spent all of our money on women, beer and cigarettes?"

"Don't be fucking stupid, of course I haven't. I've had a bad run on the horses lately as well."

"Why have you come in here?"

"I don't know. I just needed to go somewhere to shout at someone." Kevin stormed off as quickly as he'd arrived.

Steve looked at Peter when he was sure that Kevin was out of earshot. "I wouldn't like to be this Chris when Kevin gets hold of her, he can be a right nasty bastard."

"What do you mean?"

"We were in the Jericho arms some time ago, and a bloke tried to chat up his girlfriend when Kevin went for a piss. Kevin grabbed this guy by the throat and would have killed him if we hadn't been there to drag him off. It took four of us."

"Are you sure that was all the other guy had done?"

"Yeah, I'm certain. Kevin's got a terrible temper, and a very short fuse."

Peter made a mental note to give this information to Susan when he got home that evening, and carried on working as if nothing had happened.

As usual, Peter arrived home after Susan, but had to start dinner straight away. Susan came into the kitchen to get the Gin and tonic water out of the fridge for a top up.

"I've got some information for you to add to your list."

"Why would I need information on my list?"

"Steve told me at work today that Kevin tried to strangle someone in the Jericho Arms a few months ago, and they had big problems pulling him away."

"Why do I need to know that?"

"Because when the police interview you about my disappearance, you can tell them about it. It will draw attention to his temper, and enforce the point about him killing me with his bare hands, meaning that there would only be a small amount of blood at his house when he killed me."

Susan took the list out of her pocket, and updated the notes. "Make sure that nobody ever finds that note, or we could be in real trouble. As soon as all this is over, rip it up and burn it."

Later that week, Peter had something else to take his mind off his worries. Something that he didn't expect Susan to tell him. "Remember our anniversary?"

What part? The car crash, Jaeger dying, Mark dying? God, was it only four weeks ago?

"Of course I do. Why do you ask?"

"Can you remember the part in bed?"

"Yes." Peter started to blush.

"Well, I think that I'm pregnant."

"How did that happen?"

"I thought you said that you remembered the part in bed?"

"Oh." Peter was short of words to say. "Does that mean that we're not going through with your plan?"

"Of course we're going through with it. Why shouldn't we?"

"But you're having a baby. I can't leave you if you're having a baby."

"It would be better for the plan if you disappeared now. No-one would believe that you would leave me if I was pregnant, so it will be easier to persuade everyone that Kevin has killed you."

"No, I can't leave you if you're pregnant."

"You have to. You said yourself, if we stop now, you could go to prison, and we could lose everything."

" But I can't leave you if you're pregnant."

" My parents will be there for me, and I will join you when the baby's born, as soon as I can travel. Your friend can set me up with a new identity, and we can disappear together."

"But you'll never be able to come back and visit your parents after you leave."

"Of course I will. No-one's interested in me, I'll be able to come and go as I please."

Peter went for a walk to think of a way to change everything that he had put into motion, but he knew that it was too late to pull out.

Steve didn't make it to work for the start of his second week, so Peter was left in peace to get on with his clandestine activities. A contrite Kevin paid Peter a visit later on the Monday morning.

"Dad, you know that you wanted to keep this office?"

"Yes."

"Well, if you do me a favour, I'm sure that you could keep it."

"On my own?"

"Of course, on your own. Steve can move out to the Finance team area. He's fucking useless anyway."

"What do you want me to do?"

"Remember when you used to give me the names of winning horses?"

"That was years ago. I doubt if I could still do it. It takes a lot of concentration, and used to make me ill."

"Well, if you want to keep your office, the name of a winning horse this Saturday will swing it."

"Just one?"

"Just one, and that's it."

"I'll phone you on Saturday morning."

The last problem area was resolved. If the horse lost, Kevin would be deeper in debt, and have another reason to steal the money, and Peter would have a reason for Kevin to invite him to his house, to provide him with the name of a winner before his bookmaker became too impatient. The final part of the plan was well and truly on. Peter processed the final invoice to be paid, and waited for the weekend.

ELEVEN

As most punters will tell you, it's easier to choose a losing horse than a winner. All Peter had to do was make it look like the horse had a chance, and Kevin would believe him. Within minutes of the horse losing, Kevin was on the phone.

"You ker-nob. What happened?"

"I found out some new information after I phoned you that meant that the horse wouldn't win. I tried to phone you back, but you'd left, and your mobile was switched off."

"Well, you can give me the money I lost."

"I can only draw out £100 at this short notice. I take it that you lost more than that?"

"Too fuckin right I did. You can put your own money on next time."

"I can't do that, I don't have an account with your bookmaker. Look, it's not a problem, there are some big races tomorrow; I can come round and give you the name of a decent priced winner tonight. I won't be able to get there until nine o'clock though."

"Right, don't be late."

Peter had never liked the sight of blood, especially his own, and had to look away as Susan cut his thumb, and caught the blood in a small container. When she'd collected enough, she put a plaster on Peter's thumb, and screwed the cap on the container. He put the blood container in his bag, along with the knockout juice, the wig and false beard, his change of clothes, including the big-heeled shoes, and his false documents. He told Susan what she had to say to the MD, and she took a few notes to remind herself.

"Go and visit the MD personally on Monday morning. Make sure that you look upset enough to make it believable."

At five to nine, he parked his small car out of sight of Kevin's house, picked up his newspaper, and checked that the knockout juice and the blood were in his pocket. He walked briskly to Kevin's house, and rang the doorbell. The sound of loud rock music diminished, and the door opened. Kevin stood in front of him with a small bottle of beer in his hand. The beer was quite clearly not his first, and he was not a happy man, but Peter hoped that soon he would have other things to make him even more pissed off.

"I need to open this out on a large table." Peter followed Kevin into the dining room and opened the paper to the following days racing page, and spread the paper out on the dining table. "Put your beer bottle on top of the paper to stop it from moving please." He started to stare at the page, but gave up after a minute.

"Could you get me a glass of water please?" As soon as Kevin had left the room, Peter emptied the fluid into Kevin's beer bottle. Kevin re-appeared with a glass of water and two beer bottles that he's emptied earlier, and exchanged these for the half-full one. He paced up and down for a minute, taking a drink every time he changed direction.

"Well?"

"Give me a few minutes, and I'll have a winner for you."

"Just hurry up, it's Saturday night, and I'm usually in the pub by now."

Kevin put the empty bottle on top of the paper and went off to get himself a fresh one. He was half way through the new bottle when he became unsteady on his feet, and had to take a seat at the dining table. His eyelids drooped, and his head crashed onto the table. Peter walked around the table and pulled Kevin's head up by his hair. He was well and truly gone.

"Payback time, you bastard."

Peter walked back to his car and picked up his bag. He took the bag into the house and took out a thin pair of gloves. He wanted to leave his fingerprints in the house, but not in areas where they would not be expected. He went into Kevin's bedroom and found the blow-up doll that he'd been bought for his stag night. The adrenaline was pumping through his body, and he inflated the doll in record time. He took the doll downstairs and dressed it in his own clothes, with a large scarf covering its face. He dressed himself in his old Oxford bags and his big-heeled shoes, and spilled most of his blood from the container onto the dining room carpet. A few pullovers underneath Kevin's blue raincoat made him almost the same size as Kevin, the darkness outside would make up for the difference. The false beard and wig completed the disguise, and Peter collected Kevin's car keys, a pair of Kevin's shoes and carried the inflatable doll to Kevin's car. He gave the dustbin a huge kick as he passed it, knocking the lid onto the ground, making even more noise. A light came on in next door's porch, and a head appeared at the front door. Peter kicked the dustbin lid once more for effect.

"Keep the noise down, I've just got my baby to sleep."

Peter kicked the lid again, as he tried to get the back door of the car open.

"What are you doing?"

Peter put on his best 'Kevin' voice. "Keep your nose out, you ker-nob. I'm taking him home, he just can't hold his drink." Peter opened the back door of the car, and laid the doll on the back seat. He watched the neighbour go back inside, then went to the garden to check the garden fork and spade. As expected, they were still in there, so Peter picked them up and put them in the boot of the car.

He started the car, and headed for Woodstock, ensuring that he was going fast enough to activate the speed camera as he went past it. He turned left after the petrol station and the pub and navigated his way through the narrow windy roads towards Charlbury, turning off right into the woods surrounding Ditchley Park. He drove up the lane before pulling over to the side of the track, and extinguishing the headlights. He opened the boot, took out the spade and Kevin's shoes, and walked into the wood until he found an area to get some of the local mud on the spade and shoes. He ambled back to the car and put the spade and shoes back in the boot. He took out the small container and emptied the remaining few drops of blood onto the back seat. He deflated the doll, and put it in a bag on the back seat. There was still time to kill; he needed to stay there for the time it would actually take him to dig a hole and fill it in again, in case the neighbour saw him return. He sat on the fence on the side of the track, checking his watch every few minutes, his mind racing with the thoughts of which parts of the plan had failed, and whether Kevin was waiting for him on his return. When half an hour had finally passed, Peter got back into the car to drive back to Kevin's house.

Peter was much quieter arriving than leaving. He let himself into Kevin's house as cautiously as possible, and was hugely relieved to be met by the loud snores coming from the dining room. He put the racing paper and the bottle containing the remnants of the drugged beer in his bag, put the deflated doll back in Kevin's wardrobe, and hung Kevin's coat back on the hanger inside the front door. He noticed that Kevin's blue raincoat was torn at the shoulder, and hoped that Kevin wouldn't get any untoward ideas from the damage incurred. He changed out of his old clothes back into Susan's version of Peter, and took off the false beard and wig. The adrenaline rush had worn off some time ago, and he had started to shake again. He managed to steady himself enough to gather his things together, let himself out of the house, walked to his car, and drove to meet with Susan at the Holiday Inn car park at Pear Tree roundabout. As arranged, they kept out of sight of the security cameras.

Susan was also a bag of nerves. Unlike Peter, she could only guess what was happening, and whether there were any problems. She could hardly talk when his car pulled up next to hers.
"How did it go?"
"Exactly as planned. I even got the next door neighbour to come out and speak to me."
"Did he think that you were Kevin?"
"Definitely."
Peter gave Susan a mobile phone. "When you need to talk to me, use this. My new mobile number is entered into the phonebook under the name Chris. I would expect the police to check the home telephone for calls from or to my mobile, so don't try to contact me using our phone at home. If you have problems with this phone, just buy another cheap mobile and send me a text."
"When can I tell my parents?"

210

"Not for some time. We want everyone to look worried so they don't give the game away. Text me when it's safe for me to call you on the new mobile on Monday evening. Don't forget to phone Kevin tomorrow before you report me missing to the police."

"I love you."

"I love you too, but you need to be brave for the next few months. Look after our baby."

Peter drove north on the A43, wondering what he'd got himself into. Susan had problems driving home, as she rubbed the tears from her eyes.

Kevin came to his senses as slowly as his brain would allow them. He had difficulty finding a part of his body that did not hurt, especially his head, which sent lightning bolts to his brain in time with his heartbeats. He felt much sicker than he usually did after a long night of beer and any other spirits or substances on offer. His tongue was drier and felt much larger than normal, and a drink from the half empty beer bottle on the table next to him made no improvement on any of his ills. His love of betting had no interest in the race taking place in his body to get rid of the contents of his bladder or his stomach as he staggered upstairs to the bathroom, but he would normally have been thrilled of the closeness of the photo-finish between him throwing up in the sink and the stream of piss into the toilet, whilst trying his hardest not to fart until he was seated on the bog, as he was certain that he would follow-through. The take-away curry he'd eaten earlier was not as hot on the way back as it was going down, and he didn't enjoy it half as much either. He rinsed his mouth with water from the tap and spat it out into the sink, but needed to run the tap, and poke his finger in the plughole to clear some of the larger lumps of vomit. When he felt that he had thrown up all of the contents of his stomach, he sat on the bog and his blurred mind tried to work out the reason for what had happened to cause his current predicament. He fell asleep again, and when he awoke half an hour later, he felt safe enough to edge his way to his bed, where he lost consciousness again.

The constant ringing of the phone brought him back to life some hours later. His body no longer ached, and the headache had subsided to an almost bearable level. His tongue was still too big for his mouth, and had now changed to a lump of rubbery plastic

The phone finally stopped ringing when he reached out of bed and fumbled it to his ear. Susan spoke to Kevin for the first time since the day that she ran out of his house, after seeing him in bed with her mother. "Is Peter still there? He didn't make it home last night, and I can't get him on his mobile phone."
"No. He was here last night, but he must have left when I fell asleep."
Susan hung up without further conversation, which was no surprise to Kevin, although he was glad that she did. Kevin found it almost impossible to talk. He tried to move his tongue around the inside of his mouth, but the sensation and the taste were alien to him, which he found difficult to understand; but the plastic non-taste was the least of his problems.

A small piece of the jigsaw puzzle flitted into Kevin's fuzzy memory of the previous night, and he struggled downstairs to check whether Peter had left the name of a winning horse to save him from his debts. He even checked underneath the table in case it had fallen to the floor, but he found nothing. Kevin was far more interested in getting the name of the horse from Peter than he was of Susan's fear that Peter had disappeared, but when he tried to phone Peter's mobile it was switched off, as Susan had told him. Kevin finally believed Peter's warning that eating warmed-up take-away food would give him food poisoning; he drank a glass of water, shrugged his shoulders, blew out a huge sigh and stumbled back to bed.

After Susan had hung up, she phoned the police to report Peter as a missing person. A policewoman came round and took some notes, and was worse than useless.

212

"People go missing all of the time. He probably wants some space, and he'll be back within a few days."

"But his blackberry is switched off. He never switches his blackberry off."

"He would switch it off if he didn't want to be contacted for a few days. Don't worry; I'm sure he'll turn up."

"My husband was worried about fraud in the Company he works for, and went to report his concerns to Kevin Stevens, the Finance Director, and he hasn't been seen since. You might be sure that he will turn up, but I'd be a lot happier if you spoke to the Finance Director before making such insensitive comments."

Without Peter and Jaeger, Susan found the house very quiet and spooky. The impact of yesterday's events finally took their toll. She couldn't trust herself to speak to her parents without telling them what Peter had done, so she went for a walk in the park to keep herself occupied. Memories of Jaeger came rushing back to her as she saw the open areas that he used to love to run around in, and she sat on a park bench, sobbing uncontrollably. People were looking at her, and an old couple asked her if she needed help, but Susan shook her head and walked to an area where she could be alone to compose herself before going home. It was no better at home; she had no appetite, had no interest in the programmes on the television, and would have dearly loved to lose herself in the oblivion provided by a bottle of gin, but had promised herself that she would not drink until after the baby was born. She sat alone and cried herself to sleep.

Susan awoke the following morning feeling no better. Her body ached from sleeping on the sofa, and she was shivering from the lack of blankets in the early morning chill. She looked in the mirror, and a tired old woman with red eyes peered back at her. She would normally have rushed upstairs and covered her face with makeup, but decided that her appearance was that of a person who was gravely concerned for her missing husband. She went upstairs and ran a hot bath to warm her body, and to take away the ache that seemed to penetrate right through to her bones.

She finally felt strong enough to visit James, the MD.
"I'm sorry Peter's missing, Susan, but I'm sure that he'll turn up."
Was that all anyone could say?
"Why would Peter leave when we've just found out that I'm pregnant? He's wanted to be a father for years."
James was the first person that she had told of her pregnancy, as they wanted to keep it secret until the results of the initial scan, but she thought it might stop people making stupid comments about Peter's disappearance, and the surprised look on James's face showed that it worked.
"Peter was worried that there were strange payments being made by the Company, and he went to see Kevin on Saturday night to discuss it. That was the last time that I saw him."
James picked up the phone and spoke to the payments department. "Have we made payments to new accounts lately?"
"Yes, but they were all authorised by Mr Stevens."
"How much have we paid to them?"
"I'm not sure, about two hundred thousand."
The MD's mouth opened wide and he hung up. He phoned Kevin. "Could you pop into my office please, Kevin."
Susan went white. "I don't want to speak to him. Peter wanted to warn you about him, you're just going to cover this up to keep the Company out of the news."
"No Susan, I'm taking this very seriously, I assure you. If you don't want him to see you here, you can leave out of the door that leads to the car park."

That evening, two policemen came to interview Kevin at his house, one of them was much more interested in Kevin than the other one.
"We would like to know where you were on Saturday evening."
"I was here, at home all night."
"Is there anyone who could vouch for you?"
"Peter Stevenson was with me earlier that evening."

"It's his disappearance that we are investigating, so unfortunately, he can't give you an alibi."

"Why would I need an alibi?"

"Because we're investigating the disappearance of Peter Stevenson, sir, and you were the last person to see him. Could you please tell me what time he left?"

"I'm sorry, I don't know. I was talking to him, and then fell asleep. I've been really busy lately with my job, and I had food poisoning from a re-heated curry. When I woke up, he'd gone."

"Does he often visit you at home, sir?"

"Not very often, no. We spend most days together at work, so he doesn't normally have to meet me outside work."

"So why did he visit you on Saturday night?"

"He was giving me horse racing tips."

"Horse racing tips?"

"Yes, what's wrong with that?"

"Mrs Stevenson was under the impression that you were talking about work."

"Well, he was probably too embarrassed to tell her the truth."

"Did you both bet on the horses then sir?"

"No. I did, but he didn't?"

"So why did he give you tips, if he didn't bet himself?"

"He just did."

"And is there anyone who can verify that you were here for the rest of the night, after Mr Stevenson left?"

"No. I told you earlier, I went to sleep."

"Have we had dealings before sir?"

"I very much doubt it, I don't have much interaction with the police. I'm the Finance Director of a large company." The policeman smiled as he finally remembered their previous meeting.

"Thank you sir, that will be all for now, but we would like to speak to you again soon."

The policemen left, and went back to their car. The policeman with the supposed 'super powers' was like a dog with three cocks.

"I've met that bastard before, when I pulled him over for dangerous driving. I'm sure he's guilty, and I'll prove it. I'll teach him to take the piss out of me."

He ran a check on Kevin's car registration number, and couldn't believe his luck. At ten past ten on Saturday night, Kevin's car was caught speeding in Woodstock.

The next day, the police made a visit to Kevin's neighbours. "Did you see Mr Stevens on Saturday night?"

"At about ten o'clock, he carried his friend to his car and put him in the back seat. He said that his friend had drunk too much, and he was taking him home."

"Gotcha, you bastard!"

The evidence was overwhelming. Kevin had debts with the CSA and his bookmaker, he was seen carrying Peter to his car, and his car was caught speeding. A check of Kevin's house found the blood on the dining room carpet, that matched Peter's blood type, but unfortunately for Kevin, not his own. There was also the same blood type in the back of Kevin's car. There was also money missing from the Company that had been authorised by Kevin.

Kevin was, in his own words, "fuckin' annoyed, and amazed" when the police arrested him the next day.

Kevin's solicitor could not understand why Kevin was still pleading not guilty with all of the evidence against him. "If you change your plea to guilty, the sentence will be much shorter."

"Look, I'm not guilty of anything, and it's your job to sort this out."

"All of the evidence shows that you owed a large amount of money, and you stole from your Company to pay off the debts. It also points to the fact that you killed Peter Stevenson to stop him from telling everyone. There's a witness who saw you carry him from your house on the night that he went missing, and bloodstains matching Peter's blood group on your carpet and in the back of your car. And you have no alibi. Why do you think that you will be found not guilty?"

216

"That's your job, not mine. I haven't done anything wrong. As long as I tell the truth, they have to find me innocent."

"But all of the character reports back up the evidence, especially your temper."

"I can't understand that. People are just jealous that I've done well for myself, and raised myself from working class to be Finance Director."

"But what about your reported treatment of Peter?"

"Well, that's bollocks for a start. I've been his best friend since we were at school together years ago."

"Mr Stevens, it's my duty to tell you that there's no possibility of you being found not guilty, and to convince you to plead guilty, otherwise you will end up with a long sentence, with a reduced chance of parole."

"That's it. You're fired. I'm sure that I could do a better job myself."

"You'll have to get someone qualified to represent you. You'll be better off if I carry on, as I know the facts of the case. No-one can get you out of this mess but yourself. Just own up and accept the consequences."

As usual, Kevin thought that he knew better than everyone else. He was annoyed and amazed when he was arrested; he was much worse when he was found guilty.

TWELVE

Although Kevin was treated with the respect that common criminals gave to convicted murderers, he hated every minute that he was locked away from his regular nights of drinking and women. He employed an investigator who spent a large amount of money trying to prove that Kevin was innocent of all charges, but the case against him was airtight.

Peter had covered his tracks well, and his new identity enabled him to disappear without a trace. As expected, the Police felt that they had no need to look for Peter; his body would turn up sooner or later. Kevin's investigator's check of the airports, trains and ferries for information regarding Peter's whereabouts revealed nothing, as did his colleague's clandestine analysis of Peter's bank account and credit card. His surveillance of Susan was dropped soon afterwards to allow him to carry out work for other clients that would result in a more positive and lucrative outcome.

The man and the woman walked past the dome-shaped greenhouse to the front door of the house. The man carried the young child, due to the woman having her hands full of her hair dressing equipment. She'd made quite a success with her new hair and beauty salon since she'd rejoined her husband, including house visits. The strong Hebridean wind made it difficult for them to keep their balance, but they were getting used to it. She knocked on the door, and an old man answered it, and invited them inside.
"My wife's waiting in the kitchen."
The woman looked at him fondly and smiled. "Before we go any further, you really need to explain what a Mock Turtle is."

28680458R00129

Printed in Poland
by Amazon Fulfillment
Poland Sp. z o.o., Wrocław